The Accidental Pinup

The Accidental Pinup

Danielle Jackson

JOVE

New York

A JOVE BOOK
Published by Berkley
An imprint of Penguin Random House LLC
penguinrandomhouse.com

Library of Congress Cataloging-in-Publication Data

Names: Jackson, Danielle, 1985- author.
Title: The accidental pinup / Danielle Jackson.
Description: First edition. | New York: Jove, 2022.
Identifiers: LCCN 2022001076 (print) | LCCN 2022001077 (ebook) |
ISBN 9780593437339 (trade paperback) | ISBN 9780593437346 (ebook)
Subjects: LCGFT: Romance fiction. | Novels.
Classification: LCC PS3610.A3475 A65 2022 (print) |
LCC PS3610.A3475 (ebook) | DDC 813/.6—dc23/eng/20220124
LC record available at https://lccn.loc.gov/2022001076
LC ebook record available at https://lccn.loc.gov/2022001077

First Edition: July 2022

Printed in the United States of America
1 3 5 7 9 10 8 6 4 2

Book design by Daniel Brount

To Dr. Cheryl R. Jackson
If I hadn't stolen your romance novels when I was
far too young, none of this would have happened.
Thank you, Mom!

ONE

"This is going to be uncomfortable, but trust me, totally worth it." Cassie coaxed Dana to arch her back higher, squeezing everything just so. "You look incredible."

"It feels weird," Dana said. "I'm starting to sweat."

"Totally normal," Cassie said. "Hold it, right there." The angles were just right; the light streaming through the open windows cast the perfect amount of shadows and ethereal glow. Dana's naturally red curls glinted with gold undertones, and the lace chemise she wore was sheer enough to showcase the constellation of freckles across her unbelievably unblemished skin. Maybe it was the blush or the body shimmer placed just so, or the fact that Dana was sweating, but she was sparkling all over. A corny person would say she was glowing from within. And that's exactly what Cassie wanted to capture.

She took in the entire scene for another moment, stepping back a few paces to admire her work. "We're ready. You are ready. You're a goddess." The second she saw Dana's eyes light up with the compliment she gave her—which Cassie genuinely meant—Cassie pressed the shutter release. "Bingo."

They shot for another thirty minutes. A seasoned pro, Dana was able to twist and exaggerate her body in exactly the way Cassie had envisioned for this photo shoot. Starting a new series was always daunting, but it was the first time in a while that she had a project of her own to work on. Not that she could complain about her boudoir photo shoot business—Buxom Boudoir—but Cassie longed for more time to do whatever she wanted. She was lucky that Dana, a plus-size model, had a new line of pinup-inspired lingerie, and luckier still that Dana was her very best friend in the whole world. Because working on the national ad campaign for Dana's collection of sexy underthings was exactly the type of thing Cassie *wanted* to work on to take her career to the next level.

Beyond the pretty makeup and sexy lingerie, Cassie enjoyed her job the most when Dana stopped sucking everything in, exposing body rolls and dimpled legs, let out a sigh, and stuck out her tongue in exaggerated exhaustion. Cassie took a few more rapid shots until Dana flicked her off. And Cassie had a hunch that would be the shot they loved the most.

Cassie connected a USB cable from her trusty Canon EOS 5D camera to her laptop, giving the images a minute to upload. She gazed at Dana, who had pulled on a silky floral robe, the same one she and all the bridesmaids had worn the morning of Dana's wedding. Cassie hadn't seen Dana look so happy and relaxed and beautiful since that day until now. Knowing she was going to be a part of her best friend's biggest dream—starting an all-inclusive lingerie line that was smashing the patriarchy one thong at a time—was beyond fulfilling. The early online support from Dana's announcement of her collaboration had been overwhelmingly positive, and Cassie knew her vision for her pinups with a twist would be well received.

"Jesus Christ, Dana," Cassie said, focusing on the photos. "Your boobs are, quite frankly, the tits."

Dana's fair skin bloomed in a crimson flush. For someone who had spent most of her time in front of a camera scantily clad, she blushed so easily. "Thanks, doll face. I couldn't have done half of that without you. Only you can get me in those positions." She joined Cassie in front of the laptop screen as Cassie scrolled. Sure, there were a few duds here and there, but when the photos worked, they really worked. Cassie knew the angles of her best friend's body better than anyone—except maybe Dana's wife, Riki—and she knew the vibe she wanted to convey.

"Undies with caution tape emblazoned on the trim do require a certain panache," Cassie teased. "And I think we got it. I cannot wait to see the underwear you designed on a model's ass on the side of a bus."

Dana's collection, under the Luscious Lingerie brand, was called Dreamland. Everything was lacy and sheer, with gorgeous pastels and deep jewel tones, but just like in the middle of an incredible dream, there were random things that didn't quite make sense— yellow caution tape trim, skulls and crossbones in the middle of lace patterns, hand outlines on the cups of bras. Not to mention the size range: everything from XXS to 6XL. Anyone and everyone who wanted pretty undergarments could find them in Dana's Dreamland.

Dreamland came to Dana after she had spent years wearing plain, boring bras that offered the support her ample bosom needed, and she wanted to wear the sensationally sexy and vibrant designs she saw fellow lingerie models wearing regularly. While they got to wear lacy, sheer, strappy teddies and playsuits, Dana—and similarly, Cassie—was confined to blasé basics.

When Luscious Lingerie burst on to the scene a few years earlier, they had made their mission to create lingerie and undergarments that made everyone look and feel supported and sexy, no matter what. And Dana wanted to model and design lingerie that looked and fit like a dream.

Cassie had spent many a night creating vision boards and scrolling through Pinterest to define what it really meant when something "fit like a dream." Dana wanted everything to fit perfectly but also be brashly sexy and fun . . . which lingerie could absolutely *not* be when a body didn't fit into what "traditional" sizing deemed appropriate. Dana's Dreamland and Luscious Lingerie were taking the unconventional and necessary steps to make garments that could appeal to anyone who wanted to wear something vivacious and pretty.

And with the help of the Lucious Lingerie designers, adding cheeky touches like mesh cutouts, bright patterns, and the aforementioned caution tape bands, Dana's idea of a quirky, off-kilter lingerie dreamscape went to the next level. Dana's Dreamland line ranged from supportive bras and sheer panties in a variety of cuts to relaxed bralettes and cozy boy shorts, from plush robes to gauzy chemises and supremely sexy teddies—all made to fit and feel great on different body types.

"You know, I designed the caution undies with you in mind," Dana said, gently poking Cassie's side, knowing it made her squirm. "When was the last time anyone has been down there?"

"Ha ha, thanks for that," Cassie said, rolling her eyes and swaying her ample hips. "Admittedly, it's been a while, but I'm okay with that. I've got a job to focus on and a few more projects in mind—plus BB is doing really well."

"People love taking off their clothes and getting photographed," Dana said, shimmying over to a privacy screen to change.

Buxom Boudoir was Cassie's dream come to life. A few years earlier, once Dana had started gaining traction through her social media following as a plus-size model and body-confidence advocate, she and Cassie had started their luxury boudoir/pinup photography studio in the heart of Chicago's River North neighborhood. Cassie had photographed Dana for as long as she'd been interested in photography—they had been best friends since middle school. Initially bonding as the first two girls in class to get boobs and attracting all the attention from dumb preteen boys, Cassie and Dana were each other's ride-or-die, BFF, sister from another mister, and so forth.

Starting her own photography business wasn't exactly what Cassie had planned, however. She knew that she was a great photographer, she had an interesting point of view, and people would be interested in what she wanted to show. But more doors closed than opened when an inexperienced, Black female photographer came knocking. Cassie was tired of the rejection and decided to combine her love of all things vintage into a full-service boudoir photography studio. It took some convincing, but with her parents as early financial backers, her meager savings from the various photographer jobs she did land—including copious amounts of engagement photos, weddings, and family portraits—and Dana's support as well, Buxom Boudoir (affectionately called *BB*) was born.

At first, it had been just Cassie and Dana—between the two of them, they could handle scheduling, styling, hair, makeup, set design, and, of course, the actual photography. But as clients started gravitating toward Cassie's professional and easygoing demeanor and their following grew. They brought on Kit Featherton, a petite, effervescent Brit who dressed entirely in prim pastels and barely wore any makeup herself, but who tackled makeup and hairstyles with gusto and flair. As whimsical as her name, Kit spent more time attending hair shows and beauty seminars and practicing techniques on willing clients (and not-so-willing coworkers) than anything else. Cassie admired Kit's devotion to learning as much as she could about how to care for and style a variety of different hair types, and she had become an indispensable part of the Buxom Boudoir team.

With the addition of Kit to the team, their popularity skyrocketed, and Cassie couldn't be happier. BB started to get some recognition from local businesses to do photo shoots for social media content, small-scale ad campaigns, marketing materials, and a Chicago bridal magazine had even hired the team a few times for editorial spreads. But best of all, BB was a boudoir studio run by a Black woman, with all-female employees, producing beautiful content that left their clients happy and empowered. Cassie was her own boss, had an incredible team, and wanted even more.

Bringing on Samantha Sawyer—a young, recently graduated marketing major with a photography minor—had been the icing on the cake. Sam's business acumen, social media savvy, and ability to aptly assist with photography equipment made up for her grumpy disposition. Youngest of them all, always bored, prickly on her best days and seething on her worst, Sam was painfully blunt, took no shit, and made the BB team complete. With Sam in place to concentrate on scheduling, check clients in, make sure everything was prepared, and help Cassie throughout shoots, Buxom Boudoir was a force to be reckoned with, and Cassie had more time to take on freelance shoots and daydream about her own more conceptual projects.

Several months ago, Buxom Boudoir had found its new home

when they moved from a small storefront into a new, bigger loft space located on the top floor of an old warehouse that had been converted into workspaces. Cassie loved this studio because it had been a blank slate and they could do whatever they wanted to it. They had views of the skyline, natural light came in just right from virtually all sides, and there was enough room for everyone to have desks, a large area for shoots, and a spot they called the Glam Zone, which consisted of two salon chairs, mirrors for hair and makeup, and thrifted shelving repurposed for all of Kit's beauty products, curling irons, and bobby pins. Dana had clothing racks lining the makeshift walls of her "office," with options for the different types of photo shoots they did—sultry and sexy or cheeky and cheery. Their studio had become Cassie's sanctuary—she spent more time there than her own beloved apartment, which was within walking distance. She owned and ran a photography studio on her own terms, and she was finally saving money.

And yet, she still wanted more. Cassie had successfully carved out a niche in the boudoir scene, but she wanted to book national ad campaigns that were torn out of magazines to put on inspiration boards or were pinned thousands of times on Pinterest. She wanted the freedom to explore her own personal photography endeavors and work on high-concept artwork that she could show at galleries across the country. She wanted to use her platform and to boost up curated collections of artists she admired so they could find success, too. Which meant Cassie still had a long way to go, and art directing and photographing the campaign for Dana's line would be a clutch gig for her.

"I can't believe this is one of the last times I'll be photographing you like this for a while," Cassie said when Dana emerged from behind the partition. She looked gorgeously refreshed in a white bodycon dress that hugged every single curve, including the teeny tiny bump only someone who spent a ton of time taking pictures of Dana in minimal clothing would notice.

Dana smiled, her hand immediately cradling her belly. To anyone else, she looked like her normally curvaceous self, but Cassie's best friend was finally, blissfully, eagerly on her way to motherhood. After years of trying to conceive and miscarrying until she was diagnosed with cervical insufficiency, a condition that prevented some women from carrying pregnancies beyond the first trimester, Dana and her debonair wife, Riki, were finally going to have the baby they so desperately wanted. This time around they were armed with the knowledge of what they needed to do to carry this pregnancy to term. They had also spent months searching for a sperm donor whose background matched Riki's Japanese heritage, and they had recently found an anonymous donor through a local sperm bank.

But with her diagnosis, Dana would have to go on bed rest sooner rather than later, to keep that baby cooking for as long as possible. And as much as Dana wanted to star in her own lingerie line's campaign, she also knew how important this line would be to so many people and that it needed to move forward, which meant someone else would model in the ad campaign. Their timing may have been less than ideal, but Dana was determined to have it all and make things work from the safety of her cozy bed.

Which was why it was integral to the success of Dreamland that Cassie was in charge of the campaign. She had been a part of the process since the concept initially creeped into Dana's mind— ethereal lingerie with a twisted edge. Dana trusted Cassie with her work and her life, and Cassie was ready for this giant step, art directing a well-known lingerie brand on a hotly anticipated body-inclusive lingerie line.

Amply bosomed herself—*36H, thank you very much*—Cassie

was full-figured and proud of it, but she understood the struggles of finding affordable, pretty, and fun lingerie. Dreamland was going to provide this to women of all sizes. Dana had worked countless hours on the prototypes, making sure someone with a negative-A cup or an XXXL derriere could find the same negligee but cut to accommodate different body types.

"I'm just glad everything will be in your hands. But I will be watching," Dana said, laughing a mock-evil laugh.

Cassie chuckled, knowing Dana would figure out some way to oversee every step of the process.

"The set I wore today is just the start and will be an awesome way to get my followers riled up. We should have samples of the full line soon, and once I approve those, we'll be in full production, your shoots will be underway, and our campaign will finally happen."

My shoots. Our campaign. Cassie's chest swelled—she was proud and exhilarated to bring recognition and momentum to their careers. Sam and Kit were also going to be on hand for styling and makeup, and their involvement with a national ad campaign for a popular lingerie brand would give them professional boosts, too.

"Have you heard from Luscious Lingerie lately?" Dana asked. "Rebecca something or another is handling all the marketing and should be in contact soon."

"Aside from those initial emails you sent with me copied on them, I haven't heard from her directly," Cassie answered. "Anything I need to know before stuff ramps up?"

"Well, she mentioned having you come in and do a trial run at one of their studios. I guess the higher-ups want to see what you do with the prototypes and a model or two they had in mind for the full campaign."

Dana's fiery red hair was covering her face as she rummaged

through junk mail on the front desk. Cassie knew she was avoiding her gaze for a reason. Her heart started pounding as she dreaded whatever bomb Dana might drop next.

"You mean I have to go in and prove myself, don't I?"

"No, Cassie. No. I told them, it's you or no one at all."

Cassie knew this was too good to be true, too easy. Every other step of the way to this point in her career had been a fight, and so was this. Except this time, Cassie was determined to make the most of it and come out of it with her goal in hand. More times than not, when she was up for a campaign on a larger scale or at the national level, Cassie was passed over for someone the company had worked with already. Having run her own business for close to five years now, she understood the appeal of going with an already trusted colleague and knowing what to expect in regard to their quality of work. But that didn't mean that Cassie wasn't willing to give people a chance or go out of her way to support other women and people of color who had been in her shoes, just starting out and looking for a break. Hell, Cassie was still at that point now—she knew the only reason she had this job was because her BFF was calling the shots. And she wasn't going to let someone else walk in and take this away from her when it was so close.

"Out of curiosity, do they have another photographer in mind?"

Dana began shuffling through junk mail again, suddenly very interested in a local pizzeria's menu, though Cassie knew she already had it memorized because they ordered from there pretty regularly.

"D?" Cassie asked, adding an edge to her tone. "Who is it?"

"Reid Montgomery," Dana mumbled quickly. Cassie closed her eyes in frustration.

Reid Montgomery was like an eyelash that got stuck in Cassie's eye right after she had just drawn a perfect cat-eye flick, so she couldn't actually rub it out. She and Reid rarely ran into each other in person, but she knew his name well—they were constantly being compared. On a surface level, their aesthetics were alike—vintage, pinup, retro—and they often competed for similar jobs in the city. But Reid Montgomery utilized retro as a style, while Cassie made a point to use it with a wink and twist its message into something more powerful, or at least cheeky—Rosie the Riveter giving the middle finger instead of making a fist, a re-creation of *Bye Bye Birdie*'s iconic phone scene but with smartphones, or a hiked-up skirt revealing not lacy underwear but full leg tattoos instead.

But she had to admit that Reid had a good eye for angles, cropping, and composition. And he was a white dude, so everyone automatically took him more seriously. He'd been Luscious Lingerie's go-to photographer for the last couple of years for virtually all of their major ad campaigns. They did editorial shoots throughout the year to include in catalogs and on their social media, and there were usually projects with special collections with other influencers and celebrities, like Dana's Dreamland line.

And now he was more than likely going to take this job away from her if she didn't perform to LL's expectations.

No way, lady. Don't count yourself out before it even starts, Cassie coached herself against that nagging, pessimistic voice in the back of her mind. Still, Reid Montgomery was the thorn in Cassie's professional side. Two months ago, Cassie had been passed over by *Chicago* magazine to do a relatively straightforward and tame cover shoot with the new mayor. They went with Reid Montgomery, of course, who gave them a perfectly fine set of photographs that would probably be used for years to come. In that same issue, Cassie had done a great photojournalistic set on Le Diner en Blanc.

A year earlier, Cassie had all but secured taking new photos at the Frank Lloyd Wright Home and Studio for their brochures, on-line presence, and more, but at the last minute, they decided to go with, lo and behold, Reid Montgomery. Prior to all of that, when Cassie was still out there, submitting her work to agencies and ap-plying for photographer positions day in and day out, she was con-stantly compared to Reid's aesthetic, told they already had a guy who did this type of work, and rejected.

And now here he was again.

Except this time, Reid would be the one wondering why he was looked over for someone else, someone better.

"Well, whatever. It's fine. Maybe he's the guy they want, but I'm the woman they need to run this campaign smoothly and make sure your skivvies look the absolute best they can," Cassie said, pepping herself up.

Dana would usually chime in with either an unprecedented level of enthusiasm or a loud, ridiculous whoop, but when Cassie looked up from her laptop, Cassie saw Dana was standing stock-still.

"Hey, D, what's going on?"

Dana suddenly hunched over, and a surprised groan erupted from her mouth. Cassie ran over to Dana as she slumped down, easing her to the nearby couch. Cassie put her hand on Dana's, which had gone straight to her lower stomach.

"Cassie, call Riki. Something's wrong."

Reid Montgomery's phone started vibrating as he pulled up to the State Street studio of a local TV news station. It wasn't his usual clientele, but after he photographed the mayor in *Chicago* magazine earlier that year, he was suddenly the new guy all the local, strait-laced Chicago celebrities wanted to take their photos. Reid had made his mark in the photography world by mimicking poses and stylings of classic pinup photography. If he could spin something in a vintage way, he'd do it no matter what, even if the subject or model wasn't even remotely interested in the pinup aesthetic. It was just what he did. There were other photographers out there who made a lot of money from specifically doing this sort of thing for regular, everyday people, but Reid had gone after national ad campaigns from the start and had been successful. And that had worked to his benefit, because now he was the go-to rockabilly photographer with a reputation for getting the job done above and beyond expectation.

Or so he told himself.

There were times when he wanted to walk around and take photos just to take photos, and he was lucky that he could afford to take days off here and there and do whatever he liked. Not every photographer could, and he knew it was a privilege to work on his own terms and his own time.

Things had changed for him after working with Luscious Lingerie, a Chicago-based undergarment company that was always in the fashion world news because of their support of the body-confidence movement. It gave Reid an opportunity to collaborate with big-name influencers, and other clothing brands had taken notice. Surprisingly, so had someone at the mayor's office, because he was astounded when someone from *Chicago* magazine called him with a gig to photograph the city's new Latina mayor, who was tenacious and took no BS from anyone. The magazine cover made the rounds from morning-news programs to prominent placement in convenience stores on every corner. Mayor Rodriguez looked powerful and charming and, most of all, important. Reid was still riding that high.

His buzzing phone brought Reid back to the present, standing outside the studio's side entrance to be let in for the photo shoot, but he ignored it. He had a full day ahead of him and had called in a couple of favors with some art galleries he'd shown work in over the last year to bring in an office assistant and intern to help out. He mainly worked solo, but the various teams of newscasters who worked different times during the day made this shoot more complicated. Luckily, everyone was already in hair and makeup, since most of them either had been on air or would be later in the day.

From the beginning, Reid had always felt alone. His entire life, he had known the only person he could rely on was himself. His parents had been aloof at best. Once he hit elementary school, Reid learned independence was a survival skill in his family. His parents generally felt like they had better things to do, were sporadically at home because of odd jobs, or spent time with their skeezy friends, and Reid often preferred it that way.

But when Reid was almost eleven and his younger brother, Russell, was born, he suddenly had this other person he had to make sure survived. From the outside, it might look like Reid raised Russ, but really, he just made sure the kid didn't kill himself by accident or get involved with something shady. Beyond that, Reid and Russ were never close.

His proclivity for solitude made it easy to focus on his career, get ahead in life, and save a ton of money. It also added to his overall bad-boy persona. He didn't love being labeled a devious rockabilly in the Chicago art scene, but he liked that he had an image people noticed, and he kept to it. Reid's perceived detachment kept expectations low, and since he was good at his job, his clients kept coming back.

After a couple of hours of cheesy group shots of local reporters (who would all likely need their heavy makeup retouched in editing), he decided to take some candid shots while they milled about. He winked at the meteorologist and watched their cheeks immediately flush red. *Click.* He saw the sports and special segment reporters laughing with a camera guy over something on one of their phones. *Click.* One of the lead anchors set to retire later that year sat off to the side by himself, looking over notes. *Click.* These were the moments he wanted to capture more than anything. More than the bright lights and overstylized pinups hiking up their legs, more than the power stances against city backdrops. These fleeting moments no one paid attention to—that's what he wanted to see.

Scrolling through photos on his camera's monitor, Reid felt his phone buzz yet again. Without looking at it, he knew it was a text from Russ, who'd been relentlessly texting him for the past few days. A week ago, Russ had called him saying he had gotten into some gambling debt due to a few terrible hands at an underground poker match in Colorado—whatever that meant; Reid tried not to get too involved—and needed Reid to wire him some money. Which he had, and Reid assumed that would be the end of it. If this text was any indication, Reid anticipated a frantic, pleading phone call from his younger brother soon, and, as usual, Reid would send him funds.

Just as he was going to read Russ's text, however, his phone genuinely rang. It was a call from Rebecca Barstow, the marketing manager for Luscious Lingerie. He had heard through the grapevine that a new special collection was coming soon, so he anticipated this call would be a new offer for a national ad campaign.

It was a hard job taking pictures of models in their underwear, but someone had to do it.

Ugh, he felt sleazy for even thinking it. To be honest, after spending two years as the lead photographer on many of LL's ads and some of their product merchandising shots, Reid had seen just about everything when it came to lingerie photography, and it had become just another part of the job.

"Bec," he said, knowing she hated when he shortened her name. "How are you?"

"Reid, how many times do I have to ask you to call me Rebecca, my *actual* name?" she said. "What's your schedule like later this week?"

"Nothing that can't be rearranged for you, *Rebecca*."

"Charming. Great. I need you to come do some test shots for a new line. Local influencer, size inclusive, yada yada, you get the idea."

Reid could hear her typing on the other end of the call, like she was talking to him but was also doing three other things at the same time. Knowing Rebecca, she probably was.

"Cool, email me the details, and I'll be there. Any reason why there are test shots and you aren't just hiring me outright?"

"We have another photographer in the running, and she has ties to the designer. The execs would much rather go with you, but we're saving face because this line could really be big for LL. She's a model and influencer with a huge social media following and is exactly the type of creator we want in our special lineup."

"As long as it's my usual fee or higher, I'm game. I'll see you later this week."

"Sure thing. I'll keep you posted on what's going on with the other photographer, and we'll go from there," Rebecca responded, the clack of her keyboard going quiet. "Maybe we could get drinks after . . ."

Reid knew it would come up eventually. He and Rebecca had hooked up a few times post–photo shoot. He tried not to make a habit out of sleeping with clients, but they worked together regularly, she was his main contact at LL outside of their accounting department, and she was cute. But he wasn't really looking for anything aside from the very, *very* casual, and Reid didn't want things to get messy. Luckily for him, neither did Rebecca.

"Yeah, maybe, we'll see," he said, trying for coy and not outright dismissive. He didn't want anything to jeopardize his cushy working relationship with LL.

Plus, this job was probably in his best interest right now. Knowing his brother, Reid fully expected to eventually answer Russ's call or text and hear a plea for some kind of financial support. A few months ago, Russ needed help when he was selling CBD oil in Maine, and before that it was protein powder in Vegas, then came the gambling trouble in Colorado. This time, who knew? Melatonin chocolate treats in Seattle? Maybe this time Reid wouldn't even ask about whatever "quick moneymaking" scheme Russ was involved in; he'd just send the cash and get on with it. The last thing he needed right now was to get worked up or worse—actually worried.

When he ended the call with Rebecca, packed up his gear, and made the requisite rounds to everyone before he left for the day, he finally opened his messages on his phone and started to scroll through a litany of unclear, rambling texts from Russ. After his third reread, waiting for his rideshare, he finally gave up and called Russ.

"Hey, Reid, it's about time."

"What is it, Russ? What do you need now?"

"So, when was the last time you went to the house in Tinley Park?" Russ asked.

Reid hesitated; he couldn't actually remember the last time he'd been home to the southern suburb they grew up in. Before he let guilt creep in, he answered, "It's been a while, why do you ask?"

"It's a complete shithole. The wallpaper is peeling, I'm pretty sure there's water damage to the first-floor ceiling, and the basement smells like something died—"

"Russ, what are you talking about?" Reid was confused. Why did Russ care about the house? He was halfway across the country. Unless . . .

"I'm home, big brother."

"Why?" Reid blurted before he could stop himself. "How long have you been here? Does Dad know? Are either of them there?"

"Relax, Reid," Russ said. "I've been here about a week, which you'd know if you responded to my texts or answered my calls." He continued telling Reid about his journey from Denver and his lackluster welcome back to Illinois.

"So, Dad's cool with you staying at his house?" Reid asked.

Their father wasn't going to let Russ stay there without some kind of benefit for himself. He may have been an absent parent, but Robert Montgomery was always on the lookout for a hustle. And knowing how eager Russ was to please their parents because he never got much attention as a kid, Reid feared their dad would take advantage of this situation.

"Yeah, that's the thing," Russ said, hesitating a beat before launching into a long-winded explanation to justify whatever it was their father demanded. "With Mom gone, no one is really here to handle bills and all that. So he said if I want to stay, I have to pay.

And you know I had to leave my last gig because of the whole poker thing, so . . ."

Reid rubbed between his eyebrows as Russ continued to come up with more reasons to drain his funds. Mortgage payments, utilities, food . . . The list of responsibilities their father had suddenly given his twenty-two-year-old brother seemed endless. And if the house was in such terrible disrepair after long stretches of vacancy, it probably needed work.

"Look, Russ, are you okay? You don't have a bunch of hippie mobsters tracking you down, right?"

"Uh, I don't think so."

"All right, fine. And Dad is definitely downstate on the farm?" Their father had left his "city living" and supposedly worked on his cousin's soybean farm, making a decent living. Without his family. And this was just the sort of thing he'd insist on if Russ wanted to stay at the house. "Have you heard from Mom?"

"Dad says he's not coming back anytime soon, and I haven't heard from Mom for almost a year."

God, what assholes. Reid let a few moments pass before he talked himself out of doing the right thing.

"All right, I'll help you with bills at the house in Tinley, but you have to work. Once you're on your feet, you take over paying for everything, or you can leave again," Reid said, realizing that offering to pay for these things was going to cost him. The extra cash from this Luscious Lingerie job would definitely help out.

"I can do that," Russ said.

Reid knew he'd have to babysit Russ and make sure he was holding up his end of the bargain.

As Reid listened to Russ drone on and on about how he'd built tiny houses from old train cars, Reid checked his email with his brother on speakerphone. Looking at Rebecca's email, his eyes stopped on one name in particular—the other photographer in consideration for this ad campaign.

Cassandra Harris.

Hers was a name he had seen and heard more and more lately. Apparently, they had similar styles with a vintage edge, and she ran some kind of boudoir business as her main gig. Boutique photography was cute, but it wasn't exactly lucrative. What did he have to worry about?

Nothing, aside from his brother. Securing this LL job now would be ideal, knowing he'd have to clean up whatever his brother's mess would be this time.

"Reid? Are you still there?"

Closing his email, Reid turned his focus back to his brother.

TWO

Cassie walked through the doors of an old warehouse in Pilsen that had been updated into studios not unlike the one she worked out of herself, feeling at ease in the open floorplan with a ton of light pouring through tall windows on one wall. She checked in with the woman sitting at the front desk, who was so chipper, it was alarming. But then again, Cassie was used to Sam's deadpan and sarcastic demeanor. It made her wish she had the entire Buxom Boudoir team with her—Sam's determined drive to keep everything on schedule, Kit's light and creative touches, and Dana's boisterous laugh filling everything between the floor and the rafters.

Dana, who had to bump up the start of her bed rest, was at home, propped up by many pillows and wearing the softest new cashmere pajamas that Cassie had gifted her after her recent hospital stay. Dana had essentially been prescribed to stay calm and off her feet—two things Dana did not do well. She thrived on waiting until the last minute and running around to find a missing shoe for her personal blog or the perfect top for a boudoir client. And Cassie knew from experience that Dana despised being told what to do.

When it came to what fashion trends were considered appropriate for plus-size women, whom she could or couldn't date—let alone marry—and how she went about her life, Dana did as she pleased. It was one of the things Cassie loved most about her best friend.

But she also knew the pain Dana and Riki endured for years before Dana's diagnosis had come through. And the baby they had hoped to have for so long was finally on its way, so Cassie knew Dana would do whatever had to be done to keep them both safe.

Between making sure Dana was okay and taking on her styling jobs for upcoming appointments at BB, Cassie barely had time to think about her test shoot and interview with Luscious Lingerie. She also didn't have time to continue overthinking that Reid Montgomery was the other photographer under consideration for this job—the job she already considered hers.

The perky receptionist behind the front desk told Cassie it'd be a few minutes before Rebecca came out to get her, so she busied herself by getting a cup of coffee in the waiting area, which also gave her a sneak peek into the space where she'd be working. Peering through the doorway, Cassie saw it was pretty typical: blank backdrop, a couple of tripods for cameras, monitors nearby to look at work throughout the shoot. And so many fricking spotlights and flash reflectors and other artificial modes to make the lighting look "better." She knew it was necessary, especially when there was a product to be featured, but Cassie preferred using as much natural light as possible when it came to her work.

Going back to the coffee station, Cassie heard the familiar sound of a shutter click and a bright flash reflecting off the wall of windows next to her. Commotion came from a similar work space across the hall. Someone was already in there taking photos.

Cassie felt her shoulders hunch up as she gathered her camera bag and the coffee, which she had made to occupy her waiting time more than anything. Would they bring her in when the other photographer was already there? Was he there?

Okay, if Dana were here, she'd bring you back from this brink. Cassie took a deep breath. *If Dana were here, she'd already be in the room scoping it out.*

So she went in, keeping to the back of the space to stay out of sight.

Sure enough, Reid Montgomery, who had the audacity to look pretty hot from behind, was in the room taking photos. The model, who was quite pretty and also quite slim, was wearing a white chemise, with sheer peekaboo cutouts in the shape of handprints.

"Now pop your hip," Reid called out. He moved around the model, getting different angles. The model, whose name Cassie's didn't know yet, flipped her long blond hair over her shoulder and posed. In a minute she'd probably kick back her leg and purse her lips.

"Okay, kick back your leg and purse your lips," Reid said.

Cassie rolled her eyes. *Typical.*

Cassie then grabbed her phone to take a few photos to both remember the layout of the room and to send a pic to Dana, to let her know the artistic direction LL apparently thought they could take without Dana's input.

Dana's response was swift and accompanied by an eye roll emoji.

> I'll take care of this.

"Cassandra Harris? There you are," came a voice. Cassie recognized her from the avatar in her email signature as Rebecca Barstow,

Luscious Lingerie marketing manager and her main point of contact so far.

"Call me Cassie," she replied, hand outstretched. "I didn't realize things had already started."

"Right, well, Reid was already here for some catalog shots, so he got started early. It's really just a formality," Rebecca said, firmly shaking Cassie's hand and then leading her closer to the action. "He should be wrapping up soon."

"I can hear you, Bec," Reid said, quickly glancing over his shoulder at them. Cassie could have sworn she saw him give her a once-over, but she decided to ignore that. Even if she was suddenly keenly aware that he had the brightest green eyes she'd ever seen. But none of that mattered because she was there to make sure her best friend's lingerie campaign ended up in creative, capable hands—her own.

"Once he's done, Cassie, we'll give our model Natalie a short break and then you can get started," Rebecca explained, taking a few steps back.

Cassie decided to continue to observe her competition as he took a few final shots. She liked how much he moved to get the right angle, not staying in one spot for too long. Reid encouraged Natalie to change poses, but not forcefully. He suggested a lot of classic pinup poses, but Cassie also noticed he took photos of Natalie as she rearranged the chemise, fluffed her hair, or when she took a breath before starting to pose again. Those were the types of shots Cassie was interested in seeing in his portfolio, not the overstylized, hypersexual, too-bright photos the LL execs would choose. But she had to admit, he had an easy rapport with Natalie, and she could see how that would be beneficial when working with models day in and day out. But there was no panache, nothing subtle about what Reid had Natalie do. She arched her back, stuck out her boobs, and he told her to keep her face "happy but serene." Considering the reason Luscious Lingerie wanted to work with Dana in the first place was to bring something new to the market, Cassie started to feel like she had an edge over Reid. But she also knew she was going to have to push herself to do something that would impress Rebecca and everyone else making major decisions about Dana's line.

More and more, clothing and beauty companies—conspicuous consumption of any type, really—wanted to appeal to a wider range of clientele. Just because they portrayed an idealized body type didn't mean that the people shopping their products looked like that, and with the rise of social media, the whole world was finally watching and had the means to call them out. So the smart companies, the ones who wanted to succeed and continue to grow, tapped into a section of the market that had been overlooked—the average consumer.

Now, the stay-at-home mom and savvy businesswoman could find the companies that fit their personal brand because the people showcasing products in the campaigns actually looked like them—not just the people advertisers assumed they wanted to look like.

Cassie loved what she did when she worked with her boudoir clients—she not only made them feel pretty and comfortable but also proud. Whether she had someone in full dominatrix leather or a simple lace camisole, Cassie knew her customers wanted to feel as good as the Buxom Boudoir team made them look.

And having a plus-size, Black photographer with a ton of hair and the perfect cat-eye flick helped, too.

Within the current settings, however, Cassie realized her photos would turn out looking almost identical to Reid's, which was the last thing she wanted. As Reid busied himself packing his stuff and Natalie pulled on a robe to get her makeup touched up, Cassie surveyed the room. Her eyes kept flicking to the front desk area. It was mostly blocked by a wall, but after noticing the light that had filled that part of the waiting area earlier, Cassie knew what she needed to do.

"Rebecca, what would you think about taking this photo shoot outside?" Cassie suggested, loud enough for everyone in the room to hear. She stole a glance at Reid, noticing that he was definitely trying to listen to what was going on. His expression was blank, but his eyebrows were perked up high.

Good, Cassie thought. *See why I'm the right person for this job.*

"I'm not sure we're equipped to move everything out there right this second," Rebecca said, looking up from her phone.

"I don't need anything other than my camera," Cassie said as confidently as possible. If she was being honest, a tripod would have been awesome, but she was trying to be spontaneous and—more important—different from Reid. Utilizing natural light had always been something Cassie strived to do, and Chicago had been blessed with warmer temps that week, sunny with enough cloud cover to balance out anything too harsh. If they could find a blank brick wall, Cassie would be in her preferred element. "Can we get access to the roof?"

As soon as Cassie asked her question, there was a spark of genuine excitement on Rebecca's face, and she quickly went to check that it wasn't off-limits.

She gets it, Cassie thought. She looked at Reid again, who had finished packing up his stuff and was now lingering and probably being nosy.

Let him keep watching, she thought, raising her chin. *Better yet, put him to work.*

"It's Reid, right?" Cassie said, walking a few steps in his direction. "Is that your tripod?"

Reid looked over at the equipment by the set. "Not mine. Everything that's left was already here. Cassie, did you say?"

Like he didn't know her name. Well, actually, there was a possibility he didn't know her name, or who she was, because she was always hearing about him after he had taken jobs from her. She'd been aware of Reid for a few years, having seen him at artist networking events and gallery openings in the city. And he likely had no idea that he'd been chosen for opportunities over her. Either way, Cassie liked having this slight upper hand of creativity right now.

"Nice to meet you," she said, lying through her teeth and extending a hand to him.

He gave her hand a firm shake, and Cassie couldn't help but notice how his hand engulfed hers and that he was very, very tall.

Rebecca came back as the handshake ended. "We're good to go. There's an elevator back here. Natalie, you good?" Natalie ruffled her hair again, nodded, and followed Rebecca.

"Would you mind terribly bringing that tripod up to the roof? I need to check a few things on my camera before we get started up there," Cassie said, unbuckling her bag to prep.

"I thought you said you only needed your camera," Reid said. He glanced up from securing his own backpack closed. He was reaching for a helmet on the floor that Cassie hadn't noticed earlier, as well as a classic black leather jacket. "But I'll bring it up and hang out, since you watched my shoot as well."

Cassie felt her eyebrow raise. "Fine. Thank you," she said, placing her camera strap around her neck and gathering her bag. She'd fiddle with the settings once they were in the elevator.

Reid dropped his helmet and bag near the front desk, winked at the woman sitting there, who smiled back at him like no one had ever given her the time of day, and they headed toward the elevator at the same time. Cassie knew his type: cocky, handsome, and considered himself too good for the work he was doing. Cassie knew this because she was the exact opposite: a hard worker, overachiever, always prepared and put together, and a people-pleaser, particularly when that crowd was her clients or an ad exec with an agenda. And here he was, doing her a favor, but not without a slight smirk, a motorcycle helmet, leather jacket, dark jeans, and a slightly too-tight T-shirt.

And seriously, did he really not know who she was?

Annoyances aside, Cassie reminded herself that this job meant everything—recognition of her craft, a respected company showcasing her work, supporting her best friend, who would in turn be supporting her, not to mention a huge payday. Cassie wasn't going to go softly like Reid probably expected.

The chime of the elevator brought Cassie out of her thoughts, ready to work. Rebecca and Natalie were already up there, standing near an exposed-brick half-wall barrier that would work perfectly for what Cassie wanted to do. The Buxom Boudoir studio also had direct access to the rooftop of their building, and it was one of Cassie's go-to spots for an easy and awesome backdrop utilizing the best source of light—full sunshine. Some photographers shied away from working in the elements, but Cassie just saw it as a welcome challenge. People, objects, clothes, bodies, skin . . . they all looked different in sunlight or in shadow. They changed in the hazy early-morning light and the sharp, waning light of dusk. This is what Cassie loved about capturing images.

And she was going to do just that, right then, to prove to everyone why she was the photographer for this job.

Walking out into the warm air, Cassie found a spot for her bag and turned to take the tripod from Reid. Much to her surprise, he was setting it up for her, across from where Natalie and Rebecca were chatting. "Does this work for you?" he asked.

"Sure, if I even decide to use it," Cassie said, trying to keep a straight face. "I just wanted to have the option of a static shot. But because the theme of this collection is dreams, a little extra movement on my end will make for more interesting photos."

"That's an excellent point," Rebecca said.

Cassie wasn't sure if she was trying to diffuse the situation or if Rebecca agreed with her idea. Reid stepped away from the tripod and moved back a few feet, still in Cassie's peripheral vision.

"Natalie, hi," Cassie said, reaching out her hand. "I'm Cassie, and I'm really glad to work with you today."

"Likewise," Natalie said, shaking Cassie's hand. "Ready when you are."

Cassie nodded, backing up a few paces and putting the camera viewfinder to her left eye. Natalie began posing similarly to how she did inside—predictable, calculated allure.

"Don't arch your back as much," Cassie directed. "Remember, this is supposed to be a dream. It's not perfect, it's not shiny, it's a little messy, more disjointed."

Natalie hesitated and rubbed the back of her neck, her elbow jutting up at a funny angle.

"Wait—hold that," Cassie said.

Natalie stilled, looking a little surprised at the pose Cassie responded to so vocally.

"Slump a little and stick out your other arm. Don't move, just follow me with your eyes." Cassie circled around Natalie, taking photo after photo. No one else on the roof mattered at that point. With that movement, Natalie had suddenly become the muse Cassie needed to take this photo shoot to the next level. She knew her movement would blur some of the images, and that's what she wanted.

Several weird poses followed, and Cassie was pleased to see that Natalie eventually caught on to the direction she had for Dreamland. The photos would be pretty enough, but Cassie would have to suggest they hire a plus-size model for this campaign, which was imperative to fulfill Dana's vision for her line.

"And that's my time, I believe," Cassie said, glancing down at her watch.

"Cassie, I could have watched you work for longer than the allotted thirty minutes," Rebecca said, handing Natalie her robe. "That was awesome. I've never seen anything like it. The light was perfect, the rooftop an inspired backdrop. We may even be able to use some of these test shots."

"I believe Dana insisted on a plus-size model for the campaign," Cassie said, making sure Rebecca was paying attention. "It's really important to her brand that body inclusivity be the main focus of whatever we do since she's out for the time being."

"Absolutely," Rebecca agreed. "We'll start scouting for a lead model immediately."

Before Rebecca could continue, her phone rang. Cassie went back to her camera bag and began securing things in place. She was about to scroll through the photos on the screen display of her camera to take a look at some of the pics when she heard a not-so-subtle cough nearby.

"Still here, I see?" she said.

"Indeed."

Cassie wasn't going to give Reid Montgomery, of all people, the satisfaction of asking what he thought of her shots. She also wasn't going to spend time going through pleasantries about the nice weather or the benefits of having a central location of a photography studio near an L stop. Instead, she decided to breeze through the awkward silence and wait to chat more with Rebecca. She was the only person Cassie needed to worry about. Besides, she had killed it in the photo shoot; Rebecca clearly understood and liked the dreamy concept, and Cassie did not need the distraction of green eyes and dark hair belonging to a very tall man in a leather jacket.

"That was smart," he said, sidling up to her. "Moving to the roof. To give them something different. They'll like that." He stopped himself from going on, which Cassie assumed he did on purpose, to get her to acknowledge him. He wanted to come across as aloof and unassuming, but Cassie knew better—every move Reid made was on purpose.

"But?"

"But that's not what LL does. They keep to their usual styles, make the shoots easy and straightforward and less expensive, and their clients know what to expect."

"You severely underestimate the clientele Dana's following will bring to this venture."

"I looked your friend up and you're right, she has the influencer thing going for her," Reid said. "But that'll only go so far."

Cassie wanted to retort with something quick and snappy, but she wasn't sure what to say. He had a point, both about Dana and about LL's business-as-usual mentality when it came to their marketing and advertising. But couldn't this be the time to try something new, something different, something better?

"Do you both have a few minutes? Dana and I have an idea," Rebecca said, breaking up what could have turned into a very heated discussion. "There's a small meeting room on the first floor."

Reid agreed, heading toward the door that led back to the elevator. Cassie gathered up her bag and jean jacket and started to worry he may prove her wrong.

"Absolutely not," Cassie said. In the time it had taken them to get back downstairs and find an iPad to include Dana in the meeting via video chat, Reid had been sizing Cassie up. The boudoir photographer everyone loved and thought was cool, Cassandra Harris was a name he had tried to ignore especially because his last few clients had mentioned her work to him—mostly on smaller scale ads and local photo shoots.

Plus, she was hot. Knowing Dana Hayes was a plus-size style influencer with a devoted following, Reid understood that the model they found for this test shoot wasn't going to cut it. In fact, more than once, while Cassie was telling Natalie how to move up on the roof, Reid imagined Cassie in front of the camera, wearing next to nothing, and him taking those photos. If his assumptions were right, Cassandra Harris had a banging body underneath her cool-girl style. She wore a chambray button-down shirt that was tied at the front, accentuating her hourglass shape. The black skinny jeans she had on hugged every curve. Her full mouth had barely smiled that day, but he could tell if she did smile, her entire face would light up because those dark brown eyes were so damn expressive. She'd be terrible at poker based on how high her left eyebrow raised whenever she wanted to make a point. She had tied her hair up in a red bandanna, Rosie the Riveter–style, and Reid also noticed a few errant black curls hanging out of the back, which his hands itched to pull as if he were a kid on the playground teasing a cute girl.

Basically, Cassie was a knockout, and she should clearly replace Dana as the model in the campaign—which is exactly what Dana had just proposed.

"Absolutely. Not," Cassie repeated again. She was standing at one end of the conference room table with her hands on her hips, tapping her foot. Reid could feel her nerves building with each staccato tick.

"Um, absolutely," Dana said from the screen. Reid could see she was propped up with what looked like at least nineteen pillows, and she was wearing the fluffiest robe he'd ever seen. She still had on a full face of makeup, however, and seemed to be in good spirits for someone confined to a bed for the remainder of her pregnancy. "Rebecca, do you have that email I sent you?"

"Yes, let me just pull it up," Rebecca said, bringing over another tablet.

Reid noticed that the color had drained from Cassie's face, like she already knew what was going to be on that screen.

"Oh, D, you didn't," she murmured.

"Oh, I did," Dana replied, barely stifling a laugh. "I'm doing this for the sake of my line. You know, the one I've been working toward for my entire career."

Rebecca looked at Cassie before giving the tablet to Reid. Cassie nodded and avoided his gaze.

"Whoa," he said before he could stop himself. He scrolled through a series of photos of Dana and Cassie posing together in simple black tank tops and jeans before getting to photos of just Cassie. "Who took these?"

"Our office assistant, Sam. For Dana's birthday earlier this year," Cassie reluctantly explained. "I only did it because my former best friend insisted on it as a gift and we were day-drinking— You know what? Never mind. You've seen them now. It's all irrelevant."

"Cassie, these are really good," Rebecca said. "You both look incredible and completely at ease. These outtakes of just you at the end are really gorgeous, too. What do you think, Reid?"

Reid nodded in agreement. "Yeah, I could see this working."

"I don't want to lose this campaign because someone"—Cassie glared at the tablet with Dana's grinning face on it—"decided to send over a bunch of random photos that I was promised no one would ever see. Ever."

"You'll still be art director," Dana replied. "I already told Rebecca it's the only way this will work. There's no one else I can trust to not only bring this vision to life but to actually embody it, too. These garments were made for someone like you, Cassie. Someone people will see and relate to and want to be."

Reid watched Cassie closely and saw she was slowly letting out a long, deep breath.

"Art direction from a model?" he said. "Wouldn't she be too close to the products to really get the overall scope?"

"First of all, I'm not a model," Cassie said. "Second, I know the merchandise better than anyone aside from Dana. I've seen every iteration, every sketch of every single thing in this collection. Third, I fully understand and support Dana's vision for this line to cater to customers of all shapes, sizes, and orientations. If anything, I'm overqualified to art direct."

"And she was the actual muse for the entire collection, and she's a total babe under those cute clothes," Dana chimed in. "Oh, yeah, and all those other credentials she said."

"I'll need a couple of days to get the powers that be on board, but I think this could work. It solves the model search, we've hired Cassie's boudoir team to provide styling and cosmetic support, and we have a photographer," Rebecca said.

Reid knew Cassie was glaring at him before he looked at her. And when he did, he just shrugged. This campaign's payday was exactly the break he needed with his irresponsible brother's financial troubles looming over him. "My schedule is relatively clear. Plus, we have some time before principal photography starts."

"I haven't agreed to any of this," Cassie said. "I'm just not sure . . . I just really wanted . . . I need a day. Please."

"Yes, of course. I'll need to know ASAP, however. We want to get the ball rolling on this," Rebecca said, glancing at Reid. "We can figure out how it will all work. You'll both be involved from the start."

Cassie let out a short, unamused laugh through her nose and waved goodbye to Dana, who blew a giant kiss her way and gave a cold glare to Reid. Rebecca ended the call quickly and told them both she'd be in touch over the next day or two. Cassie all but ran out the door toward the exit. Reid picked up his helmet, zipped his jacket, and headed out as well.

It was going to be a great afternoon for a ride with no particular destination, one where he could hopefully enjoy the post-rush-hour traffic on side streets and make his way back to his apartment in the Gold Coast. He had parked around the corner earlier in the day, so he was headed that way when he heard a familiar voice.

"D, you really don't get it, I don't want to . . ." Cassie's voice trailed off as she spoke into her phone. "I don't want to think about it. I want to be the one taking the photos." Just as she was saying those final words, her gaze met his. "I'm going home. I'll come by soon. Just let me think this over. On my own, all right?" The look she gave him as she put her phone in her pocket wasn't exactly welcoming.

"Everything okay?" he asked. Apparently, conversation wasn't his strong suit that day.

"Peachy," Cassie said. "Looks like you got yet another great campaign."

"Looks like I get to work with this up-and-coming model no one has ever heard of," he said. "And an art director who is going to make my life pretty difficult."

"At the very least." A few beats of silence passed between them.

"I don't know what Dana's trying to do, but I think—"

"Don't move," Cassie abruptly cut in. "Just stay right there." She pulled out her smartphone and started taking photos in quick succession. She moved closer to him, and appeared to be photographing his . . . leather jacket?

"Uh, Cassie?"

"Just a second," she said, completely focused. "Can you turn to the right a smidge?"

She was so close to him now, Reid could see her barely breathing to keep her hands steady. He wondered what was different about right then versus earlier. Here she was concentrating, determined, and powerful. Not that she hadn't been upstairs, but there was something urgent bubbling beneath the surface. Her brown eyes were rimmed in black and so shiny he could almost see himself in them. She smelled good, too, like flowers and sunshine and the beach.

"Okay, that's all," she said.

"What was that?"

"The light came through that building's window over there, and every single crease in your jacket was visible. The texture was perfectly on display, and I wanted to take a picture. Don't you ever just see things and want to photograph them? Even with a phone?" She waited for an answer.

"Yeah, I guess so. You were just a little intense about it, that's all."

Cassie shrugged and started to walk away. She was heading in the same direction as he was parked. When she noticed he was following her, that cute eyebrow arched up in question.

"I'm parked over here," he said, pointing in the general direction they were heading. In the time since the rooftop photo shoot, a crisp breeze chilled the afternoon air, promising a cool fall evening. Cassie pulled a scarf out of her bag and quickly wrapped it around her neck.

"Well, good luck with everything," she said, and then stopped. She looked like she wanted to say more but decided against it. Then she noticed the bike. "Wait, that's your bike?"

To be fair, Reid's bike was an actual bicycle. With his leather jacket, vintage moto helmet, and all-around vibe, he knew people were surprised—and by surprised, he definitely meant disappointed—to see a sensible dark blue bicycle parked out front of wherever he was working. When he moved back to Chicago from LA, he knew he wanted to get back into biking, and he'd treated himself to a top-of-the-line aluminum bike from his neighborhood hipster bike shop, along with a top-of-the-line lock.

"Yeah, what were you expecting?" he said, making light of it.

"Something louder."

"I thought about getting cherry red but didn't want to be too flashy."

There . . . He saw it—an actual smile from Cassandra Harris. And now that he'd seen it, he wanted to see it again.

"Well, I have plans, so I guess I'll see you around," Cassie said, about to turn away.

"Leaning toward taking the job, then?" Reid asked. "As the model?"

She looked back at him and slowly smiled, but it was laced with tenacity. It was alluring and maybe slightly terrifying. And Reid was instantly obsessed with it. If she did agree to model, he was going to have fun figuring Cassie out while they worked together.

"Wouldn't you like to know."

"I would, actually, so I know what my role is through all of this."

"Simple. You'll be there to push down the shutter button. I'll be there to do everything else."

THREE

Cassie walked into the BB studio the next morning with a carafe of coffee and a box of croissants from Good Ambler. She normally reserved treats for their weekly staff meeting, but after that weird afternoon with Luscious Lingerie and Reid frickin' Montgomery, she decided to channel her stress into carbs and share them with her friends.

As expected, Sam was already in the office, sitting at her desk right by the entrance to the loft. Her giant noise-canceling headphones were on, but she acknowledged Cassie with a nod. Cassie held up the treats and box of coffee, which received a slight smile. Coming from Sam, that smidge of recognition was her equivalent of bouncing off the walls in excitement.

Cassie went to the small kitchen area with a long table that also doubled as a meeting space and set down her treats. She opened the mint-green retro fridge and took out cream for the coffee as well as butter for the croissants. She turned around and almost bumped into Sam, who had silently come over to get plates and napkins.

"What's the occasion?" Sam asked. She was clad in all black, and her wavy dark brown hair was in a messy half bun. Aside from a subtle pink lip stain, Sam was fresh-faced, her blemish-free light brown skin on full display, dotted with freckles from her mixed Jamaican and Irish heritage. Cassie thought Sam always looked impossibly cool.

"Yesterday was a doozy," Cassie said. "So I'm curing my wallowing with baked goods."

"Did you say baked goods?" a breathy British voice called out. Kit glided into the office, wearing a demure teal sweater and a cream tulle skirt with knit tights. She was especially cute in the mornings, blue eyes sparkling and wearing barely any makeup. Eventually, she'd get antsy and start playing around with products between sessions. By the end of the day, her alabaster complexion would be covered with neon-yellow eyeliner and sunset-orange blush. "I haven't eaten breakfast yet, Cassandra my sweet. You are a godsend."

Without further explanation, which Cassie didn't feel like getting into just yet, the ladies of BB—minus Dana, of course—sat down and enjoyed coffee and carbs.

"So, what's on for today?" Cassie asked Sam, master of the schedule.

"Nothing major until this afternoon. An easy pinup headshot set, and then later on, a wedding-gift session with a very nervous bride. She's sent at least four follow-up emails with inspiration links."

"Great, I need an easy morning and at least two more of these croissants," Cassie said, relieved.

"Oh, wait, actually there was one thing I wanted to ask you about," Sam said, jumping up and briskly walking back to the front desk. "Have you ever had someone actually set up an 'informational' meeting?"

Cassie frowned and looked at Kit, who shrugged as she continued to stuff her face with bread. "Not in a while."

"Looking at the site stats, there was a landing page from a year and a half ago, where you offered job consulting to up-and-coming photographers and influencers . . . I assume that last part was for Dana," Sam said, scrolling on her laptop. "Anyway, someone booked thirty minutes for this morning. Set to begin in fifteen minutes. Because I confirmed it." Sam grimaced when she realized how close it was to this supposed meeting time.

"Is there a name?" Cassie asked. Of course she would have an inconvenient meeting in the middle of an otherwise free morning. But she had to admit she was excited that someone was coming to her for advice, so she decided to go into this situation with an open mind. Anything to keep her mind off the events of the day before and especially the person she had had to deal with . . .

"Just a company name: RM Photos?"

You have got to be kidding me.

"Cassie, love, goddess on earth?" Kit asked. "Are you breathing?"

Cassie let out a slow breath. "Thank you for the reminder."

"What?" Sam asked as innocently as she was capable of doing. It came across as defensive, but Cassie had to assume she didn't know who RM Photos could be. And why it was so annoying.

"Reid Montgomery."

"The douchey pinup guy?" Sam said. "Why is he coming here?"

"Well, one, because you confirmed the appointment," Cassie said, rolling her eyes. "And two, because Luscious Lingerie and Dana and said 'douchey pinup guy' are all trying to convince me to model in the Dreamland campaign."

Kit's mouth dropped open, and she looked over at Sam. They

shared a moment of understanding. On the surface, broody Sam and fluffy Kit were total opposites, but more times than not, they were very much on the same page. Cassie did not have time for their shenanigans.

"What?"

"It's not a *terrible* idea," Sam said.

"It's a downright brilliant one. You're, like, a total babe," Kit said, donning a very poor Valley girl accent.

Cassie sighed and looked down at her checkered Vans sneakers. Then she looked at her watch. She had ten minutes to get herself together, find a way to save her career-defining opportunity, and figure out what to do about Reid Montgomery coming to her studio.

"All right, to the Glam Zone," she said. She marched over to a chair with Kit and Sam right behind her. "Kit, I need you to make my makeup flawless—nothing over the top, just enough to look severe and nonchalant. Can you handle it?"

"On it." Kit grabbed brushes, blush palettes, and lip gloss, and pulled on an apron.

"What do you need from me?" Sam asked.

"Remember the jumpsuit from the Rosie the Riveter update we did for Dana two months ago? I need that, plus shoes that give me some height. I'll make do with the scarf I have on. We have eight minutes to get in formation."

Without Cassie having to beg or explain why this was so important to her, Kit and Sam got to work. Closing her eyes as Kit brushed on shadow and patted color into the apples of her cheeks, Cassie attempted to calm herself. She could say some sort of meditative affirmation but decided to just breathe steadily. When she opened her eyes again a minute or so later, her cheekbones were like whoa, her lips were poppin', and she felt refreshed and confident. Sam walked over with the navy-blue coveralls, cut perfectly to accentuate her curves, along with simple dark brown ankle boots. Cassie quickly retied her hair with the bright, abstract floral scarf she already had on that day and pulled out a few curls to frame her face. It was just the splash of color to accent the outfit.

"Ready for battle?" Sam asked, her maniacal smile evoking Wednesday Addams.

Kit nodded in agreement.

Just as Cassie went behind a privacy screen, a few of which were set up all over the BB studio for easy wardrobe changes, she heard the buzzer go off. Reid was on time, which was appreciated. He could stand to wait a minute or two while she readied herself. Plus, he had to walk up four flights of stairs first to get to the top floor.

Cassie loved that her Beauty Avengers had assembled into action and saved the day. She wasn't wearing a power suit by any means, but she knew she looked good, and that made her feel great. She was ready to face down the man who was standing in her way to success. The exposure that would come from a job at this level was paramount to moving forward, building the profile of herself and her business. Kit was going to get major makeup and hair recognition with this ad work, and Sam would gain invaluable experience being a part of the team that styled a national campaign. A lot was riding on this going right, and Cassie was ready to fight for them all.

She heard him come through the large sliding warehouse door and check in with Sam. She rolled her shoulders back, took a deep breath, and walked toward him, her heels clacking against the hard floors, each step full of purpose and importance.

"Reid, what a surprise," she said. "Welcome to Buxom Boudoir."

"Cassie," he said, almost as though he was inconvenienced by this meeting. "Nice place."

"Thanks," she said. "To what do we owe this unexpected visit?"

"I thought I'd come by to see what you thought about the campaign and working together," he said, avoiding looking at her directly and carefully studying the loft. As he looked over at the windows in front of them, Sam scowled at his back. But then Cassie noticed her eyes dip down, presumably to Reid's derriere, and she noted that Sam's scowl softened into appreciative perusal.

Same, girl. Cassie hadn't forgotten what that butt looked like. It was pretty great. But also, beside the point of this unnecessary meeting.

"Did Rebecca send you to do her bidding?"

"Not exactly," he replied. "I liked the work you did yesterday and wanted to find out more about your vision for Dreamland. It seems interesting."

A forced cough to cover up a laugh came from Kit's makeup station. The top of her white-blond head peered around a mirror, even her most innocent smile failing to cover up her skepticism at Reid's remarks.

Cassie motioned for Reid to accompany her to the table where the remnants of Cassie's carb fest were still out. "Coffee?"

"Uh, sure," Reid said, taking the mug she had grabbed from a cabinet and extended toward him. "Thanks."

The silence bristled between them while they both focused on their coffee cups.

"You know, you didn't have to make a vague appointment through the website," Cassie finally said.

"So you would have just seen me without question?"

"Oh, no, I would have questioned it," Cassie said, pleased when she saw the corners of his mouth tick up. "But you could have been more straightforward."

Reid paused before replying, looking down at his coffee and then back up at Cassie. He met her gaze and held it. It was strangely easy to look him in the eye, but also unsettling when Cassie realized whom she was staring at.

"I knew I had to do something to get in front of you without too much pushback. Yesterday wasn't awesome," he said. Cassie couldn't disagree there. "Dana's suggestion for you to model was surprising."

"To say the least," Cassie said, catching herself before she noticeably winced at how sharp her tone was. She didn't need Reid to know how riled up she had gotten over the idea of modeling. Specifically, in front of him. And in her underwear.

"Right. So I wanted to hear more about your vision. When things get started—"

"*If* things get started."

"If things get started," he echoed. "I want to be on the same page as you. And your team." He said that last bit louder to make sure Sam and Kit overheard him as they continued to mill about in random parts of the studio so they could eavesdrop.

Cassie sized Reid Montgomery up yet again. He'd come into her studio, wearing dark jeans and a nice sweater hoodie and perfectly worn-in chukka boots, and was being nice? Something didn't add up. Sure, Dreamland was a big campaign for everyone involved. Dana had a huge following online, and the interest from a few posts she put up about early designs had received a lot of buzz.

"Everything in Dreamland is off-kilter," Cassie said, fiddling with a napkin on the table with one hand and toying with a curl that had escaped the back of her scarf with the other. "At first glance, things look hazy and ethereal, but up close, things just aren't right. The colors are oversaturated, but there are harsh shadows from the sun. Or everything is perfectly in place, but the makeup is smudged and runny."

"Like a dream," Reid said, derailing Cassie's train of thought.

As she was speaking, she had started to gaze out the windows across from them. When she looked toward him as he spoke, snapping back to reality, she saw how intently he looked at her.

"Exactly," she said. "A really weird and sexy dream with caution tape–lined undergarments."

"That you'll be wearing."

"That I'm possibly considering wearing," she said, sitting up straight. "I haven't given my answer yet."

"I think you know what you want to do."

"I think I want to figure this out on my own," Cassie said, standing up. "And I don't need you or LL trying to sway me either way."

Much like Cassie's vision for the dreamy ad campaign, she couldn't shake the feeling that something wasn't right with this entire situation. Reid was here, in her studio, without warning, seemingly trying to convince her to model, though he was both encouraging and defensive at the same time. Nothing made sense.

"Well, I like your ideas. I'd like to be a part of it in some way. But like you keep reminding me"—Reid stood as well; how quickly she forgot he was much, much taller than her, and she felt like a dweeb for finding that incredibly attractive—"it's totally up to you. Good luck with your decision."

Reid put his coffee mug on the counter near the sink before extending his hand to Cassie. She shook it firmly once, letting go and balling her hand into a fist in the deep pocket of her jumpsuit, convincing herself that she did not care one bit that he shook her hand, not one bit at all.

He turned around and nodded at Kit as he walked by her, and he simply met Sam's glare as he made his way to the door but didn't engage further.

Smart man, Cassie thought, following him to the door.

"Here's my card," he said as he made it to the doorway, holding out a black business card. "My cell number is on there. Keep me posted on things."

"We'll see," Cassie said, placing the business card in her pocket. Reid waited a minute, as though he expected Cassie to give him one of her cards. Instead, she just stood there, waiting for him to leave so she could shut the door.

"Okay," he finally said. "See you around."

Cassie waited until she heard his descent down the stairs, and she quickly slid the door shut. She let out a huge sigh of relief and leaned back against the door.

"What. Was. That?" Sam said, her words stilted.

"I have no idea," Cassie said, avoiding eye contact.

"I have an idea," Kit said, stifling a giggle. "But I will keep my thoughts to myself for now."

Thank God for Kit's inherent politeness.

No sooner than he had left that awkward meeting with Cassie and the women of Buxom Boudoir, Reid had a text message from Rebecca Barstow, asking him how things had gone. He thought back to the day before—as he'd made his way home from the test shoot after the idea of Cassie modeling had come up, Rebecca had called him with a strange request.

"I've got the execs almost on board, but they aren't thrilled with the idea of Cassie running the show," she explained. "They'd much rather work with you, like they always have. They know what to expect and can count on you to keep things moving in the right direction."

Reid didn't really know what their hang-up was about Cassie, but he did know that Luscious Lingerie liked working with people they already trusted. It's why he had been a regular photographer for them for the last couple of years. "What does that mean for this campaign, then?"

"It means that they're willing to let Cassie and Dana think they're running the show, but you'll be keeping tabs on things and making sure everything goes according to LL's usual standards."

"You want me to spy on them or something? Try to hack into their computers? Bec, this sounds sort of ridiculous," Reid said.

"I agree, and believe me, I'd much rather have someone like Cassie in charge, but they're really counting on this campaign and the launch of the line going well. They don't want any big risks."

"So what exactly do you need me to do? Call you with weekly reports?"

"Nothing so severe. Just let me know if you foresee any problems, and maybe—" Rebecca hesitated.

"And what?"

"You could go to her studio to try to get a better idea of what they have planned. I've only heard concepts, so I'm curious if there's anything more concrete."

"Well, they'll probably want an actual model."

"That's the other thing," Rebecca said. "Turn up the charm a bit, and try to get Cassie to model. She's actually perfect, and it would be one less thing for us to have to get done."

"So you want me to spy on them, find out what their plans are, and encourage someone who doesn't want to model to actually model, all while making her think she's in charge when she isn't?"

"Exactly. Easy-peasy."

"Hardly," Reid replied. "You think I can just walk in there and get straight answers out of her?"

"Just bat your long lashes and say something cute," Rebecca said. Reid could hear her teasing smile through the phone. "We'll make this worth your while, as well."

Now this was something Reid was actually interested in. "Time and a half."

"I'll check, but that should be doable."

"And I want the difference up front."

"You're driving a hard bargain, Montgomery. My reputation is on the line, too, you know."

"You want me to babysit? I want to be compensated."

"Fine. But Cassie has to be on board with modeling in the campaign."

Knowing he could make some serious cash on this, Reid was willing to play nice with LL and do their bidding on the Dreamland campaign, no matter how ludicrous. It had potential to be huge, and Rebecca's bosses were finally coming to that realization. Reid decided he would do what he could to make sure it all came to fruition and rashly made an informational meeting appointment through BB's website that night, hoping he could turn on enough charm to ensure Cassie would go through with this.

Too bad he wound up botching everything and left Cassie more annoyed than she already had been.

He thought about checking in with his friend James, a Chicago restaurateur and the only person who put up with his loner ways, to grab a drink or something later on, but decided against it. He'd order something for lunch and settle in for a long afternoon of editing and uploading photos for a few different clients he'd shot the week prior. But just as he closed his apartment door and hung up his jacket, his phone buzzed again, this time with a phone call. *Russ.* Reid let out a sigh because he had hoped for at least a few minutes of peace before he had to deal with the other headache in his life. He picked up and didn't even get a chance to say hello, because Russ was already talking.

"Russ, slow down, I can barely make out anything you're saying," Reid said as he walked through to his kitchen. "What is going on?"

"I missed a payment and now Dad is threatening to kick me out," Russ said at lightning speed. "He's pissed, Reid. Really pissed."

"You already owe money?" Reid asked. He wasn't too surprised that their father had figured out some way to pass a money problem on to Russ, but he didn't realize Russ was going to bungle everything from the start.

Paying off Russ's rampant gambling debt had been more than Reid expected. He knew Russ was both gullible and always looking for a quick way to make cash, but getting in over his head with an underground gambling ring was a lot, even for him. Reid's once-comfy savings account was seriously in need of a boost.

And the quickest way to get those funds would be through this campaign with Luscious Lingerie.

"I didn't know, Reid," Russ said. "I didn't know it was going to be this much or this hard. He didn't tell me everything."

Per usual. Robert Montgomery was happily ensconced on a farm downstate, away from the city life their mother had supposedly persuaded him into. Or, at least, that's how he'd always painted it for them. Reid didn't know what was fact or what Robert was embellishing—it was probably some combination of both. Either way, Reid had made the decision long ago to not let his parents' issues with each other or the lives they ended up with impact his choices.

He could not, however, say the same for his brother.

Neither of them said anything for a minute. Reid wished he knew what to say to Russ, who was so needy for encouragement.

"I just wish I could get them both out of my life," Russ said, admitting something Reid had never heard before. And he knew what his brother was feeling. The last time he had felt something similar was when he was twelve and Russ was still a toddler. Reid remembered the empty feeling he had when he saw their mom, Rose, act so loving and affectionate with Russ. Back then, every move she made was for Russ's well-being. Something he didn't remember ever getting from her. And then, he later felt a pang of disappointment when he was eighteen and Russ was almost eight, and Rose started fully ignoring her younger son. Russ could do his homework without much assistance, make a simple cheese sandwich for his own lunch, and wanted to spend more time in front of the TV watching cartoons than snuggling and reading with her. She didn't feel needed, and Reid recognized the things Rose had done with him when he was around the same age. Reid always thought that could be the thing he and Russ bonded over. Their ten-year age gap left them with so little in common, but Reid assumed he could try to teach Russ that their parents left a lot to be desired. Instead of accepting this independence, though, Russ grasped at whatever attention he could get from their parents, Rose in particular. Sometimes, she'd humor him and listen to whatever he had to say about his day at school. But most of the time, she'd cut the conversation short, leave the house, and they'd both wonder when she'd come back. And at the time, Reid was more concerned with how he was going to get the hell out of there.

Hearing Russ's admission, finally, after so many years of trying to impress them or, frankly, find out where they were, made Reid angry and a little sad, too.

"What do you want me to say, Russ?"

"I don't know." Reid could tell from Russ's reply he was annoyed and angry, too.

"What, should we buy the house from him?" Reid said the words before he could think about what he had suggested.

"Uh, maybe?" Russ said. "It would take Dad out of the equation completely. He'd probably leave us alone forever."

Russ did have a point there. If there was no reason for their father to depend on Russ to pay bills and the mortgage, then they wouldn't have to deal with him again. And who knew where their mother actually was at this point. She wouldn't feel any type of way about losing that house, because she rarely showed emotion toward them at all.

"Russ, I spoke too soon, I don't know if I—if *we*—can afford to do that," Reid said, backtracking rapidly. "I just paid off your last expensive idea."

"It was your idea, Reid. You suggested buying the house," Reid reminded him. "I could stay here, earn my keep by fixing stuff up. I've done enough random construction jobs to do basic repairs. And I'll try to find a job—"

"Like I said from the start, you are definitely getting a job."

"Yeah, fine, I'll get a job. And I've been thinking about going to college."

"One thing at a time, okay, Russ?"

"Yeah, sure, okay," Russ said. "So you want to do this?"

Reid didn't say anything for a moment. This was more than just helping Russ by sending him cash. It was going to be a lot of work, and Reid would be the one responsible for it all, even if Russ was the one living there and working. He heard Russ softly clear his throat, interrupting Reid's train of thought while he tried to work his way through this wild idea. He ran a hand through his hair and let out a long, slow breath.

"I need a couple of days to get things in order and figure out if it's possible. So until then, don't talk to Dad. And look for a job."

"You got it."

Again, silence settled between them. This was probably the longest conversation they'd ever had.

"Thank you, Reid," Russ said. "I'll let you go."

Russ hung up before Reid could say anything in return.

Reid stared at his phone for a moment, wondering if he was really going through with this. Before he lost his nerve and decided to let Russ fend for himself, he started a new text.

REID

Bec-Just got done meeting with Cassie at BB. She's not totally on board yet. If she does model, I'll do what you and LL asked. But I need the money ASAP.

FOUR

The next morning, after an extra cup of coffee and a special treat from Firecakes Donuts, Cassie headed toward Bugles, the bar where Dana's wife was the manager and they also lived behind. Cassie was equipped with donuts to share with her pregnant best friend and her pregnant best friend's wife and, of course, herself.

The sun was shining, and she was listening to her workout mix even though she was just walking as an attempt to stay upbeat. She had made up her mind. At least she thought she had.

The idea of being in front of the camera usually terrified her. In this case, though, she knew Dana was telling the truth: she had designed her Dreamland collection with Cassie in mind. Cassie had spent countless hours with sample fabrics, feathers, and buttons held up to her décolletage and across her butt for months. But to actually model? In her underwear? And outside, in the winter?

To be fair, doing the photo shoot in the winter was her idea, to save money at locations and for the sharp winter sunshine she loved so much.

And, more important, Cassie had to consider her photography career. Because while modeling was never something she'd thought about seriously—tipsy birthday photo shoot notwithstanding—she now had to deal with the fact that Reid Montgomery would be the photographer of this campaign. Art director or not, Cassie's dream campaign was slipping through her fingers.

She hit the ringer on Dana's apartment behind Bugles. Instead of buzzing her in, Riki greeted her at the door.

"Hey, Mama," Cassie said, smiling sheepishly. "I brought donuts as an apology."

"You don't need to apologize at all, Cassie baby," Riki said as she took the donuts and led the way upstairs. "Blame it on hormones if you want, but suggesting you take Dana's place is a big ask." Putting the donuts on the dining room table, she beckoned Cassie into the kitchen. "Try my new brunch special drink, debuting tomorrow: elderflower blood orange mimosas."

Bless Riki Sakai and her cocktails for every hour. Cassie sipped the beverage and closed her eyes in appreciation, then gave an exaggerated chef's kiss.

Riki and Dana started dating after college, after they met online. Riki was calm and collected, the opposite of her vivacious, extroverted wife. Cassie knew almost from the start Riki and Dana were a good match. Riki had a preternatural way of bringing Dana down from whatever ledge she found herself standing on. Dana was loud, and not just when it came to her fashion choices. There wasn't a bar top in Chicago that Riki hadn't convinced Dana to climb down from. But Cassie knew Riki listened to Dana and understood when her confidence needed a boost after a particularly grueling photo shoot. And Riki had been Dana's rock through their journey into motherhood. Cassie had been in that role for so long in her friendship with Dana, and it was nice to have someone who really understood the beauty in all of Dana's chaos. Cassie and Riki, in turn, had also become quite close over the years.

Dana rushed out of the bathroom in a flurry. To anyone else, she looked beautiful and perfectly fine, but Cassie could tell her best friend was struggling. For starters, her signature red matte lip was smudged, and nary a highlighter or contour could be seen on her cheekbones.

"Is she wearing leggings? And a sports bra?"

Cassie noticed that Riki was giving her wife the same once-over.

"The first trimester is a bitch, okay?" Dana said, putting on an oversize sweatshirt. "The moment, and I mean the exact moment, I finish putting on lipstick, I am plagued with morning sickness. My eyes are watery, I'm pale, and no concealer can cover up the bags under my eyes. This little jerk better be worth it."

Riki put an arm around Dana's shoulders. "They will be, I promise."

Cassie watched as Dana pouted through a sweet smile.

"I'm going to let you two talk. And you're in luck, D, Cassie brought donuts."

Dana stuck her tongue out and pretended to dry heave. "Food before noon makes it worse. But please, don't not eat on account of me."

Riki grabbed two thickly frosted donuts and her mimosa and went to their office.

Cassie looked down into her drink, avoiding eye contact with Dana. Before she could muster up the courage to speak, Dana began.

"Cassie, I know it wasn't fair what I did yesterday, and I'm sorry I sprang so much on you all at once and in front of everyone. It was selfish, and I should have talked it over with you first. But when I saw that model in my stuff, I wanted to take action."

"I appreciate your apology, D. It's a lot for everyone, but most of all for you. Your dream of your own lingerie line is happening. Your dream of becoming a mother is happening, too. Each of those things on their own would warrant a little craziness."

"I know you well enough to know that when you come bearing gifts in food form, you have more to say, so let me have it."

Cassie took a deep breath, a swig of mimosa, and decided after she let this out, she'd have the apple cider donut. "You know how much shooting this campaign means to me. It would put me out there on a national level, and I've been working so hard to get something like this. I love you, and I'll do anything for you, but I don't know if I can let this go, D. I want it too much."

Cassie could see the concern on Dana's face, but she wasn't sure if it was because Dana was nauseous or if she felt guilty for putting her friend's career on the line with her idea. "You'll be in complete and total artistic control."

"Except I won't be, Dana. I'm not used to being in front of the camera. It's completely different. I'll be half-naked and cold and unsure of what to do."

"I will give you a crash course in modeling. It's not as hard as everyone makes it out to be," Dana said with a wink. "Reid will just be there to hit the shutter. I'll make sure there's something in the contract that if he starts to art direct, he's fired and will be immediately escorted off the premises." Dana nudged Cassie's side and watched Cassie smile.

"Modeling *is* hard," Cassie said. "And it will be the middle of winter in Chicago. And most of my location ideas had you outside, weather permitting."

"Hey, I'd do it if this tiny monster would let me move any farther than to the bathroom or from the bed to the couch. I still want to look and feel sexy. You have no idea how horny pregnant women get."

Cassie raised an eyebrow.

"We have needs, too, Cassie. I'm growing a human, not a chastity belt."

Cassie laughed, a real, deep, cathartic laugh. She needed it.

"If, and just *if*, I do this, you swear I'll be in charge? Tell me the truth, Dana. The maid of honor in your wedding, the godmother of your unborn child, and your best friend since middle school."

"I told them if you weren't in charge, then they wouldn't be manufacturing my line," Dana said, holding out her pinkie finger. Cassie linked it with hers. It may have been juvenile, but it was still the way they let the other know they were being serious.

With her promise in place, Cassie felt like she could move on and finally talk about the unwelcome leather-clad addition to the campaign. "And now I just have to prance around in a negligee in front of a far-too-good-looking dude for the next few months."

"You think he's good-looking? I knew it." Dana's laughter pealed out and filled the room.

"Riki?" Cassie called. "I'm going to need several more mimosas before my modeling course starts."

Reid didn't want to admit that after his harebrained idea to buy his childhood home, and especially since he saw those slightly revealing photos of Cassie Harris, the idea of working with her in the Dreamland lingerie was a welcome distraction. It wasn't just that she was sexy—she was more than that: determined, tenacious, beautiful . . . But there was something else going on behind all those curves. Hopefully she wouldn't make things difficult and he could coast through this extra surveillance job for LL. He needed the money, and he'd signed a contract from Rebecca just that morning. She had assured him over email that an additional signing bonus was moving through their accounting department as they spoke, and he should see a direct deposit in the next few days. All he had to do was take great photos—easy—and keep Cassie placated enough to go through with the vision of her campaign, become a model overnight, and not cause any issues because she wasn't behind the camera—not so easy, but doable if he could focus on her lush body and work on his charm. If she even decided to do the campaign as a model and art director.

Beyond all of that, however, Reid had a few days before he had another photo shoot or needed to make any major life-altering decisions, like buying a house from his deadbeat dad to save his wayward brother. He spent some much-needed solitary time editing projects, including a couple of smaller scale but still national-level ad campaigns—one for retro-style shoes and one for an over-the-top YouTuber who was starting his own rockabilly fashion line. Both perfectly in Reid's wheelhouse, so it was easy busywork. Over the last few years, the clients he took on were on a much higher caliber and he could charge a premium price. He wasn't about to take on extra work or start shooting wedding photos again to make ends meet any time soon.

But as he stared at his double monitors filled with images of wing tip shoes with tassels, Reid knew he wasn't in the mood for work. He decided to get on his bike and ride a bit to clear his head. Riding through the Gold Coast, the neighborhood he lived in, Reid's mind floated back to his brother and the mess Russ had made—and dragged Reid into, too. Before Russ came back to Illinois, they would go months at a time without contacting each other, but then out of the blue, Russ would be in Nebraska or Louisiana, asking for a little help toward rent, money to take on an extra sales gig, or something along those lines. Russ meant well and had a lot of big ideas, but he never quite followed through on any of them.

Thinking about Russ almost always put Reid in a bad mood. Not to mention that the pressure from LL to essentially spy on this new campaign wasn't settling well in his mind, either.

Luckily for Reid, there was actually one person he could count on aside from himself for counsel: James Campbell. He was the one friend who seemed to stick. And he had coincidentally biked toward James's job, so he continued riding to see what he had going on.

They met in grad school at University of Illinois Chicago—Reid had been coasting his way toward an MFA in photography, and James was studying to become a film director. While James's professors pushed him to apply himself fully, Reid always skated by doing the bare minimum. He made extra money by doing headshots of most of the theater majors, as well as taking cast photos for the various plays. He'd met James and found him both easy to photograph and easy to talk to. Reid used James in a lot of his early work. James was a tall, Black man with deep brown skin who kept his hair meticulously cut—he went to the barber every two weeks—worked out like a maniac, and had one of those smiles that never failed to attract attention. Photographing James for much of his early portfolio work had been easy, and Reid was grateful that James was sufficiently full of himself to be a model at a moment's notice.

After grad school, Reid bounced around from New York to LA for a year or so, but he knew he'd always have a friend and a place to stay with James in Chicago. When Reid decided to move back to the city because he kept finding consistent work that sent him there anyway, he stayed with James for a few weeks before finding a small, shitty apartment to call his own. That was almost four years ago. He had since moved into a newer, better place, but without James's generosity, Reid wasn't sure where he'd be at this point.

Around the time when Reid moved back to Chicago, James decided to go into the restaurant business—turns out he didn't direct plays or films very well, but he could "direct" a busy restaurant— and Reid was the first person he asked for advice on everything, from how food tasted to the floor plan. Reid didn't have any experience in interior design or the culinary arts, but he had a good eye, liked food, and James trusted Reid to be up-front with him.

The previous year, James had successfully opened his own restaurant—Simone's, named after his grandmother—in the heart of River North. James called Reid to do any and all promo shots for the restaurant, and when *Chicago* magazine came calling to do a feature story on the new hot spot, James insisted Reid take the photos. That relationship led to a great contact at the magazine, which eventually led to Reid's recent mayoral photo shoot.

As he walked into Simone's, Reid's eyes adjusted to the dim lighting and cool ambience. Exposed brick along one wall combined with dark rafters and ductwork gave the restaurant an industrial feel, but the lush fabrics in the drapes, upholstery, and tapestries helped soften the cacophonous sounds that came with a bustling restaurant that had a long wait list for reservations. The absolute best part of the restaurant, however, was its year-round rooftop bar. Reid loved it for the people-watching opportunities, something any photographer enjoyed having. It was high enough that the view was broad and wide across the neighborhood, but it was low enough that people weren't ants. The foot traffic was ideal, and on a busy weekend afternoon, it was a prime spot to see what was happening in River North.

Reid nodded at the host as he wandered through to the back staircase to go up to the rooftop. James was working the bar, using every ounce of his charisma chatting with two patrons who were more than happy to flirt back with him. Reid had to admire James's devotion to always taking an opportunity to talk to women—and they were always willing to talk to James. In addition to his good looks, he had a seemingly easygoing demeanor, though Reid knew every move James made was on purpose. It might be to move his business forward or to have a casual fling, but there was always more than met the eye with James Campbell.

"Reid, what's good?" James said, placing a coaster down at the corner of the bar where Reid always sat. It was the perfect spot to see both what was going on in the restaurant and what was happening at the street level. "The usual?"

Reid shook James's outstretched hand and nodded. James handed him an IPA from Reid's favorite Chicago brewery, Revolution, and then turned back to his adoring fans. He laughed with them as he poured and delivered two cocktails made in record speed, and, just as quickly, James turned back to Reid, unloading recently cleaned glasses onto a counter behind the bar. Reid also noticed a bucket of limes that James would probably slice while they talked.

"Don't you have minions to do this sort of thing?" Reid asked.

"My most recent minion quit and now works for Bugles down the street," James replied, frustrated. "I've lost a few good people to Bugles, but Riki runs a good operation."

Reid suddenly put two and two together. "Riki, who is married to Dana Hayes? The model?"

"Yeah, you know them?"

Reid explained the basics of the situation, leaving out the part where he was running surveillance on Cassie's input. "Do you know anything about Cassandra Harris?"

"I know she's making waves in the art scene. We had a local artist mixer a while ago, when you were in New York for a photo shoot, and she made an appearance. She knows a lot of people. And a lot of people know her, too. Especially in the neighborhood." James took a minute to greet a new customer and had to run down to the first-floor bar for a specific bottle of liquor.

Reid felt his phone buzz and expected to see his brother's name flash across the screen. But he was pleasantly surprised when it was an unknown number suggesting they meet up in a few days at the Rookery in the Loop so they could start scouting locations.

This is Cassie, by the way.

Reid felt himself smile, which he tried to tamp down into a smirk, but he knew he was grinning at his phone like some kind of giddy loser.

REID

Does this mean you're going to do the campaign?

CASSIE

I suppose you'll get to see me in caution tape lingerie after all.

He wondered what changed her mind. From what little he knew, Dana could be convincing, but he also suspected that Cassie knew an opportunity when she saw one, even if it wasn't exactly what she wanted.

And he'd be damned if he didn't take the opportunity to work with Cassie while she was wearing next to nothing.

Knowing that James would tell him to keep his money if he tried to pay for the beer, Reid quickly finished his beer and left enough cash to cover the drink, a normal tip, and then some, and headed down the outdoor staircase that led to the street. Before unlocking his bike, Reid sent another text to Cassie, agreeing to meet her. He thought about sending something extra charming, but he didn't want to push his luck with Cassie. Reid had a feeling she would be able to see through him from a mile away.

A few days later, when they met outside the historic Rookery building in the Loop, Reid felt strangely nervous.

"Hey," she said, walking up to him while he locked his bike.

"Hey, yourself."

"They're setting up for a wedding tonight, but the event coordinator said we could look around as long as we don't touch anything."

Walking into the Rookery, with its signature Frank Lloyd Wright architecture, impressive winding staircases, and distinct windowpanes, Reid felt like he was transported into a crystal palace. He immediately understood why Cassie wanted to shoot part of Dreamland at this location. It was ethereal and full of shadowy pockets that would showcase the texture and design of the clothing . . . or lack thereof.

"I love right here," Cassie said, gazing upward. They had walked through the building and up a short staircase. She stopped in front of a pretty famous spot where the grand staircases seemed to overlap, casting shadows yet still leaving enough light to reveal or conceal just enough. "The evening light will be perfect."

She was wearing that jean jacket again, and in the midday light, Reid could see it was authentically frayed, not manufactured to look that way. He wanted to take her picture just then, looking over the staircase, half of her face concealed in shadow. He imagined the jacket over lace and satin, not the green T-shirt and blue jeans she was wearing. Reid cleared his throat, trying to take his mind elsewhere.

"I had this idea for a silhouette shot. When it was Dana doing the modeling, I didn't have a problem with it, but now that it'll be me . . ." Her voice trailed off.

"What did you have in mind?"

"There's a lace bra, completely sheer, and it looks like two hands covering up the . . . cups."

Reid could see a flush start at the base of her neck and start to rise up.

"But with the right light, I think she could—"

"You mean, you could," Reid said, walking closer to her.

"Yes, I could be facing toward the front, but holding the bra out, dangling from my fingertips. Provocative, but still showcasing the hand motif."

"Very . . . provocative indeed," Reid replied. They both avoided making eye contact. "The venue's perfect."

"I agree," she said, walking toward the staircase. "It's just . . . never mind."

"What?" he asked as she shook her head and kept walking. "Look, we're going to be working together, and it's going to be pretty intimate, so you may as well say what's on your mind." Reid had trotted down the stairs in front of her, and turned around, stopping so Cassie was standing a couple of steps above him, making them the same height, and he could look her directly in the eyes to be as convincing as possible. "You can trust me."

Cassie chuckled to herself. "It's weird thinking about me as the model instead of Dana."

"You think about Dana a lot."

"She's my best friend," Cassie said, brow furrowing. "And I take her picture a lot. For as much as she claims that I'm her muse, she's actually mine."

"You definitely have muse potential."

"What does that even mean?" Cassie said, putting her hands on her hips.

"That, right there. This power coming through. Don't move," he said, taking out his phone.

"Reid—" she started to protest, but he held up a hand and, surprisingly, she stood still.

"You're pretty cute most of the time," he said, moving around her. "Don't move your head, just move your eyes." He continued to move in a half circle, up a step, then back down. "But then there are these glimmers of pride and fury that come through in bursts. I've wanted to photograph those moments ever since we met at the studio. I might not be in charge of this shoot, and I'm just pushing a button. But you're definitely a muse." Reid slipped his phone back in his pocket.

"Amusing, maybe," Cassie finally said, continuing to walk, navigating the bustling event setup.

"Call it what you want, but we could attempt to have a good time while we're doing this," he said, catching up to her. He watched Cassie's gait slow down ever so slightly, as she did her best not to look at him. Her deliberate dismissiveness made Reid realize that charming Cassie was going to be harder than he thought, but keeping her happy would make the entire situation easier and hopefully move everything along quickly. "I'm starving. Lunch?"

It was his turn to lead the way, out of the Rookery and into the brisk October air. As he unlocked his bike, Reid suggested heading back to Simone's. He knew Cassie's studio was in the vicinity, so heading back near River North would also bring him closer to his apartment as well.

"You don't have to go to lunch with me, you know," she said to him as they walked toward the L station. "And the other places I wanted to check out are farther away, so we don't have to go anywhere else. We can meet up again a different day."

"And you should know, two new colleagues sharing a meal is acceptable," Reid replied to Cassie's indignance. "We can discuss other places you had in mind and when we can meet again to take a look at a few more spots."

The L ride and walk back to their neighborhood was interesting. Cassie was quiet and barely made any conversation, but Reid noticed that there was a hint of a smile on her lips most of the way there. He was going to attempt some small talk when the familiar vibration of a text message came from his phone in his back pocket.

> How goes the scouting? Any issues
> with our model so far?

Reid frowned at the screen, wondering how he was going to stay sane during this campaign. Between trying to please Rebecca and the Luscious Lingerie execs with regular reports—which he had been assured he didn't have to give unless there was some kind of issue—attempting to make nice with Cassie and her team, and ignoring his newest urge to make Cassie smile again, Reid had a lot going on. For now, the simplest way to keep Rebecca at bay until he had something to actually report was to keep things enticingly vague.

REID

Nothing to worry about so far, unless you count not falling for my charms.

REBECCA

Turn it up a notch. She'll warm to you eventually. I didn't like you at first either.

REID

Gee, thanks, Bec. Will keep you posted . . .

After he hit send, Reid put his phone back in his pocket and prepared to get off the train with his bike in tow. He liked to think Cassie was impressed with the ease he maneuvered his bike up and down the platform steps, but her steely demeanor suggested otherwise. Once they were at ground level, the walk from their L stop to Simone's was just a few blocks.

"I saw your photos of this place in *Chicago* magazine," she said as they walked near Simone's entrance. "I'm intrigued by year-round rooftop dining."

The weather was crisp and the sun was shining, and while Cassie walked, Reid wanted to capture the hints of copper and gold in her coiled hair. She had done the same thing to him when she took photos of his jacket, right? And he'd already called her a muse.

The wall outside of Simone's was whitewashed brick, and he certainly wouldn't be the first person to take a series of photos in front of it. Many a Chicago influencer had taken photos in front of this restaurant. Reid didn't like those generic, trendy shots that were so often used on Instagram for empty likes and comments, but he thought this backdrop could be the perfect spot to continue to get used to working together.

"Hey, do me a favor?" he said, nodding her over to him as they came up to Simone's.

"Okay, sure," she said, reluctantly coming closer. "What's up?"

"Hold my bike, right there." As soon as she took the bike, hands nestled on the handlebars, leaning slightly forward, bright sunshine illuminating her face, Reid understood why Cassie liked working with natural light so much. She was glowing against the light bricks. He quickly pulled his actual camera out of his messenger bag and took a speedy succession of shots before she could protest too much.

"Reid, I wasn't—"

"You're going to have to trust me at some point," he said, peeking over the viewfinder.

"You're right, but are you going to be in your underwear, too?"

"That could be arranged if it would make you feel better."

Click.

He got the shot he wanted: Cassie smiling a real smile. And he knew it was real because she started laughing. He took pictures of that, too. Reid was starting to understand the appeal of taking pictures in front of this wall.

"Oldest trick in the book, right? Imagining people in their underwear." Cassie giggled.

"The thought of me in my underwear is funny to you?"

"Oh, come on, underpants are always funny," she said.

"The last thing I'll be doing is laughing when you're in front of my camera," Reid said, suddenly serious. He didn't mean to change his tone.

"Reid," Cassie said. "Don't."

"Don't what?" he said, moving closer, still taking pictures. Even when she was serious, she was gorgeous. Her face told a story, and he wanted to read the entire thing.

Cassie hesitated. "Is this what you do with all the models? Flirt and say cute things to make them feel at ease?"

"Not all of them," Reid answered. "I can only think of one that I've felt compelled to flirt with and say cute things to."

"Well, it's very . . . unprofessional." Cassie walked his bike to a nearby lamppost and waited for him to lock it up.

Reid took one final shot of her profile because now she was deliberately not looking at him.

"I like being unprofessional with you." He was taking another risk, saying something direct, knowing it would make Cassie uncomfortable, but it might be a way to get her to at least talk to him. "Maybe you could loosen up a bit, not be so professional all the time."

She did turn and look at him then, handing over his bike and putting her hands on her hips. "I have to be professional. The utmost professional. It's why I'm so good at what I do and why people respect me. I'm professional."

He'd struck a nerve and clearly didn't understand what she meant. She sped by him and walked into Simone's. Reid latched the lock on his bike and let out a sigh of relief because she hadn't left.

Is it weird that I like unnerving her just as much as I like seeing her smile? he asked himself as he walked in. Cassie was waiting near the host stand, but he motioned for her to follow him to the bar.

"Reid, back so soon?" James said from the main-level bar, glancing between the two of them. "The rooftop is open, the heaters are on, and only stragglers from the lunch rush are left."

"You know the way to my heart, James," Reid replied. "This is Cassandra Harris, photographer, model, and owner of Buxom Boudoir down the street."

James extended his hand. "Nice to meet you, Cassandra."

"Call me Cassie. Nice to meet you, too. I've admired your facade for a while now and attended a networking mixer here a few weeks ago," she said.

"Next time you need a makeshift gallery space or a photo shoot backdrop, please let me know," James said, passing a knowing glance between the two of them.

Reid knew if they dallied much longer, James would start asking more direct questions.

"I'll send up some drinks and apps, on the house."

"Much appreciated," Reid said, following Cassie toward the staircase to the roof.

James was correct, there were only a few people up on the rooftop. He and Cassie sat at a table near the far end of the bar so they could watch the busy street down below.

"How do you know James?" Cassie asked, marveling at the cocktails and charcuterie board a server had brought them.

"We're good friends; he's a former model I used to work with early on, and we kept in touch," Reid answered. "I've known him since grad school."

When he mentioned grad school, Reid noticed Cassie's eyebrow raise. That one eyebrow would be the death of him.

Reid and Cassie ate in silence for a few minutes, as the hustle of the street below minimized the awkwardness. There was still a lingering fog between them after their earlier confrontation. He could tell something he said had bothered her, and as he was about to apologize, she started talking.

"Earlier, I came off a little harsh, but being professional is kind of a sore spot for me," Cassie said, playing with the damp cocktail napkin under her water.

"You're so . . . even-keeled all the time. Don't get me wrong, you're pleasant and to the point, and I like that in someone I'm working with, but don't you ever just lighten up a little? When we start principal photography in a couple of months, it's going to be a lot of stress and work. I'd hate for you to dread doing it."

"I'm working on getting used to the idea. I've spent years behind the camera, so it's going to be an adjustment," she replied. "I don't have a big personality like Dana. I want to be a photographer first and foremost. This is just an opportunity on the way to bigger things."

"Cassie, when it comes down to it, we're artists. Don't you just want to make some cool art sometimes?" Reid thought back to the day she had given him a similar argument, after she'd taken his, or rather, his jacket's photo.

"Of course I do. And I know you do, too. But you get to have that kind of approach to things, not me."

Reid was reeling because he didn't understand what she meant. He must have looked confused, because Cassie started to look annoyed.

"Come on, Reid. Really?"

Obviously, he needed to figure this out. But aside from wanting to take great pictures and show them off, what else was she worried about here?

Cassie let out a sigh, and then spoke again. "In my career, I've had a lot of men make me feel unprofessional or tell me how to do my own job. And more often than not, it was a white guy whose entire demeanor changed when he met me in person after talking through only email or over the phone."

"So you've worked with some crappy people—"

Cassie held up her hand. She wasn't done.

"It's not every single dude who comes to a photo shoot; I've had my share of run-ins with well-to-do, nice women who will seek me out just to make themselves feel better. Doing what I do—it's always political in some way."

"But aren't some people just jerks? We all have to work with shitty execs or pompous designers or . . ." Reid trailed off, because he started to realize, the tiniest bit, what Cassie went through to get as far as she did.

"That is bullshit," he finished.

"Or toxic masculinity, systemic racism, the patriarchy. There are lots of names for it," she said, rolling her eyes as she rattled off a litany of terms Reid never had to consider for himself. Cassie moved to pick up her drink, but Reid grabbed her hand, surprising them both.

"That really sucks, Cassie."

Cassie looked from their hands to his face. "I appreciate that."

She adjusted on her chair, in an attempt to take her hand back, but he held on to it. "Reid, you don't have to—"

"I know you think I'm messing with you, but I meant what I said earlier today," he said, realizing it was actually the truth. "Let's try to at least have fun working together."

FIVE

Cassie spent the next couple of weeks on similar neighborhood jaunts with Reid—an afternoon traipsing through Bucktown, a morning in the Ukrainian Village, and absolutely refusing to go to Wrigleyville. Wandering the city, Cassie explained her vision of the literal Dreamland she wanted to create. Time of day mattered as much as the weather or what she'd be wearing. Dawn, dusk, cloudy and foggy days . . . those would make all the difference in the scenes she saw so clearly in her mind.

Imagining herself in those scenes, however, was a bit less clear.

To be fair, the way she caught Reid looking at her sometimes made her feel like she could almost belong in the dreamscape she was determined to bring to life. After the handholding incident at Simone's—that her mind kept playing on repeat—Cassie found hanging out with Reid both intoxicating and infuriating. He did seem to understand where she was coming from once she explained her approach to professionalism, but then he'd find yet another way to tell her she was a muse or they should just have fun.

Cassie didn't buy it. At the initial LL shoot, he was aloof and dismissive. He clearly wanted the job with a company he had already worked for in the past, and he probably wanted a payday that was probably considerably higher than what she was expecting to get. But now, all of a sudden, he was nice and supportive and understanding? Something didn't add up. Was he actually flirting with her, or did he talk to all models like this?

Well, I guess I'm referring to myself as a model now.

Reid was right about that—she needed to reframe her narrative. She was still a photographer first and foremost, but Cassie had to admit what Reid said about her being muse-worthy was nice to hear. Was it weird she enjoyed that a hot near-stranger said she was his muse? Maybe. But was it also kind of awesome? Definitely.

Still, the idea of being a model versus actually modeling was a persistent worry in Cassie's mind. She knew that it was hard work, having heard firsthand from her best friend. She also knew how difficult it was for some of her boudoir clients to look relaxed and sexy while wearing next to nothing.

But you also do a damn good job making everyone feel at ease. It was one of the top comments in the feedback section of her website and various review sites on the web. She wanted her clients to trust her. Could she do the same with Reid? And with herself?

Admittedly, she had a hard time looking at him and speaking in sentences that weren't tinged with sarcasm or annoyance—their lunch at Simone's had been weird. Something about him got under her skin, in a good and a bad way. Cassie didn't know how to feel about him and was struggling to get to a place where she could be comfortable around him. And this was while she was fully clothed.

Since agreeing to Dana's crazy plan of both art directing and starring in the Luscious Lingerie Dreamland campaign, she'd changed her mind at least a half dozen times, and Dana had to coax her back into doing it. Then, when Kit and Sam found out she'd agreed to model, they wouldn't let her back out. So here she was, scouting locations and having every inch of her body measured and remeasured to be sent to LL for the actual lingerie she'd be modeling in a couple of months. Oh, and also working with the man who had all but hindered her career to this point.

With Dana on bed rest, Cassie was grateful to know the rest of the BB crew would be on hand for the Dreamland photo shoots. Kit was charming, a little kooky, and unabashedly British, but she also had a voracious mind, creativity that knew no bounds, and she'd stand up to anyone for her friends. Cassie knew Kit came across as sweet, but she'd seen her handle difficult clients and fend off unwanted attention without missing a beat. And the fact that she kept a smile on her face the entire time made her a little deranged and alluring at the same time.

Meanwhile, Sam had become the reason for Cassie's ability to juggle more projects than ever before. Her tenacity for organization and marketing savvy saved Buxom Boudoir from overwhelming paperwork, scheduling issues, and social media responses. Did Cassie wish from time to time Sam would look like she actually wanted to be in the same building as everyone else? Sure, but Sam was devoted and loyal to the work they were doing. Her acerbic wit and interest in all things macabre sometimes seemed to avoid confronting feelings, but Sam genuinely wanted to learn everything she could about photography as well as running a business. Cassie sometimes worried about the day Sam would find something bigger than being BB's office assistant, though she wanted her friend—and all of her BB friends—to thrive and have successful careers.

It would have been all the sweeter if Dana had been the model and Cassie the photographer. Cassie would never malign the fact that Dana was putting things on hold to have a baby. Cassie couldn't wait to meet the little person growing inside of Dana, but she knew she was going to miss having her best friend, best colleague, and best cheerleader by her side through this process. But she was the CEO of Buxom Boudoir, her work was awesome, and she was going to do whatever she could to make Dreamland the best lingerie collaboration Luscious Lingerie had had to date.

With Reid frickin' Montgomery.

What a weird few weeks.

Cassie followed enough local models and influencers to know that Reid had a type. A model type. She wasn't it. They did a lot of wandering around Chicago, the perfect city to get lost in, looking for hidden gems to photograph her half-naked ass in front of. Murals, mosaics, parks, vacant lots . . . the opportunities were endless.

"Have you gotten any more prototypes from Dana?" Reid asked over coffee in Logan Square.

"A few more have come in, and even more arrive later this week. If anyone comes at me with a measuring tape and a needle one more time, I'm going to scream."

"How is Dana doing, otherwise?"

Cassie appreciated that he was asking about her friend. "She's coping. We've done a ton of impromptu photo shoots from the safety of her bed, she's ordered countless robes and nightgowns online, and she is slowly going out of her mind. Poor Riki; Dana is insufferable when she's told what to do."

Click.

Cassie was so busy talking about Dana that she failed to notice that Reid had started to take pictures of her while they sat.

"Don't do that," she said.

"You have to get used to this view of me," Reid said, giving her that irresistible smirk from behind the viewfinder. "But I was think-ing, maybe, before it's bitterly cold, we should do a test shoot."

Cassie's heart skipped a beat, and her face must have fallen be-cause Reid put his camera down. Cassie knew the day would come when she'd actually have to model, but this was happening. For real. And earlier than expected. Before her nerves took hold, Cassie replied, "That's a great idea. Really, it is. I'll talk to the team and see if anyone can come with to help out."

"Good," Reid said, looking smug.

"We could do it on the studio roof after Friendsgiving," Cassie said.

"Friendsgiving?"

"Oh," Cassie said, realizing she was thinking out loud. "We do a Friendsgiving event at the studio with the whole team, friends, some of our best clients. It's low-key and we take care of everything when it comes to food."

"Sounds festive."

"It is, actually," Cassie said. She picked at the cardboard sleeve around her coffee cup, and Reid looked out the window next to them. "Do you want to come?"

"Are you inviting me?"

"Well, we are—how did you put it? Colleagues, right?" Cassie wanted a sinkhole to swallow her whole. How awkward could things get? "You could bring James, too, if you even want to come."

Cassie had thought a lot about what they had talked about at Simone's. She hadn't expected to have that conversation with Reid, nor did she think he'd actually admit to not understanding where she was coming from when it came to professionalism. Reid struck her as the type of person who didn't want to readily acknowledge his faults, so the way their conversation progressed—handholding notwithstanding—made Cassie think there was more to Reid than his flashy photography style and cute butt. Friendsgiving could give them another opportunity to get to know each other better, and hopefully ease the nervousness she felt around him.

"Really?" he asked, not hiding a pretty goofy smile.

"Yes, really, Reid," she said, hating that she sounded annoyed, but she was a little bit. She wasn't about to beg him to attend a nice event at her expense. "Four p.m. at the BB studio, Friday after next."

"Can we do the shoot that Thursday, instead of after it?" Reid asked. "I'm helping out my brother with some stuff, and we both have some time off before the holidays ramp up for everyone."

Cassie hadn't heard Reid mention a brother before. Her plan of getting to know him better before their photo shoot was thwarted, but she decided to go with it. "Sure. But knowing Chicago weather, it'll be thirty degrees at that point."

A week later, on a positively balmy day, Cassie and the BB team had brought their studio out to the roof. Drawing inspiration from the initial photo shoot she had done with LL, the roof was a great starting point.

Cassie was sitting in a tall director's chair while Kit did her makeup. While she worked, Cassie studied her friend, who was wearing head-to-toe lavender. Kit performed cosmetic magic on clients and models alike and made everyone feel welcome with her light and airy demeanor.

Sam, outfitted in all black and her favorite combat boots, was organizing a clothing rack of samples from the Dreamland line, her trusty clipboard with the schedule on it nearby. She was a typical twentysomething and acted like she had much better things to be doing than working at a cool photography studio.

Cassie was grateful to have them both there. She had been on pins and needles all morning. The rooftop had a partial view of the Chicago skyline as a superb backdrop, and there were fewer prying eyes way up high instead of out in a park. Cassie knew her preferred locations would work well, even if they had to rent out a space or pay for designated time to have a location, but that didn't mean they could block people from going about their usual business or watching what was going on. At least up on the rooftop, they could put up a sign on the door that deterred the other tenants from coming out there.

Kit perfected another one of Cassie's spiral curls while Cassie herself touched up her blush.

"You look unbelievable, my sweet," Kit said in her singsong voice. "And this weather! Seventy-two degrees in November. What are the odds?"

"Um, thank global warming and then consider your carbon footprint." Sam's voice floated over from somewhere behind a rack of Dreamland samples.

"This is crazy, right?" Cassie said, peeking at herself in Kit's mirror one more time. "It's so weird. Usually it's Dana sitting here naked under a robe—"

"But it's not Dana, it's you, Cassie darling. You are going to bring Dreamland to life! Fantasy to reality," Kit said. "It's going to be glorious. You will be glorious, like this glorious morning."

"Say *glorious* again," Sam said. Tucking her dark hair behind her ear, she continued. "She's right, though. You'll be great or something."

"Samantha, was that an actual word of encouragement?" Kit said.

They were all chuckling when the rooftop door opened and Reid walked out. Cassie suddenly sat up straight, painfully aware that she wasn't wearing anything aside from a silk robe and flip-flops. Thank God her hair and makeup were already done; hopefully the blushing was kept to a minimum.

"Good morning, ladies," he said casually, surveying the space. "This weather, right?"

"Glorious," Kit responded, winking at Sam. "And our gorgeous girl is here, too. Sam, what's up first?"

Sam flipped through her clipboard to a specific page. "Caution tape plus sheer robe, followed by the pink nightie, and then white lace romper. Three should be good for today, since it's a pre-shoot and all."

Cassie stood up and instantly felt more exposed but attempted to appear collected.

"I'll get the first outfit on, then."

Reid nodded in agreement and started unloading his equipment. Kit had lugged up a privacy tent that they had used at outdoor photo shoots so Cassie could comfortably change. Before she zipped the "door" shut, she looked at the scene. Kit was organizing her makeup, making sure she had touch-up materials at the ready, Sam was sweeping the floor where Cassie planned on standing, and Reid was . . . well, he was looking right at her. He looked serious, and maybe a little nervous, too.

They hadn't spoken or texted much since she asked him to Friendsgiving, and they definitely hadn't discussed their talk or the handholding before that. And as much as she wanted to avoid it, she was still nervous. She was about to model, in sexy lingerie, outside, in front of this hot guy who was making a point to be nice to her about everything. She had tried to explain this conundrum to Dana, but Dana just laughed and told her to enjoy the moment. Some help she had been.

Cassie snapped out of her thoughts and quickly zipped the tent shut. She poured herself into the caution tape bra and panty set and laughed at the filmy sheer black robe that complemented the black tulle-lined bra cups. She took a deep breath and was about to walk out—in front of *him*, in her *underwear*—when her phone buzzed twice in quick succession.

The first text was from Dana: Good luck my glamorous goddess! A glorious day for a photo shoot! Cassie smiled—of course Dana used the word *glorious*. Cassie typed in a quick thank-you and the sunglasses emoji before moving on.

The second was from, of all people, Reid:

REID

Is Sam always like this?

He included a candid, blurry photo of Sam literally scowling at him.

CASSIE

Yes.

REID

Are you ready? We're ready when you are. It's going to be . . .

CASSIE

If you say glorious, I'm staying in this tent forever.

REID

Great. I was going to say great.

CASSIE

I'm nervous.

Cassie hesitated in that small dim tent, which was ridiculous because Reid was probably thirty feet away from her at most. Admitting vulnerabilities to someone via text when they were close enough to talk in person was unsettling. Then she heard footsteps.

"Cassie love? My darling, beautiful woman, are you ready?" Kit called. "We can't wait to see you. We can also leave if you need us to. Just let me know, all right?"

Cassie took another deep breath, squared her shoulders, and opened the flap. She let her eyes adjust to the bright sunshine, but she soon saw Kit's stunned face, mouth agape.

"What? Did I mess up my hair?"

"Shit, *Cassie*," Sam said, her face in a similar state of shock. "Why the hell have you been hiding all this time?"

Cassie playfully pushed Sam away from her and walked closer to the scene of the crime—ahem, photo shoot—where Reid stood adjusting his tripod. She cleared her throat. He turned around and nearly dropped his camera.

Reid could barely process what was happening. Was it Thursday or last Monday? Or maybe he was dead. He felt dead. He couldn't move. But he had to save his camera from falling in what felt like slow motion.

Sure, he'd let himself imagine what Cassie would look like in Dreamland's signature caution tape lingerie, but his fantasies didn't compare to the real deal. Cassie looked incredible. Cute and sexy and undeniably dangerous.

He, of course, was staring. And from the looks on the three women in front of him, none of them appreciated it very much.

"Cassie, you're a bombshell," the British one said. Kit—right—he reminded himself. He remembered which one was Sam because he'd nicknamed her "Sam the Sourpuss" after meeting her one time. Maybe by concentrating on other things, he would be able to keep certain things down, for lack of a better term.

"So, we should start," Cassie said. After all, she was the art director and she was in control. "Shall we?"

"Yeah, uh, yes, let's. Please," he sputtered. *Get it together, Reid. If you're nervous, she'll be more nervous.* "Let me do a few test shots, so just stand here."

Through the viewfinder of his camera, he could stare at Cassie for long periods of time without it seeming too creepy. He zoomed in on her face, which, with exaggerated eyeliner and orangey-red lipstick, was still Cassie's face. He checked the digital picture screen and said, "There's a pretty big shadow coming across, should we move? The space is more open on this end."

"No, I want the shadows. This is Dreamland, remember? Things shouldn't be perfect," she replied, moving her stance a bit. He then noticed she'd put on Sam's combat boots and unlaced them. It was just the exact amount of quirkiness Cassie had spent the last month trying to explain to him.

"You got it, boss," Reid replied, making Cassie smile a real smile. He pressed the shutter, hoping he got it. Her smile could stop traffic, start bar fights, and end arguments. And he couldn't get enough of it.

He started moving around, and Cassie shifted, too. She never quite looked at the camera, and Reid couldn't tell if that was on purpose or because she was avoiding his gaze when he looked up at her from behind the camera.

"Move your arms a bit," he suggested gently. He knew he wasn't in charge, but she had barely done anything aside from shift from foot to foot. "Maybe put them at weird angles . . . to take us to Dreamland, right?"

Cassie nodded and stuck one arm out at a right angle. It was weird, but it worked. "What if I pull my hair like this?"

"Keep going," he encouraged, hitting the shutter in rapid succession. "Now, hands on your hips, exactly. Hold that pose."

She had gone rag doll limp, hands on her hips, knees slightly bent. Her ample bosom threatened to pop out, but the look was there. Strange, not quite right, but sexy as hell, and just plain cool.

"Sam, give her your sunglasses," Reid ordered. Sam went to Cassie and placed her black mirror aviators carefully on her. Kit pranced over to fluff Cassie's hair and added something shimmery to the apples of her cheeks, as well as on her shoulders and collarbone.

"Reid, this is gorgeous," Kit said. "She's luminous."

They continued on for a few more minutes, and then Cassie called time for a break. Sam handed her the robe from earlier, and Kit passed her a water. They both went inside to the studio, and Cassie sat down in the chair where she had her makeup done earlier.

"That was . . ." Cassie said. "That was . . ."

"You're a natural," Reid said as he entered, perching on the table full of cosmetics next to her. "That was inspiring."

"You directed me," she said quietly. "Maybe I'm not cut out to do both."

Reid scooted closer to her. "You are doing it, though. It's hard work, but you're doing it. And yeah, I suggested a few poses and asked for a prop, but that's what a good photographer does. You would have done the same thing if it was me up there in front of the skyline."

"We could make that happen. That pink nightie would complement your blushing cheeks," she said. "Speaking of which, I better go change."

But before she could wander off back to the privacy tent, Reid reached out and caught Cassie's hand, pulling her back toward him. His other hand instinctually reached for the small of her back, but Cassie pulled away. She kept her distance but held his gaze. Neither of them said anything, but somehow, they didn't need to speak. He was close enough to notice the swell of her chest, quickly rising and falling with every breath she took, and he felt his own heart pounding as well.

"Friends, we found Dana's stash of chocolate—" Kit said as she walked through the roof door, with Sam right behind her. Reid and Cassie jumped farther apart. "Oh, you know, I think we left something inside . . ."

"I'm going to change, give me two minutes," Cassie called out, walking back to her tent, avoiding Reid's gaze, and to convince her friends—and likely herself—that they hadn't seen anything happening. "Let's pin my hair up for these next two, I think it'll work better."

Well, that was interesting, Reid said to himself. *Very interesting.*

SIX

After basking in the glow of feeling like a *model* for most of the previous day, Cassie switched gears back into the CEO of Buxom Boudoir for their annual Friendsgiving celebration. She, Kit, and Sam had spent the morning transforming the loft into an autumnal wonderland, with little hints of Christmas and Hanukkah sprinkled throughout, as well as some naughty details. Among the gourds and maize in the Thanksgiving cornucopia on the table, there was a dreidel, a Black Santa Claus ornament, and fuzzy handcuffs. Sam was putting the finishing touches on her evergreen branch and riding crop garland across the long stretch of windows, Kit was spreading glitter like it was her job (which it was), and Cassie was arranging the final place settings—complete with napkin rings made out of caution tape—when Dana and Riki came in.

"We three have arrived," Dana announced. They had received permission from her doctor that, as long as she stayed sitting with her feet elevated, Dana could attend the party. They had to use the freight elevator that was normally reserved for deliveries in the four-story walk-up, but Cassie was so excited to have Dana at BB's social event of the year. Dana was shimmering in a champagne body-con dress that hugged every curve. Cassie noted the slim black belt positioned above where her baby bump would eventually appear. Dana wasn't quite showing yet, but Cassie thought the effect was cute nonetheless. She grabbed a bag from Riki, who was sweating from hauling in supplies but was also beaming at her wife.

Cassie set out the postcard flyers that were in the bag on each place setting, advertising the upcoming season's specials: couples boudoir sessions, gift cards, and more. Then she saw a stack of flyers that she had not approved: COMING THIS SPRING: DREAMLAND BY DANA HAYES, A LUSCIOUS LINGERIE COLLABORATION, STARRING OUR VERY OWN CASSANDRA HARRIS.

Well, shit just got real. Sure, the announcement was only going out to a select group of loyal customers and Chicagoland pinup enthusiasts, but aside from the marketing and advertising departments at LL, the Buxom Boudoir team, and Reid, Cassie doubted anyone else knew about her modeling debut. She hadn't even told her parents, and she talked to her mom multiple times a day.

"Guess what Reid sent to me this very morning?" Dana said, beckoning Cassie over to where she was sitting, scrolling on an iPad. "Would you like to see?"

Cassie knew what she was talking about because he had shared the proofs with her as well. And they looked good. Her vision was coming to life, the dreamy landscape, the bright sunshine bouncing off her brown skin, her body contorted into classic pinup poses but ever so slightly off-kilter. The photos where Reid suggested Cassie wear Sam's aviators also turned out great.

"Cassie, you look incredible! You're a star," Kit said, waving Sam over to look, too.

"I especially like this one," Sam said, pointing to an outtake that

Reid must have accidentally left in the folder. Cassie studied the photo, wondering what she was looking at. She looked . . . hungry. There was a determination in Cassie's eyes that was both empowering and a little scary. She definitely could relate that feeling to food, but they'd had salads for lunch that day, and no matter how good that salad might have been, she'd never look at lettuce like that. Then she realized it, the gaze was slightly above the sightline of where the camera lens would have been.

She had been looking at Reid.

Cassie glared at Sam, whose lips slowly upturned into an unsettling smile like the Cheshire cat's. She was practically giddy.

"Yes, there are quite a few with a similar expression, Cassie love. It's your Blue Steel," Kit said, sharing a coy side glance with Sam.

Cassie had to admit that they did have a point. And like she'd told Dana, it had been a while since she had noticed anyone like she'd been noticing Reid. But how on earth could she ever have a crush on a stupid boy who was stealing her first major ad campaign right from under her?

Except he wasn't stupid. Reid had been helpful throughout the process so far. And she enjoyed scouting locations and going to lunch or dinner with him after. His calm demeanor helped her through the first photo shoot, and that was just some practice shots—those weren't even the real deal yet. They just wanted to get everyone on the same page, and Cassie wondered if it had worked out almost too well.

"Did Cassie tell you she invited him to our party?" Dana, not one to miss a beat, jumped on the moment to gossip with the girls. "And he said *yes*."

Kit erupted into squeals, Sam raised her hand to give Cassie a high five (which she reluctantly gave), and Riki let out a wolf whistle as she headed to the makeshift bar where she was going to be mixing cocktails all evening.

While at the moment she was annoyed they were making fun of her for noticing a hot guy, it was nice for Cassie to have the support of her friends through the entire modeling process thus far. She always had Dana, but it took a long time for Cassie to trust anyone else enough to let them in. She had worked solo for so long—her parents raised her to be independent and hardworking, just like they were. She was an only child, so she never had to share, and she was good at being on her own. Cassie gravitated toward photography because it didn't matter if there was just a model or sometimes an entire crew of people involved in a photo shoot, but as the photographer, she was the one calling the shots. Even when she wasn't the art director, or she had a demanding client, Cassie was the eye behind the camera, making someone or something look good.

But this was nice, too. A group of women whom she liked working with and loved talking to, day in and day out. They were all different, and in the beginning, Cassie thought she'd only relate to Kit and Sam through work. But Kit loved baking almost as much as Cassie did, so they were constantly sharing recipes and had a semi-regular baking night at one of their apartments each month. Sam watched TV at almost a professional level and was always ready to binge-watch the latest prestige drama or quirky comedy with Cassie on a random night off work. And Dana, of course, was always there to encourage Cassie into a new direction—moving to Chicago after college, starting Buxom Boudoir together, and now, modeling in a major ad campaign.

She hated using terms that she knew would eventually become blithely anachronistic, but they were her squad. And she wouldn't know what to do without them.

"My lingerie looks insane on you," Dana said, bringing Cassie back from her daydreams. "It looks so good. You look awesome!" Dana gave Cassie one of her all-consuming hugs, and when they finally pulled apart, Cassie noticed Dana was wiping tears from her eyes.

"Don't worry, it's hormones," Riki called from behind the bar, laughing.

Cassie and Dana laughed, too.

"Can't I just be excited for my best friend? I got her into this modeling thing. I'm your agent! I'm going to start making inquiries on your behalf!" Dana yelled, laughing at herself. She nestled back on the couch near the front door, her throne for the evening.

"After this, I'm going into early retirement," Cassie said, taking the excess caution tape back to storage. She heard the buzzer go off—probably the caterers they hired for the night, coming to set up their pre-Thanksgiving buffet. Turkey sliders, butternut squash stuffing, truffle mac and cheese, a giant harvest salad, and much more. Kit had baked no fewer than three pies, Cassie had made two types of chocolate chip cookies and a cake, and Sam had surprised everyone by bringing cupcakes. They all suspected her mom actually made them, but they looked delicious either way. And Dana and Riki provided the libations. It was the start to what would hopefully be a wonderful evening.

"We have to walk up how many flights?" James asked as he clapped Reid on the back. Reid had been waiting outside of the Buxom loft for his friend to arrive. While he waited, he surveyed the rest of the partygoers as they walked in. He recognized a few influencer types he'd worked with in the past, as well as some local artists. The rest of the lot must have been clients. A lot of them greeted each other warmly, like they were all old friends.

Since they had shared that moment on the rooftop the day before, aside from sharing some of the photos from their test session, Reid had left Cassie alone. Mostly because he didn't want to scare her off, but also because he wasn't sure he knew where things were going between them. The tension between them was there, and he wanted to explore that more—it was written all over her face in the outtakes of the shoot. He liked to continue to take photos during breaks, and he did it without looking through the viewfinder of his camera. He did some of his best work this way, not that he showed this work with anyone, aside from clients who wanted every single shot. He'd post them from time to time on social media, but mostly they just lived in a folder on his computer labeled "Favorites."

And now, that folder was full of shots of Cassie. In lingerie, in the middle of November, tawny skin glowing in the bright midday sun. Was it weird? Probably. But she was hot.

And beyond the perfectly coiffed hair, the shimmery makeup, and the risqué clothes, Reid found he liked hanging out with Cassie. He might have liked walking around Chicago looking at cool locales for future photo shoots more than the actual work and having coffee or sharing a meal with her. She was different from anyone he knew, and he wanted to know her better. This party was a great way to see Cassie in her element and hopefully to steal a few fleeting moments together, to explore that almost kiss again . . .

After the week he'd had with Russ trying to work things out with the house, Reid needed to feel anything other than stressed. They had to squeeze a deal out of Robert, but once the direct deposit from Luscious Lingerie's signing bonus for Reid's "babysitting" went through, their dad had been surprisingly amenable to their proposal—things were moving forward with the sale. The sooner they bought the house and fixed it up, the sooner they could sell it.

In the meantime, Russ had kept his word and was staying at the house, working on leaking pipes, cracked windowsills, and peeling wallpaper. Or whatever one does to fix up houses. Reid hoped Russ was also looking for some kind of job or enrolling at the local community college like he had mentioned, but Reid doubted he'd had much time—his brother had sent Reid numerous photos of piles of floral wallpaper, pristine hardwood hidden under faded carpet, and a crawlspace infested with the most spiders either of them had ever seen.

Though Russ was currently the least of his worries, Reid knew there was potential for that to change. But, in regard to his family, this was the most positive experience he'd had with any of them in the longest time. He had considerably less money, the responsibility of an entire house he would soon own that needed work on every level, and a younger brother he didn't know much about.

Family—*totally* worth it . . .

"Fourth floor, are you kidding?" James said, looking at the building's mailboxes and pressing the buzzer next to the right listing.

"It's the top floor, the penthouse," Reid replied, holding the door open for two women, all dolled up. They both thanked him, but it was James they gave the once-over, smiling.

"Looks like it will be a good night," James said, rubbing his hands together. Reid decided it was because it was particularly brisk outside and not because his friend could be both charismatic and libidinous at the same time.

They walked into the loft, its giant double doors open, jazzy music playing low, twinkle lights creating a soft glow. The space had been completely transformed from a professional photography studio into a cool party space.

"Reid, darling," he heard Dana coo. "Do introduce me to your friend . . ." Reid hung his coat up on the first of a row of coatracks, many of which were already full, and introduced James to Dana, who was holding court on a plush burgundy couch.

"How are you feeling these days?" Reid asked Dana, remembering Cassie's concern over her friend's condition.

"With the second trimester I feel like a new person, but I take it one day at a time." She smiled and rubbed her belly. There was maybe a hint of a bump, and Reid could tell she was thrilled by the prospect of having a baby.

James immediately gravitated toward the makeshift bar, where he warmly greeted Riki. Reid assumed they knew each other from being in the restaurant business in the same neighborhood. He continued his survey of the room, exchanging pleasantries with people he knew. For the most part, though, Reid didn't know most of the people there, and he found it a bit unnerving. Almost as unnerving as he felt having not seen Cassie yet.

And then, there she was. She was at one end of the bar, attempting to grab three glasses of champagne, but she was struggling. Reid saw this as an opportunity to look like the great, helpful guy, but Sam beat him to it. Cassie did give him a glance, nodding in his direction and raising an eyebrow.

"What's good, Romeo?" he heard as he approached the bar a few moments too late. Riki was armed with two of her signature manhattans, the unofficial-official drink of Bugles, which she pushed in his direction. "Our lady looks thirsty."

So, apparently, they were all aware that something was brewing between himself and Cassie. Kit and Sam *had* caught them standing closer than they perhaps should have been at a professional photo shoot, and Reid had wondered what could have happened if they had been totally alone, or if something like that had taken place when they were wandering around the city. He picked up the manhattans and went to look for Cassie again. He saw her from across the room, wearing a bright pink skirt and black sweater that was short enough to see a bit of her midriff if she lifted her arms, with the highest patent leather platform oxfords he'd ever seen—oxblood red no less. She should wear those during their next shoot, whether they matched the lingerie or not. They looked like something Alice would have worn once she fell through the rabbit hole.

Reid attempted to walk casually over to the group of people Cassie was with, sharing champagne and laughing. He recognized the two women he held the door open for on the way up and smiled at them. Another woman he didn't recognize was talking.

"And somehow, you made my ass look like it did fifteen years ago, when I was still in college and had zero cellulite. I swear you added a filter or Photoshop or something."

"I'm telling you, Barb, it's the lighting. I can't control the sunshine," Cassie said, making the group laugh. "Within reason, of course. Plus, we can all agree you've got a banging bod."

Within the lull of the conversation, Reid took the opportunity to shuffle around and position himself next to Cassie. He nudged her side, which made Cassie jump, and handed her a manhattan. "Compliments of the barkeep."

"It's an open bar that I paid for," she said. "But thank you."

"You look gorgeous," he said. He couldn't contain himself.

"You're just saying that because you've seen me mostly naked."

"To mostly naked, then," Reid replied, raising his own drink, which made Cassie smile and laugh as they clinked their glasses.

After they took sips of their drinks, Cassie asked, "How are you today?"

"Great, nothing to complain about, considering the photos I've been looking at since yesterday. And you?"

Cassie ignored Reid's compliment and answered she was keeping busy with new clients and getting ready for the party. For some reason, she was refusing to get any more personal than the professional standpoint of their interactions, so he kept it that way, too.

"What do you think of the Humboldt Park pergolas for the next shoot? The white teddy with the shoes you're wearing right now would be just the right amount of unhinged."

Cassie nodded in agreement, taking another swig of her manhattan. "Actually, I was thinking about the cheeky underpants, the sheer plaid and leopard prints? We could do those in Humboldt, but maybe one of the murals we looked at in Wicker Park would work, too."

She still wouldn't face him directly, or look him in the eye, so he moved a fraction closer, and angled his body toward hers. He followed her line of sight—she was watching her friends. Kit was in a deep conversation with James, not surprising to Reid whatsoever. Tiny and blond was his type. Sam was attempting to steal a bottle of whiskey from the bar, which Dana saw and was yelling "Oi!" at her wife, but Riki was otherwise engaged, throwing a cocktail shaker over her shoulder before pouring a dark brown libation into a highball glass.

"Come with me," he said. They had to have a few more minutes of passed hors d'oeuvres before the sit-down dinner started. He took Cassie's free hand and led her through the crowd of adoring clients and friends.

Holding her hand felt natural as they walked to a quiet corner. There was a privacy partition, shielding who knew what from the rest of the guests. Probably a mountain of Dana's intricate attire or possibly tripods and light reflectors, but Reid didn't really care. He chose this corner because it was small and it would put Cassie next to him, similar to how they were on the rooftop the day before. He had a sudden need to be near her, where they didn't have to think about anything or anyone else. Perhaps the middle of a holiday party wasn't an ideal setting, but the lighting was dim and seductive, and the mood just felt right—away from everyone else, a stolen moment together.

"This party is great," he said, breaking the awkward silence.

"You really think so?" she said with such earnestness, he almost thought she was joking. But Reid looked at her and saw she meant it and was looking for reassurance.

"It's an awesome idea, and must be why you have such a loyal following in this city."

Cassie gave him a warm smile and moved a tiny bit closer to him. He noticed she kept gazing up above her head, and then he saw it . . . something that looked like mistletoe was hanging above them, but it wasn't quite right.

"Are those . . . condoms?"

"Green latex pasties, actually," Cassie answered matter-of-factly. "And leftover blood capsules from our Halloween boudoir shoots, fashioned to look like mistletoe."

Reid looked around the room and saw that someone had placed the makeshift mistletoe throughout the loft. He caught the eye of

Kit, who smiled at him and turned back to James, who was telling a very animated story.

"Did you notice the handcuffs in the cornucopia?" Cassie asked, avoiding his gaze. She was staring at her feet, or maybe his. It didn't matter, because they were under the mistletoe and there were rules to be followed. She bit her lip, as though a Pavlovian response was even necessary at this point. They were still holding hands.

The room grew quiet, or at least it felt that way, and Reid nudged Cassie's chin to face him instead of looking away. He licked his lips, and she finally looked him in the eye before closing hers.

When their lips met, she was all softness and light, everything he wanted to capture on his camera. Her hands met his body with warmth and curiosity—one went to his chest, and the other balled at his waist. Reid had a hand at her cheek and another at the small of her back. He didn't want to seem possessive, but all he could feel was *Mine.*

They both lingered in this first kiss, sweet and unsure. He blinked with his eyes closed, unable to break the spell of this beginning, because he knew for certain that this wouldn't be the last time he kissed Cassandra Harris. He felt her start to pull away . . . it could have been nanoseconds or minutes, he wasn't sure. But his hand at her back kept her close, and their kiss deepened, a moment too long, their tongues meeting for a fleeting second before Cassie pulled away. Her eyes were hazy, that eyebrow raised just as sharply as the bulge in his pants did, but Cassie stayed close to him, and for one fleeting moment, she sighed and dipped her forehead to his shoulder.

"This is . . ." she started.

"Great," he finished.

She looked at him with heavy-lidded eyes. "Yeah, great," she huskily agreed, picking up and taking a drink from her manhattan she had apparently set down on yet another corner credenza. Their foreheads met, and they stayed that way for a moment.

"You two are so gross," Sam said, passing by. She grabbed a riding crop from her evergreen garland and dragged it across them both, moving swiftly on.

"She is so weird," Reid said.

Cassie laughed again, making him feel triumphant.

"She's the best," Cassie said. "They're all the best. This night is the best." She ran her hand up to Reid's shoulder, leaving a trail of lightning along his chest.

With that, she scurried away, but not before turning back to him and giving him a genuine Cassandra Harris smile, the smile Reid had been chasing since he first saw her.

That corner of the loft would forever be the place where it happened.

Cassie was positive everyone in the room saw her kiss Reid.

And it was *good*.

She felt that kiss from the top of her victory rolls to the bottom of her platform shoes. Her toes tingled as she double-checked the chafing dishes were warmed and fully fueled before clanging a spoon against her cocktail glass.

"Thanks to everyone for coming out tonight. We're so pleased to have done business with you over the last year," she began. "I want to commend my fellow Buxom buddies for transforming our studio into a holiday oasis. Stay tuned for big things to come for all of us this next year. And please book your next photo shoot with Sam . . .

she's technically on the clock." This garnered laughs from the crowd and a truly terrifying scowl from Sam herself.

"Dinner is served, mes chers!" Dana called out, raising her glass. A hearty round of *Hear! Hear!* and huzzahs followed, and a line formed in front of the bountiful Friendsgiving buffet.

Cassie lifted her manhattan to her lips, the same lips that had just locked with Reid Montgomery's lips. The thought raced through her mind, making her giggle to herself.

"What's happening between you and Reid?" Kit innocently asked, about an octave too high.

"What's happening between you and James?" Cassie fired back.

"Well, he is gorgeous and very attentive," Kit answered, clinking her glass with Cassie's. "You didn't answer my question."

"I know," Cassie said. She watched Reid, in his slim jeans and formfitting button-down shirt, walk right past everything in the buffet line and make a beeline for the cookies she had made. He took a bite of the classic chocolate chip, closed his eyes as he chewed, and found her gaze. And winked.

The cheek of this man.

The party was in full swing, and almost everyone was seated at one of two extra-long tables they had rented. The communal-table setup made it easy for Cassie to keep moving around. She'd make a point to pour more wine and offer to take specialty drink orders to Riki before she stole a bite of a turkey slider or a forkful of mac and cheese.

Her clients blew her kisses, her friends grabbed her hands as she walked by, and Cassie actually felt at ease after the delectable moment she had with Reid moments before making her speech.

Was it okay to make out with her photographer? Probably not. Was it okay to make out with the person she was technically in charge of during the photo shoots? Nope. But did it make her feel good as hell? Definitely yes.

While she waited for Riki to finish up a round of drinks, Cassie watched Reid interact with the room. He had taken two of her cookies in addition to the one he currently ate. He sat down next to James, who was more interested in talking to Kit on his other side, but Reid stayed perched on his seat, glancing in Cassie's direction. She pulled out her phone from the blessedly deep pockets in her skirt and snapped a wide angle shot to post to Buxom's Instagram. The limited guest list, naughty backdrops of whips and blindfolds combined with holiday decor, and the open bar made Friendsgiving an exclusive event among the artistic set in the city. She'd have to remember to post a shot later—the haze from the low lighting, the decadent display of food, and the gorgeousness of their clientele made the scene in front of Cassie all the more enticing. As she scrolled through the photos she just took, she felt Reid's warmth come up beside her.

"I'll have to approve any photos of me before you post them to social media," he murmured in her ear.

"Don't you remember? You work for me," Cassie said. "I'm the art director, so I'm in charge."

"What did you have in mind?" he asked.

"What are your thoughts on your leather jacket?"

"The same that you made me pose in within hours of our first encounter?"

"We'd met a few times before that, you just didn't remember me."

"There's no way I'd forget meeting you," Reid said, closing the gap between them.

"Are you so sure about that?" Cassie said, turning her cheek before he could lean in for another kiss. "You think we hadn't met before last month?"

Reid searched Cassie's face, which was smart on his part. "I don't recall," he said quietly. The rest of the room was loud with merriment—strong cocktails, savory food, and sweet desserts occupied everyone else.

"We have met before, you said so yourself at the LL test shoot where Rebecca 'introduced' us. I'm glad to see that I left a lasting impression." Cassie felt her shoulders haunch, and she immediately crossed her arms.

"Cassie, that's not fair," Reid said, his hand protectively at her elbow. "I'm—"

"Don't apologize for something you don't remember," she said.

"I don't know what to say," he said. "I just know that I want to go back to that corner with the blood mistletoe again. I won't forget that, that's for sure."

Cassie couldn't help herself from smiling. She handed the drinks from Riki over to Sam, and this time, she took Reid's hand and led him back to the corner where they had recently been. The rush she'd felt after that first kiss had been the most real thing she'd felt since the photo shoot. The days leading up to the test shots, Cassie had been numb with anxiety, unsure of what exactly to do and how far she needed to push, not just herself but everyone on the set that day, Reid included. Cassie was glad Kit and Sam had been there, because by the end of that first break, the one where they were close to doing something rash . . . like making out . . . Cassie was running on adrenaline. She just wanted to get through the rest of the photos and return to her normal place in the BB studio, behind the camera instead of in front of it. But then, the blur of the rest of that afternoon on the roof, some wardrobe and hairstyle changes later, Cassie felt so much more at ease, and not just with starring in a major lingerie campaign but working with Reid. What could have happened if they hadn't been discovered by Kit and Sam? She didn't want to ruin this job, but she also couldn't stop thinking about what might have gone down if they'd had a few more moments alone . . .

Which led them to this dark corner of the studio, strategically placed mistletoe and all.

Reaching the almost-secluded corner and without faltering a beat, Cassie pulled Reid down to her mouth and did nothing short of devouring him like everyone else was enjoying dinner. The dim lights gave them a bit of privacy, though Cassie knew her friends were well aware of what was going on. She was bolder than before, opening her mouth, allowing him full access to give her a kiss she'd never forget. Cassie's fingers toyed with his shirttails, while Reid's hands gravitated toward the waistband of her pink velvet skirt as he gently pulled her closer.

When they parted ways to take a breath, Cassie nestled into Reid's shoulder. Kiss number two might have been more memorable than kiss number one. She plastered herself against him, and while what they did during business hours was professional, Reid had a pretty good idea of what Cassie had going on underneath her relatively innocent outfit. Lace was involved, and probably garters, and those very high platform shoes that did things to his brain that made him obsessed with the sight of Cassie's calves.

"I have to go back," Cassie said, breaking away from him.

"Don't go," he pleaded a little too willingly. "Stay in our dark corner."

Their foreheads met, for a moment, before she looked up at him. "Wait for me?" she asked. "I can't shirk my responsibilities because a handsome man kissed me senseless. But I may be able to leave sooner than later."

She stepped away a pace or two, but he pulled her back.

"I'll wait," he basically growled into her neck.

Cassie started to walk away but gave him a small grin over her shoulder.

In that moment, Reid was a goner. Which, considering the way they had met and butted heads since, made no sense. But the coy smile, the empowered walk, the confidence and happiness that emanated from Cassie, made him feel weak in the best way possible. The last time he felt that way, Reid had been too young and too stubborn to realize it was a good thing.

"Cassie," he called out, a little too loudly because the entire table near the bar looked up at him.

Cassie looked at him over her shoulder as she took a tray of drinks to the table and kept walking. She was working after all. Reid walked back to his seat next to James, who rested an elbow on Reid's shoulder. James was watching Kit, who had gone to help Cassie hand out the tray of drinks and grab another bottle of wine to pour. Sam quickly followed them with a pitcher of water. They all stopped and chatted with Dana, who was laughing uncontrollably at Riki.

"This is a dynamic group of women," James said. He turned back to his plate of food.

Reid still had only eaten a few of the cookies Cassie had made, so he stood up to see what was left at the buffet.

Before he could get in line, James said, "Be careful with her, mate."

"What do you mean by that?" Reid said, defenses at the ready. "I like her. A lot."

"Yeah, but she's in charge of your job. Don't fuck it up. You'd be messing with her career, and she'd never forgive you. And you'd have all of them to deal with, too." James motioned to the entire Buxom Boudoir crew still laughing together over something. Cassie stole a glance at him a few times, making his pulse quicken.

"Well, take the same advice yourself," Reid said. "I also work with Kit. I don't want it to be awkward. And you know how you can be."

James was suave to a fault; women couldn't resist him, and Reid was always impressed with the number of names and dates and specificities James could remember when it came to his sex life. While Reid had had his fair share of casual encounters, the tenacity with which James operated was impressive. But James made a good point. What *was* Reid doing with Cassie at this moment? Kissing her in a room full of people—her clients—without a care in the world? Not to mention, he probably had an email from Rebecca Barstow in his in-box, asking to explain in greater detail what problems he foresaw working with Cassie and the BB team. He hadn't felt great about this from the start, and especially now that it took up space in the back of his mind whenever he looked at Cassie, be it in person or in the photos on his camera.

"Reid, be a dear and go see if Cassie needs help with the cake," Kit said, sitting back down next to James, who instantly turned toward her and away from Reid.

"Wait, there's more food?" James said, giving Kit an enthusiastic high five. This made her giggle more, and Reid shook his head at his friend. James gave him a stiff nod and motioned for him to leave.

Reid walked by the corner he wanted to get back to with Cassie, but, like James reminded him, this party wasn't about finding reasons to take Cassie away from her clients and obligations. He walked over toward the bar and heard Dana's loud cackle.

"Behold, the pièce de résistance!" she proclaimed as he walked over. Cassie was circling around a three-tiered monstrosity that smelled incredible and looked delicious.

"Cassie, you made this?" he said, actually in awe.

There were layers of fluffy white frosting with drips of some kind of sauce that was bloodred, and little chocolate trees on the top, flecked with silver and gold.

"It's a masterpiece." He gave her the highest compliment he knew how to give and brought out his phone to take a few photos.

Cassie's cheeks were pink, but he couldn't tell if it was because of him complimenting her or if it was because she was overheated or overwhelmed. Or all three. "Would you help me carry this out?" she asked him.

They both took a side of the massive tray holding the cake, while Riki lit a sparkler on the very top of the cake.

Dana, from her corner chaise, had put on a Santa hat and started singing "Santa Claus Is Comin' to Town." A little corny and on the nose, but even Sam joined in the carol. Although Thanksgiving was still nearly a week away, everyone was getting into the holiday spirit. Reid looked at Cassie, who wasn't singing but was smiling at him nonetheless.

"Thanks for this," she said, but before he could respond, she started walking, and for the sake of her gorgeous cake, he had to follow suit.

The crowd of beloved Buxom Boudoir clients and industry friends all cheered when the cake came around the corner, and the singing continued. Cassie and Riki started cutting into the cake, and Reid took more photos of the merriment. Maybe they could use them for their website or something, he wasn't sure. He just knew in this moment he should actually be helpful and not pull Cassie away for yet another interlude under the mistletoe.

SEVEN

The cake had been distributed, Riki had announced they were officially out of champagne, and guests were finally starting to make their way out of the loft. Cassie had long since taken off her shoes and was padding around, picking up plates and glasses. Sam had curled up on the couch next to Dana, while Kit, Riki, Cassie, and Reid, who decided to stick around, had started to clean up.

Reid kept trying to find something to pick up near Cassie, which she appreciated and found very cute despite herself. The kisses they shared that evening made her feel both at ease and worked up at the same time. She was happy it finally happened—she'd be lying to herself if she didn't admit that she was at least curious about him, and the man knew how to kiss. But there were a host of other things that her type A mind couldn't stop thinking about. Technically speaking, she was his boss in this work situation for the Dreamland campaign. Not to mention, outside of this project, they often competed for the same jobs around the city.

Then there was the fact that they were so different from each other. On a surface level, he was a hot white guy who commanded the room whether he wanted to or not, and she was a Black woman who worked damn hard just to get someone to acknowledge her. Of course, there were millions of relationships like this and different couplings that made it work—Cassie knew she was getting ahead of herself when it came to that.

Oh, and then there was the fact that he'd already seen her half-naked, and it didn't faze him at all. Though the way Reid had just kissed her in the middle of Friendsgiving dinner made her think perhaps he was as unnerved by her as she was by him . . . And then there was the incident on the roof when they had a few minutes alone, and . . .

Cassie was definitely getting ahead of herself.

"Guy and dolls, let's call it a night," Riki called out. "We can finish up tomorrow. The rental company is coming to pick up the tables and chairs in the afternoon."

Kit and Sam made plans to meet Riki at Bugles, but Cassie yawned and knew she was done for the time being.

"Walk me home?" she boldly asked Reid, surprising herself and everyone else. She saw her friends exchange glances and knew when she came back to finish cleaning the next day, she would be fully interrogated.

"Of course," Reid said.

She'd spent enough time with him to notice the way his shoulders were tight with excitement. They said their goodbyes and grabbed their coats.

Stepping out into the crisp night, Cassie breathed in deeply, feeling the sharp air hit her lungs. She rearranged her comically large blanket scarf and put her hands in her pockets to start the walk to her nearby apartment. Cassie had taken only a few steps when she felt Reid walk closely next to her. It felt electric, feeling him so near.

"So, I feel like I should say you don't have to come up or stay when we get to my place," she started.

"But?"

She laughed a little. "But I'd like you to come up."

He bit his bottom lip as he smiled and nodded and put an arm around her shoulder while they walked, and Cassie relished the warmth he provided.

"You're in luck, I have an elevator," she said, thinking about how everyone always complained about the walk up to the studio's top-floor space.

She leaned against him as the old elevator took its blessedly sweet time up to the top floor. Cassie could see their reflection, distorted by the stainless steel's muted sheen. His arm was still around her. Even warped, they looked good together.

The door opened, and Cassie got off while Reid stood there for a beat, leaning against the back of the elevator.

"I remember," he said, just as the doors started to close.

Luckily Cassie stuck her foot out and caught the doors before they closed completely.

"You remember what?"

"The first time we met. I remember the first time I saw Cassandra Harris."

Cassie felt her own eyebrow raise, as if it instinctively knew to question what Reid was about to say. Before she let him continue, she held out her hand to guide him to her apartment door at the end of the hallway.

Cassie unlocked her door and took a deep breath. Bringing Reid back to her apartment was significant to her, and not just because of what it implied. It had been a while since she'd brought anyone aside from friends or family to her apartment. She liked her place to be just so—tidy, but still lived in. She had picked up funny little habits from her equally meticulous mother, like the way her favorite throw blanket was slightly unfolded, and a neat but rather tall pile of junk mail and takeout menus sat on the kitchen island. There was a coffee cup on her side table, which she actually had meant to put away but it escaped her mind earlier . . .

"Hey," Reid said, as Cassie walked toward the mug. "Come here."

Cassie's apartment was like her—eclectically decorated and just the right amount of askew. Reid especially liked all the windows, and knew Cassie did, too. The older building wasn't that tall, but the ceilings were high, and her view had city scenery—buildings, traffic lights, streetlamps. During the day the entire apartment was probably flooded with light, and he wondered if he was going to get to see that view in the morning.

Cassie walked toward him while he took off his coat and then helped her out of hers.

"This little black shirt has been driving me crazy all night," he said, admittedly a little awkward and not at all smooth.

"Why, because you already know what's going on underneath it?"

Reid chuckled. "Maybe, but really, it's because when you lift your arms," he gently tugged at her arms and raised them around his neck. "I can see a little bit of your skin." His hands went to her slightly exposed waist, playing with the top of her skirt. He bent down close to her face and—

"Weren't you going to tell me something? Something you remembered?" Cassie interrupted. He could tell she was nervous from the way she quickly brought her arms back down and toyed with her fingers. But she also seemed genuinely interested in hearing what he had to say. Earlier he had struck a nerve not immediately remembering their actual first encounter. Reid was almost annoyed with himself for forgetting, because how could he forget someone like Cassie?

She broke away from his embrace and walked to the kitchen, which was huge and open to the rest of the living room. She opened her freezer and took out ice cubes and then grabbed the ingredients to make manhattans. "I'm giving you fair warning, I'm nowhere near as talented as Riki, but I know how to make a decent, basic cocktail. But please, do continue with your story."

Reid leaned on the island, watching her work. She moved briskly and confidently, and she had one of those peelers for the orange garnish. He liked watching her work this way as much he liked watching her work behind and in front of the camera.

"It was two years ago. I think I had been back in Chicago for a couple of years at that point, after I realized I kept taking jobs that brought me home," Reid began. "There was a new gallery opening, where that guy who takes all the nature-city time-lapse photos was showing a bunch of pictures of trees changing. He was a real pretentious weirdo."

Cassie handed Reid his drink, and they clinked glasses. "Go on," she encouraged, keeping her face neutral.

"You were there, and some ad manager who I'd just signed a campaign with introduced me to a group of people, including you,"

Reid said, feeling very proud of himself that he actually remembered.

It was at that same gallery opening that he had been introduced to Rebecca Barstow as well, and his regular gig as a Luscious Lingerie photographer began soon thereafter. He wondered what sort of intel Rebecca would expect from him after the test shoot and the BB party. But he pushed thoughts of all that aside, and he took a drink from his cocktail and looked to see if he had passed Cassie's test.

"Correct," Cassie said, raising her glass in his direction. "Do you want to sit down?"

They moved to her plush couch, setting their drinks on a side table, and Reid fixed a throw blanket that was almost on the floor. Cassie tucked herself into a corner of the couch, and Reid sat down next to her. The instant he took her hand, Cassie was straddling him.

Her pink skirt was pushed up, revealing the all-too-familiar garters Reid had photographed on her the day before. But in the dim apartment, the feel of them under his hands as he pulled her closer made Reid see them in a completely different light.

Cassie's mouth crashed into his, hungry and unsatisfied, and Reid knew that there was nothing stopping them now. He leaned back into the couch, pulling Cassie closer, wrapping his arms around her, hands caressing over every inch of her back, then the soft nape of her neck.

"Cassie," he breathed out. "Do you want to do this?"

She nudged his nose with hers. "Hell yes," she said, smiling. And Reid smiled, too. He moved back, intending to stand them both up so they could start to get undressed, because Reid was itching to see what other Dreamland lingerie Cassie had chosen to wear that night.

But when he stood up, he stumbled and sat back down.

Uncool, Montgomery, he chided, but he tried to laugh it off. But when he attempted to stand up again, he was met with a dizzy spell.

"Reid?" Cassie said, watching him, but also lifting her shirt. A flash of a lacy black bra brought him back to reality.

"Just, um, wait a second," he replied shakily.

"Reid, are you okay?"

"Oh yeah," he said. "Just all of a sudden very, very drunk." He started laughing.

Cassie bit her lip, the very same lip he wanted to be biting, but he soon realized she was holding back her own laughter. "Did you ever eat anything tonight?"

"Your cookies," he said, his laughter starting up again. "I mean your actual cookies, no—not your actual cookies, the cookies you made for your party." And then, he hiccuped.

Cassie's laughter rang out, a glorious sound to his muffled ears. "Oh, Reid, honey," she said, righting her shirt and going back to the kitchen. "Come sit down, and I'll make you dinner."

A bag of microwave popcorn, an undisclosed amount of leftover cookie dough, a shared grilled cheese, and a canister of Pringles later, Reid started to look less peckish and could almost make coherent sentences.

"You're so pretty," he said to Cassie, slumped over the island, his head resting in his hands. He was the living embodiment of the heart-eye emoji. Okay, maybe he was still drunk.

"You're pretty," Cassie replied. "Pretty drunk."

Reid pushed her barely touched manhattan over to her. "You

could catch up." He wiggled his eyebrows at her and started laughing at himself again.

"I can't believe you're still tipsy. I've fed you, made sure you were properly hydrated, and you're still giggling at everything."

"I don't know how you aren't as drunk as me. When did you find time to eat at the party? Every time I turned around you were toasting with someone or passing out drinks. When you weren't making out with me in a dark corner." Reid's smirk widened into a smile.

Cassie sighed, rolled her eyes, and stifled a yawn. She loved the tradition of Friendsgiving at the studio, but with a long day of setup, a fun and satisfying early evening of mingling at the main event, and then enough time to start cleaning up everything, Cassie was rightfully exhausted. And she knew that Kit and Sam were probably at Bugles with a cohort of partygoers while Riki was behind the bar. She was grateful to be somewhere quiet, with a handsome, albeit slightly drunk, man.

"First of all, we had food stashed behind the bar for each of us, so we could eat while replenishing drinks, or between random toasts. Second, most of the drinks I handed out to other people, and three," Cassie said, sauntering past him, "I liked making out with you."

"We could do that again," Reid gently reached her hand as she walked by but ended up awkwardly grabbing her elbow. Cassie still stopped and put a hand to his cheek.

"We could," Cassie said, coming closer. "But you could also make me a cup of coffee while I change into something more comfortable. Think you can handle that?"

She knew telling him she was changing would catch his attention, and had she not spent the last forty-five minutes making sure he was fed and didn't get ill or hurt himself, she would have considered trying on more Dreamland lingerie for him. But as it was, Cassie definitely planned on changing into stuff she could lounge in.

As Cassie made her way down the hall to her room, she could hear Reid puttering around in the kitchen. It might take him a minute to realize everything he needed was right next to her coffee maker on the counter directly across from where he was standing, but it was adorable that he was lost in the small space. Hopefully he didn't break anything in the process.

In her room, Cassie had a decision to make. She wanted, of course, to look cute and a little alluring, but she also wanted to be comfortable. She glanced at the rolling rack of Dreamland lingerie Dana had sent to her, and she felt a smile spread over her face. It had been a while since she had wanted to look sexy in front of someone, and the feeling was nice. Whether or not Reid actually got to see the lacy neon pink bralette and matching sheer boy shorts, Cassie liked the idea of both feeling good and looking good should the opportunity arise. A simple black tee and black leggings would suffice, and Cassie also knew that this particular V-neck had a knack for sliding off her shoulder, thus revealing the bralette, thus leading to certain other things. So she hoped.

Cassie quietly walked back to her kitchen and saw that Reid had indeed figured out where everything was to make her a cup of coffee. He had made one for himself, too, and was sitting on a barstool, looking out her windows. If he heard her come up to him, he didn't show any sign of it. She slipped her hands around his waist and liked that he instantly leaned back into her. She laid her head down on the center of his back and held him tight, feeling his abs constrict as he took in a sharp breath.

"Thanks for the coffee," she said, breathing him in.

"Thanks for taking care of me," he replied. He moved just

enough to let Cassie know he was turning but didn't want to end their embrace. "I'm sort of embarrassed about the whole situation."

"It happens," Cassie said, stopping herself from laughing at him outright. But it was pretty funny that he had gotten drunk so suddenly. "And food helps." She yawned. "So does coffee."

Cassie moved to get her coffee, but Reid only allowed enough room for her to turn around to get it. He kept her firmly between himself and the island. Just as she finished taking a long, comforting swig of caffeine—which actually tasted good, too; Reid could stick around just to make coffee—Cassie felt Reid's hands start to massage her shoulders and then the base of her neck. Firm enough to loosen muscles but still sensual and caressing. A moan escaped from Cassie's mouth.

"I was just about to ask if this felt good," Reid murmured, kissing her neck. Cassie shivered.

"You have no idea," she said, leaning back into him. The massage continued, but Reid kept kissing her neck here and there, and every touch sent chills down her spine. Cassie turned herself around and saw Reid's face—he may have had that sly smirk, but his eyes had gone hazy again, just like they were at the party when she looked at him after their first kiss. So she kissed him again, deeper than before. She couldn't contain herself.

In an instant, Cassie found herself suddenly sitting on her island. In a rush of movement while still kissing her, Reid had lifted her up and now was standing with his hands on her thighs, continuing the massage. Cassie's arms wrapped around his neck, the kiss deepening. Reid moved his hands higher and higher up, and Cassie's legs wrapped around him in response. She was completely entwined around him.

They stayed this way, kissing and touching, caressing and just feeling each other. Without an audience, with the entire night ahead of them, Cassie and Reid knew they could take their time.

Losing herself to just feeling and wanting what felt good, Cassie's kiss became more aggressive. Something like a growl came from Reid—Cassie couldn't tell because they literally had not stopped kissing since he lifted her on the island—and their momentum began to build.

But as the kiss deepened, Cassie started to overthink, unable to stay in the moment. This was how it always went when she met someone new. Things escalated too quickly, too passionately, and then they fizzled out because her libido ebbed and flowed rather than staying at the brazen level of a new relationship, or because of her dedication to work—work she was now forced to share with Reid . . .

"Reid," Cassie said, sounding breathy when she came up from their kiss. "Reid, wait." She unballed the fistful she had of his shirt and unwrapped her legs from around his waist.

"You all right, Cassie?"

Cassie figured if she looked at his face, it'd be frustrated and confused, and he should be, because this night had been full of starts and stops. But she was pleasantly surprised to see that instead of being annoyed, Reid looked concerned.

"Yeah, I just . . ." Cassie trailed off as she continued to slowly, achingly, move out of Reid's embrace. "We work together, Reid. And that's important."

"So is this," he countered, refusing to let her move far away.

"I know, and I want it to be, but I also want to make sure my career continues to grow."

Was that a cop-out? Things started to heat up, and Cassie

backed down. It wasn't the first time she had done this, but in the past, she'd take a step back after she had sex with the guy she was seeing, and he'd be upset by the fact that she wasn't an eager sex goddess 24-7.

Cassie continued her shuffle to the side until she was beside Reid instead of entwined between his legs. She reached for her coffee, now lukewarm but still drinkable and offering the jolt of caffeine that she desired, among other things at the moment.

"All right," Reid finally said. "So we keep things professional."

"Really? After everything that's happened tonight?"

He took a deep breath and nodded. "But maybe . . ."

"I don't know if there can be a 'but maybe' with this."

"Cass, I like you. And I think you like me, too. Enough to make out with onlookers."

Cassie chose this moment to take another drink from her coffee to hide the smile on her face after he shortened her name to Cass. Other people called her that, but coming from Reid, it made her melt.

"What if we agreed that on set, while location scouting, and the entire day before and after we do any sort of work, we don't interact unless it's about the campaign," Reid said.

It was a harebrained idea, but Cassie didn't hate it.

"And beyond that?" she asked.

"Beyond that, we continue to explore what else is going on between us," Reid said confidently, showcasing that smirk Cassie had come to adore. He laced his fingers with hers and brought it up to his chest. "Because there's something, right? You feel it, too?"

All Cassie could do was nod. And then yawn again. "More coffee, please."

"I can go, if you need to get to sleep," Reid said, walking back toward Cassie's coffee maker to dump out the contents and make a fresh pot.

Cassie came up behind him, much like she had a few minutes earlier. "No, I want you to stay, but can we just talk? Or watch a movie? Or stay up all night and watch the sunrise?"

"We can do all of those things, but I guarantee you'll fall asleep."

"Not unless you can think of a way to keep me up."

"I can think of about a million ways to keep you up," Reid said, correcting the shoulder of her T-shirt, Cassie noting that he paused when his fingers grazed the neon-pink lace shoulder strap. Cassie silently thanked her best friend for designing lingerie.

"Do any of these ways include clothing?"

"Some of them," Reid replied. "But I like the idea of staying up all night with you, though, no matter what we are—or aren't—doing."

"We're going to need more snacks," Cassie said, grabbing another bag of popcorn.

Reid felt like an idiot. He knew Cassie understood it wasn't on purpose, but the fact that he was stumble-down drunk in front of her was a huge ding to his ego. Still, as much as he wanted to have sex with Cassie, perhaps it was for the best he didn't. James's warning to not mess things up for her was niggling in the back of his mind, along with the fact that he was keeping tabs on her work while turning up the charm to make Cassie feel at ease—a task given to him by the company that could make or break her and her best friend's careers. Cassie's earlier hesitation to take things to the next level also gave him pause. So he decided to make the most of the night ahead of them and get to know her better, off the record.

Reid thought he had an idea of who Cassie was—a hardworking, creative, and damn good photographer with an eye for details that made him jealous—but this was an opportunity to find out more about the woman he couldn't get enough of. When principal photography began, they would only interact on a professional level, according to their new deal. After a brief pause for the busy holidays, they had a couple of weeks or so of individual shots of Cassie in the key pieces of the Dreamland line before the group photo shoots. They'd be working together consistently over the next few months, until early March at least, and then the official launch of the line at the end of May.

So yeah, with this work timeline and LL's ulterior motives behind his involvement, maybe the boundaries he'd just pulled out of his ass to make Cassie feel at ease were actually a good idea.

But kissing Cassie at Friendsgiving and making out with her in the privacy of her apartment had been a release, like a rush of pent-up emotions he'd bottled up for so long. Between the drama with his brother, his need for this job, and his agreement to play along with LL's concerns, the one thing that had kept him focused and driven during these hectic few weeks was Cassie. She had started out closed off and quiet, but something had changed. Not just at the photo shoot, where their mutual curiosity and attraction had ramped up, but also on their walks around Chicago and when she explained her thought process and ideas for Dreamland. Reid knew he had a job to do, but spending time with Cassie had been something new, something enjoyable, and something he was starting to care about a lot.

"Penny for your thoughts?" Cassie said softly, handing him a warm mug of fresh coffee. After she poured a bit of cream in hers, she handed it to him.

"None for me, thanks," he answered.

The microwave beeped, and as Cassie opened it, the delicious smell of butter and salt wafted to him again. "Salty or sweet snacks?"

"Uh, both?" he replied.

"So if I dump M&M's on this popcorn, you won't be upset?"

"I would be the happiest still slightly drunk man in the world," Reid answered. Was it possible that Cassie was actually perfect?

She grabbed the bowl of the now sweetly salty deliciousness, her coffee, and motioned for him to move back to the couch. Reid noticed now how her couch was situated—centered in front of the window, rather than in front of the TV. This woman took her lighting seriously, more so than binge-watching TV shows.

"How in the world did you score this apartment? The location, the updates to the building . . . I bet it was fully occupied quickly," Reid asked, his nosiness getting the best of him—good real estate in Chicago was no joke.

"Yeah, well, I know the people who own the building," she replied, quickly sipping her coffee. "My parents. They own the building the studio is in, too, and other properties around the city."

"Wait, your parents are GH Management?" Reid knew the name; he had noticed it on a sign outside the studio and had previously seen the same plaque on some of the most coveted rental properties in Chicago.

"Greene-Harris, that's us," Cassie replied. Greene was her mom's maiden name, and Cassie had always liked that her parents had used it as a part of their company's name. "I don't like mentioning it because people assume I'm freeloading off them, but I guarantee you I'm not. Aside from getting first choice on some spaces every now and then, I'm paying the same rent as everyone else."

"That's cool, though," Reid said. "Are you close to your parents?"

Cassie nodded. "We have family brunch every Sunday. I suggested Simone's as a new option sometime soon, actually."

"James will love that," Reid said. "Speaking of which, did you see James and Kit?"

Cassie's big brown eyes opened wide. "Yes . . . that was intense. They looked cute!"

"Just tell Kit to be cautious. James is a good guy, but he's not really the relationship type."

"Funny you say that, because as effervescent and lovely as Kit is, neither is she." Cassie chuckled. "It may work out fine."

A lull in conversation comfortably settled over them. Cassie had adorably folded her legs underneath herself, while Reid put his feet up on the coffee table.

"This is nice," he said, putting his coffee mug on a coaster.

"I like it, too," Cassie replied, scooting over and putting her head on her shoulder. "I love watching the sunrise, and it's nice to have someone with me to watch it."

"We still have at least six more hours to go," Reid said looking at his watch. "What do you love so much about the sunlight?"

He felt Cassie take a deep breath. "It's going to sound weird to you, but growing up, in photos with my friends, I was always lit weird. Either I was washed out completely, or almost a shadow. And many of my friends were white because we were out in the western burbs.

"That's not the only reason why I went into photography. I did that because I loved taking pictures of anything and everything. But when I got older, I noticed that in magazines, and even in photo exhibits at the Art Institute or at galleries, no one knew how to take pictures of anyone who wasn't white. So when I went to school, I studied why."

Reid gazed back at the woman before him in awe. Not just because she had a shitty experience, but because she decided to go out and make a difference. He didn't know many people who had that sort of tenacity. It was exhilarating and incredibly attractive.

"And now you want to change the game," he replied.

"I'd like to do so, one boudoir photo at a time, I suppose." Cassie laughed, sitting up from Reid's shoulder and stretching her legs next to his on the coffee table. "Maybe it's small potatoes, but every time a client tells me they've never seen their skin glow in a photo, I'm happy and sad at the same time. Happy that I made someone feel beautiful, but sad that they've probably never had a properly exposed photo taken of them before."

Reid thought about how he styled and edited his own photos and wondered what he did on autopilot that exacerbated the situation for the models of color he worked with. What was worse, he actually had to think about what he had been doing and how it could be considered incorrect.

"I'd love to see you work again some time," he said seriously, looking Cassie directly in the eyes. "I want to learn what I could be doing better."

Cassie smiled, one of those slow-moving, genuine smiles he coveted from her. "That could probably be arranged." And before he knew it, she had kissed him on the cheek before retreating to the corner of her couch.

Again, they settled into comfortable silence, watching the quiet night stretch on before them. Streetlights turned out, as did business signs, and suddenly, Reid could see a few stars glimmering above the high-rises.

"So, what about you and your family? Do they live around here, or are they nomads like your previous life?" Cassie said, breaking the silence gently.

Reid waited a beat before answering—it always took him a minute to explain his parents. "My mom is definitely a nomad. Last I heard from her, she was somewhere on the East Coast. My old man, well, he was never really around to begin with, but he's downstate, working on his cousin's farm. At least that's what my uncle told me about a year ago or so."

He didn't look at Cassie then, because he rarely spoke about his family so frankly. They were never around and never had been. His mom did her best to stay in one place while he was growing up, but it never lasted long. He and his brother bounced around from relative to relative throughout the suburbs for some sense of stability, and when he graduated from high school, he knew he would be on his own. Reid did what he could to take the edge off things for Russ, but Russ had taken his own wayward path similar to their mother's once he was sixteen, and by then, Reid was halfway across the country trying to make his name as a photographer.

"Hey, I'm sorry, I didn't mean—"

"It's fine, really. I've been on my own a long time when it comes to family, but I have friends who are like family. James's mom invites me over more than she invites her own son to dinner." The warmth he felt from James's family made him feel like a person again, not just a lost soul trying to figure out what to do next.

"That's really great," Cassie said softly, and just as softly, Reid felt her hand take his. He pulled her closer to him, and her head returned to his shoulder. He felt her breathing slow, and as much as he wanted to continue spilling his most hidden depths, Reid let her sleep. Hopefully, they'd have another opportunity to watch the sunrise again soon.

EIGHT

don't like her, or him, but I do like her—"

"Dana, that's a picture of yourself."

"I know what I like!" Dana's laugh rang out through her apartment. Cassie made a point to get over there at least a few times a week, if not daily, to keep Dana occupied and give Riki a few moments to herself. That day, they had their staff meeting in Dana's apartment, where they surrounded Dana on the couch with a stack of photos to start choosing the models for the group shots. With a long afternoon ahead of her, Cassie was counting down the minutes to the end of the day. She needed time to decompress after the busy December holidays had brought so many client bookings. Cassie knew people wanted to take advantage of time off throughout the holiday season, especially between Christmas and New Year's Eve, but she was going to have a serious conversation with Sam about the schedule. Cassie felt like she was running on fumes with work, never mind actually modeling, too.

Cassie was nervous about modeling with other people. In crowds, whether she did it on purpose or it just ended up that way, Cassie had a tendency to retreat to the edges. Here, she had to be the center of attention. Picking people who would make her look good was both self-aggrandizing and fun at the same time.

"I love Jakob! He's so impish and sweet," said Kit. "He's also a Brit, so he'll be delightful."

"Too small," said Sam. "We need someone more imposing. Besides, Jade sort of encompasses impish and sweet for us already."

"But Jade isn't British," Kit said, as though that was the only deciding factor.

"What don't you like about Paisley?"

"Her boobs are bigger than yours, which is no small feat," Dana said. "But yours need to be the stars of this shindig, not something in the background." She gave Cassie the once-over and smiled. "Your body is banging, babe. What have *you* been doing lately?"

"Or *who* has she been doing?" Kit said, reaching up for a high five with Dana and then Sam. They all giggled.

No matter how many times Cassie told them over and over for the past month, they still did not believe that she and Reid didn't do the deed that night after Friendsgiving. And try as she might to tease Kit about James, Kit didn't falter whenever someone brought him up or they went to lunch at Simone's and he was there. Clearly, they *had* hooked up, and could very well still be hooking up. But no one gave her a hard time about it.

Perhaps Cassie's vehement—albeit truthful—denial made it worse.

"You all are relentless," she said. "Let's just get through this casting. I'll take a few shots of Dana for her 'gram, and then we have a three p.m. photo shoot, which will be all-hands-on-deck because it's a double-couple session."

Cassie went through the motions of hemming and hawing over pretty people's headshots while her mind was occupied with thoughts of that long night with Reid weeks ago. She had wanted to have sex with him in the most desperate way possible, but she was glad they hadn't moved things too far along. In fact, she felt closer to him since they spent most of the night talking and eating copious snacks. Not making it to sunrise was disappointing because the view from her apartment was truly spectacular in the early morning, and she really wanted to share that with Reid. But falling asleep on his shoulder and waking up wrapped in his arms was nothing short of delightful.

Cassie remembered waking up slowly, the weak sunshine trying to break through the clouds. She had been between fully awake and still dreaming, listening to Reid's deep breathing and steady heart-beat, feeling the warmth of his embrace. She tried to force herself back to sleep, to hang on to this perfect moment a bit longer, but the itch to photograph him in the morning light was too strong.

Inch by painstaking inch, she moved out of his arms and tiptoed to her credenza to grab one of many cameras stored there. Before she looked through the viewfinder, she surveyed the landscape of her apartment with Reid in it. He looked good there, comfortable and at ease, peaceful.

"Hurry up, I can't fake much longer," he said, cracking open one eye. "Besides, now I'm cold because you left."

"Don't move," she said. Instead of taking a long shot, she walked closer to Reid, focusing on the cut of his jaw, stubble visible from the watery light filling the room. She took a photograph of the crook of his elbow, his hands resting on his chest, and the spot where she had been sleeping most of that night, where his neck and shoulder met.

Finally, Cassie paused when she noticed Reid trembling. She thought that maybe he really was cold until she looked at his face and realized he was trying to hold back laughter.

"Are you still giggle-drunk?" she asked.

Reid let out a laugh that was infectious, and before Cassie could contain herself, she was laughing, too.

"Not in the slightest. Your fuzzy blanket was tickling my feet," he said as innocently as possible. This made them both laugh harder. "You like to take photos of things, not just people."

"I was taking photos of you, just not a full-body shot."

"Yeah, but before with my jacket, the champagne glasses at the party, and the shots you always scroll past on your phone when we're scouting," Reid said to Cassie. "What's all that about?"

"Iconic lights."

Reid furrowed his brow. "Care to elaborate?"

Cassie hadn't told anyone about this idea she had for something a little high-concept. She hadn't had too much time to think about projects aside from what she was doing for Buxom Boudoir, local businesses, and now the LL campaign. "The things we look at every day are often overlooked. But they're still beautiful. I want to photograph them in a different way, different light, different angles, and showcase how great they are. Some things are timeless—leather jackets, glasses, clock hands, and actual light bulbs. Others, like body parts, or a specific knot in hardwood, or the cracked spine of a book, can look completely different if the light hits them just right, or you turn your head a certain way . . ."

Cassie grinned to herself when Reid put his arm around her and said, "Your brain is an interesting place. I want to know everything about it."

In the month or so since that morning, Cassie had barely seen Reid due to her busy work schedule, but she hadn't forgotten what had happened between them that night, how she started to feel closer to him . . . And how she wanted to know more.

"I saw that smile," Kit murmured later that afternoon, as they pinned the final roster of models to the giant mood board they created on a wall in the studio. "And it wasn't about the last model we agreed upon."

"Despite what you and everyone else wants to think, I was smiling because I figured something out. A new project."

"Care to share?"

"Not yet, but soon," Cassie said. "It's an ongoing thing I'm still mulling over."

Kit nodded. "Are you ready for next week?"

"The New Year?"

Kit rolled her eyes. "I'll take that as a yes."

Even though the photos they took on the roof turned out great, these upcoming photo shoots were the real deal and would be sent to Luscious Lingerie for approval and feedback. They had scheduled time at the Rookery but were also going to take their chances at the Humboldt Park pergolas in the hope no random engagement photo sessions would be taking place. Then the Fern Room at the Garfield Park Conservatory was booked for the final huge group shot, and James promised they could use Simone's anytime they wanted. It was a stacked schedule, and there were enough well-lit but out-of-direct-sight areas so Cassie wouldn't be completely exposed to random passersby. In addition to showcasing Dana's Dreamland collection, the city of Chicago would also be lovingly on display next to Cassie's décolletage.

Cassie felt her phone buzz. She couldn't stop the flutter in her stomach when she saw it was Reid.

REID

> What do you think about your
> building facade?

CASSIE

It's nice?

REID

As a backdrop. You, my leather jacket, sheer cheekys (sp?) . . .

CASSIE

So you're thinking about me, in sheer lingerie, in your jacket? (It's cheekies, btw)

The dreaded blinking ellipsis popped up as Cassie smiled to herself. Was she sort of breaking her own rule of keeping things professional when it came to the photo shoots? Perhaps. But it was fun to tease him a little.

REID

I think it will make for an interesting backdrop. And you brought up my leather jacket at Friendsgiving but never elaborated. I had to rack my giggle-drunk mind to put it all together.

CASSIE

Nice use of context clues.

To be fair, Reid had a point about her building. The bricks were a lovely burnished terra-cotta orange, with black accents on all the doors, shutters, and window frames. Her parents restored the building to its original color scheme, and the final result was bold without being too overt, classic but not boring. But it was interesting, and maybe a little concerning, that Reid was taking her quick Friendsgiving mention of his jacket and turning it into his own idea for the campaign. Wasn't she the one in charge of things?

CASSIE

My building could be an interesting background and I know what the light is like.

They made a plan to fit a facade photo shoot in the schedule, and Cassie decided to consider this a collaboration rather than him taking on one of her responsibilities. Once that was squared away, she headed home. Looking at photos of beautiful people was a nice way to spend the afternoon, but after the twentieth headshot and reconfiguration of what model would wear which garter belt, Cassie was ready for nothing but solitude.

Christmas, as always, had been a to-do. Christmas Eve with her mom's side of the family, then Christmas Day at her parents' house in the suburbs, with a combination of her dad's family and close family friends. Dana and Riki, with Dana's feet propped up on a lush ottoman the entire evening, had made the trek out to the suburbs with Cassie. While she enjoyed visiting with everyone, it was draining. With the holidays, planning her work schedule for the next few months, and working herself up over the photo shoot, she was ready for a giant glass of cabernet sauvignon, a lighthearted romance novel, and a quiet night in.

Until she rounded the corner and saw none other than Reid Montgomery standing outside her apartment building.

From the moment he saw Cassie walking with her head down and hands buried deep in the pockets of her dark purple peacoat, Reid knew coming to her place unexpectedly was a bad idea.

"What are you doing here?" she said with a weak smile.

"I was in the neighborhood, and I—"

"Have you been here since you texted me, Reid?"

He grinned before he could help himself. "Not the entire time."

She sighed, rolled her shoulders back, and said, "You can come up, but I don't think I'll be the best company today."

"Oh, I was actually . . ." He had a plan in mind, but now he was hesitant.

Cassie looked at him unblinking. "You actually what?"

"Thought maybe we could go somewhere and work on your Iconic Light series. I had this idea about objects and—"

"So now you want to take that idea, too?"

Reid hadn't heard Cassie speak with such fervor. If someone didn't know her, they wouldn't have been able to tell the difference. But there was an edge, a dark vibrancy to her voice that gave him pause. "I'm not taking anything, Cassie."

"Okay. You know, I'm tired, it's been a long day—a long few days actually. Iconic Lights is something I'm still working on at a conceptual level, so, I'm not exactly looking for a collaborator or whatever you think it is you were suggesting," she said, pulling her keys out. "I have to go. We can talk on Tuesday. Happy New Year."

Before he could say anything, Cassie was through the heavy black door of her building, and it slammed shut in his face.

Reid, thankful no one had been around to witness his belittling, unlocked his bike and set off. The warmth offered from the day's sunshine was now brisk, which was usually one of his favorite riding temperatures, but that dusky evening, it was anything but pleasant. And when the wind picked up, it was like a slap in the face.

He thought about going to Bugles to have a manhattan, but seeing Riki would raise suspicion, and it was more than likely Sam or Kit would also be there. There was always Simone's, but he didn't want to see James's smug face.

Instead, he just rode.

It had been some time since Reid rode his bike without a destination. He let instinct take over, feeling his adrenaline pumping, his pulse and body temp rising against the cold air. Rush hour was ending, and he was in luck that the side streets were clearing up. He continued his ride to nowhere and let his mind wander.

Which meant he spent most of this time thinking of Cassandra Harris.

So, he had caught her on a bad day. Everyone had them. Hell, he had them most days. But ever since starting the Dreamland campaign, Reid had to admit his days were better—annoying younger brother aside. And not just because he got to see Cassie's beautiful face on a regular basis. He was also becoming a part of a team of people who did good work, trusted one another, and, in fact, trusted him, too. At least enough to include him on a group text, which usually devolved into sharing stupid GIFs and funny memes.

Too bad he was still keeping tabs on them for LL. So far, Rebecca had left him to his own devices, and seemed placated with his vague texts here and there regarding Cassie's visions. But with the real photo shoots starting the following week, Reid expected Rebecca would want to chat more with him, and make sure things were still going in the way LL expected them to go.

He weaved his way down a one-way street, taking advantage of the expanse of space offered to him without foot traffic, opening doors, or speeding cars. Reid had never had a loyal group of friends—or family for that matter. He usually found someone in the cities he migrated through, someone he could turn to for help when he needed something trivial, like moving a couch or borrowing a tire pump. But aside from James, who was loyal almost to a fault and did most of the heavy lifting in their friendship, Reid was both happy and confused at the current space he occupied professionally and personally.

Then there was Cassie. She was awesome; there was no other way to describe how he felt around her. She was running her own successful business and determined to take her career to the next level, had taken on not just the concept and execution of a major ad campaign but was also starring in it, and still had the mental capacity to come up with an interesting personal project to continue to explore creative outlets.

No wonder she was tired, Reid thought. When Reid thought of Cassie and her work ethic, her tenacious desire to continue to grow as a photographer and a business owner, he was inspired. For much of his life, Reid had operated for himself as he tried to get away from shitty parents with too much on their plates and make sure his brother, who had decided to idolize their absentee father because he didn't know any better, didn't completely ruin his life, all the while coasting through everything because he was preternaturally charming. Cassie had a drive he'd never seen before, parents who wholeheartedly supported her, and clients who adored everything she did for them. And yet, he was the one booking national jobs and making more money than necessary.

Letting Cassie in his life had been easy, almost too easy. Without the job and the photographs, and all the stuff behind the scenes, Reid knew he'd want to spend more time with Cassie no matter the circumstances.

Reid had things and people in his life making it worthwhile to wonder and hope nowadays. He liked knowing Russ was nearby, as much of an incredibly expensive nuisance he had been so far. Something had changed, and he liked knowing Russ was doing all right. It was a weird feeling to have about his brother, but it was there anyway. Whereas Reid adapted to being on his own—relished in it, even—Russ needed some kind of affirmation that he was doing the right thing. And up until Reid had started helping him over the last few months, the only person who Reid knew had shown Russ the smallest amount of affection was their mother . . . and that had been the bare minimum.

Now that Reid was starting to care, he wondered why it had been so easy for their parents—but especially their mom—not to want to continue caring for their sons, even once they had grown up. Was he so easy to put aside? Was Russ?

Reid was happy that the two of them had genuinely connected for the first time in their lives, but what did it mean? Reid realized he needed to think about what was going to happen after the sale of the house. Maybe he wanted Russ to stick around . . .

And all these thoughts and confusion had come about because

he needed the job, of course, but also because he wanted to make Cassie Harris smile.

Perhaps she was the key—the reason he was willing to go that extra mile to help his brother. The reason he wanted to succeed and see her do well, too.

Overwhelmed with his own thoughts, Reid pushed himself to ride farther, feeling his lungs burn from exertion until his mind didn't comprehend anything except to keep pedaling.

Reid finally came to a stop, realizing he was farther away from his apartment than he intended. But he took a moment and decided it was time to change things. For himself and for Cassie.

Walking into her building, Cassie was seething. She didn't realize how heavily she was breathing until she felt warm air fill her lungs. With each deep breath she inhaled, she felt her blood pressure lower upon exhaling. Would she never be rid of someone trying to take something away from her? Cassie hadn't worked as hard as she did to let people walk all over her, but here she was again—not just fighting for a job that wasn't exactly the one she wanted, but now her creative outlet was also being taken over by the same person who made her question how well she really could do everything.

Not to mention he was also making her wonder about other things, too.

Cassie was confused. Her feelings told her to cautiously give him a chance, and her mind screamed to keep her guard up, no matter how handsome he was when he smiled.

Even her mind knew what was really going on. Cassie *liked* Reid. She couldn't deny it. But that didn't mean she had to completely resign herself to falling over like a flower every time he breezed into her day.

Iconic Lights was her idea. The concept for the Dreamland campaign was, too. And she was not going to let a man who leaned exceptionally well across her kitchen island convince her otherwise.

Cassie also realized if she spent one more moment in her apartment, she was going to lose it, because the only place she could go that didn't remind her of Reid was her bathroom. The living room made her think of their late-night talk, the kitchen made her remember how tipsy he was. And even if she went in her bedroom, though he hadn't been there, she'd remember how she overthought what lounge clothes she wanted to wear in front of him and how terribly she wanted to bring him there and do more than just snuggle on the couch.

Cassie had it bad.

There was only one person she fully trusted to bring her out of this funk.

> D, I need an intervention. Can I stop by?

Barely a second went by before Dana replied.

> You never have to ask to come over. I'm terribly busy watching old episodes of America's Next Top Model at the moment, but I'll take a break for you, my lovely.

Cassie smiled at Dana's response, took one final look at her apartment, and walked out the door. Hopefully, with some much-needed sensible advice from Dana, Cassie could return home with a clear head and not simply pine away after the man who invaded her thoughts.

Cassie walked a few blocks to Dana and Riki's, where Riki met her at the door. "Bonsoir, ma chérie," Riki said, holding a large plate of perfectly round, still warm chocolate chip cookies. "Fresh from downstairs."

It was milk-and-cookies night at Bugles, a wholesome concept with the promise of seeing someone's cookies during a burlesque show.

This of course made Cassie think of Reid's drunken laughing fit over cookies after Friendsgiving. She took the plate from Riki and headed into the living room, where Dana had set up shop.

"I thought I heard someone wonderful," Dana said, patting the sofa cushion next to her for Cassie to sit. She set down the cookies and gave Dana a tight squeeze as she sat.

"How are you both doing?"

"We're going crazy. But I felt le bébé move! It's like gas."

"Sometimes it is gas," Riki called out, walking toward the door. "Heading back down to the bar, see you both later."

"Everything good with you two?" Cassie asked cautiously, noticing Dana and Riki weren't their usual affectionate selves. Normally, they kissed each other goodbye before Riki went down to Bugles, but she abruptly left.

"Riki wants to move to the Wild West." It was how they referred to the suburbs.

"What? Because of the kid? Kids grow up in cities all the time!" Cassie was not thrilled with the idea of not having her best friend within walking distance.

"Not just the kid thing, though I don't disagree with her about having more space and whatnot," Dana continued. "Bugles wants to expand, and they want Riki to come up with a way to do so, somewhere in the suburbs."

"I mean, that's great, but you'd be so far away."

"Just a train ride, doll. We might even buy an SUV or something wild," Dana said. "It's not set in stone, and we have a lot to think about. She could run everything from here, because like I said, it's just a train ride."

"Well, please keep me abreast of any major developments," Cassie said entirely on purpose. She was staring at Dana's chest, which looked larger. Much larger.

"Oh, please don't. They're huge and getting huger. It's hormones. I haven't gained that much weight. And I'm just now reaching halfway. I'm scared to measure myself to figure out what size they are."

Cassie looked down at her own ample bosom and then back at her best friend's. They both started laughing. In middle school, one of the first things they bonded over was developing early and "with reckless abandon," as they put it.

After their cathartic laughter died down, Dana turned to the task at hand.

"So, what's going on, Cassie? You seem out of sorts."

Cassie told Dana about Reid's surprise visit, and the way she slammed the door in his face. "I like him, D. But there's so much riding on everything going right. I don't know what to do."

"Honestly, I haven't dated in almost a decade. I have no idea how this works anymore," Dana said. "But I think the fact that you—normally calm and collected, albeit a little anal retentive—are so worked up is because everything means a lot to you. Including Reid."

Dana reached a hand to Cassie, who breathed in deeply and took Dana's hand in hers. "Thank you for listening. I just have a lot to think about." Cassie moved the plate of cookies between them on the couch, and they both chowed down.

"I haven't properly thanked you, Cassie, for what you're doing with the campaign," Dana said once they both had their fill of dessert. "It's not easy, and I know it's totally out of your comfort zone. But I hope you know I wouldn't want it any other way."

"Aww shucks, honey, don't tell me you got pregnant just to ensure you couldn't model so I'd have to do it all," Cassie said, lightly smacking Dana's arm.

"What can I say, my timing is impeccable." Dana replied. "But I always had you in the back of my mind for every piece. Would Cassie wear this? Would Cassie think that was cool? You really did inspire me, girl."

If anyone asked, Cassie had something in her eye at that exact moment. Hearing Dana vocalize her feelings and gratitude was more than she could take after her long day. "In a way, I'm glad it all worked out like it did," Cassie said.

"I'm sure you are," Dana replied, giving a very obnoxious wink. Cassie retorted with an over-the-top eye roll that gave most of the Real Housewives a run for their money. "Also, I wanted to tell you that LL has asked me to expand the collection to include swimwear."

Cassie swore she heard a record scratch.

"Wow, that's huge, D. Congrats," Cassie said, after a beat too long. This was a big deal for Dana, but Cassie felt like this was only going to add more for her friend to juggle, and she was already overwhelmed. "And you're okay with this?"

"Oh, yes. I talked with Reid and—"

Reid frickin' Montgomery, yet again. The range of emotions this man made her feel was going to give her whiplash.

"Why would you go to Reid before me?"

"Cassie, he has experience with swimwear. He's done all the catalog work for the LL swim division and—"

"He literally puts people in front of a blank background, and they stand still while he takes pictures," Cassie said. "Really crucial artistic involvement."

"He knows what looks good to LL execs, and the turnaround was quick on this," Dana said. "It's only going to be a few swimsuits, a one-piece and then bikinis with a few different top styles, bottoms with a bunch of rises, cuts—all mix and match. I wanted to get his technical opinion on what he thought would work. Rebecca suggested I call him."

"Well, he hadn't mentioned it," Cassie said. Not that she'd given him the chance to say much of anything earlier. She now realized that she had unfairly accused him of taking her idea for Iconic Lights and had snapped at him without letting him explain anything. Exactly like she was doing with Dana. She ran a hand through her hair, snagging on a curl and pulling just a little too hard. Even her own nervous coping mechanism was out to get her.

"I asked him not to, so I could tell you. You know, like a good friend does."

"A good friend doesn't continually spring random things on another good friend. Lingerie is one thing, but swimwear is a whole new ball game." Cassie winced. She really needed a nap. Or wine. Or both. And maybe, just maybe, ahead of principal photography starting, Cassie also needed to make peace with Reid and decide how far she wanted to go with him.

"Can I at least tell you about it, slugger?" Dana asked.

Cassie nodded, taking another cookie. A sugar high would have to suffice in place of sleep and alcohol.

"Basically, I want it to look like you've been dipped in black lava."

NINE

The morning of day one of principal photography, Cassie was nervously pacing around her apartment. Somehow, someone—cough cough, *Sam*—had accidentally booked a boudoir consult, including hair and makeup, for the exact start time of the shoot. This meant that Sam and Kit would have to cover the appointment, so instead of heading out to Humboldt Park to make the most of a sunny morning under the pergolas, they decided to move forward with Reid's idea of using the deep red-orange bricks of Cassie's apartment building as a backdrop, which was more feasible without a crew.

Kit had come over early and done Cassie's hair in Bantu knots with silver tinsel-like thread coiled around them. They almost made a halo around Cassie's head. One of the reasons Cassie wanted to work with Kit was her vast knowledge of different hair types, despite being a tiny, pale Brit. And, when Kit didn't know something, Cassie knew she was willing to find and hire an expert who could. She remembered Kit came back from a Black hair expo a year or so ago, amazed and determined to be better and learn more and also expand her portfolio of local Chicago hairstylists who specialized in Black hair care. Cassie's makeup was minimal, save for the very bright pink blush in almost perfect circles on Cassie's high cheekbones.

"This meeting shouldn't take more than forty-five minutes. You won't even know we aren't here," Kit reassured her. "Sam goes to all the consultations with you anyway, and she's going to be great. And I'll be there to soften the mood. I made double-chocolate biscotti just in case Sam's particularly prickly this morning and to placate everyone involved. Tell Reid I say hello and good luck. Same to you, my darling!"

With that, Cassie was left alone. She was wearing a silk robe, sheer leopard-print cheeky underpants, and a bralette in the same filmy fabric underneath. Her ass was mostly exposed, and the robe's thin fabric didn't offer any sort of modesty. She was slipping into her own terry cloth robe when her buzzer went off. Reid was exactly on time.

"I'll be right down," she said, hitting the buzzer just long enough for him to get in the main doors but not through the stairway door that would lead him up to her apartment. Her fellow building dwellers had been notified of the photo shoot, but aside from the guy on the second floor who worked from home, everyone else was at work anyway. Earlier that morning, with Kit's help, the lobby of her building had become a catch-all of modesty screens, a small hair and makeup touch-up station, and a clothing rack with the day's looks along with extra options. It was a furious mix of lace, tulle, glitter, and rouge in various forms.

And then there was Reid, standing in the middle of it, holding a vibrant bouquet of dahlias and a cup of something that smelled like chocolate.

"Hey," he said, averting his eyes ever so slightly but not enough that Cassie didn't notice he was taking in her barely dressed state.

"Hey, yourself," she said, walking toward him.

"These are for you," he said, holding out the flowers and beverage.

Okay, so things are going to be weird.

But Cassie had to hand it to Reid. He was apologizing for their last interaction when she should have been the one doing so. With making out at Friendsgiving, attempting to stay up all night talking, and then how she had dismissed him a few days earlier, Cassie appreciated his kind approach.

"Thanks, they're really pretty," she said, taking the flowers. "And a much-needed coffee."

"A mocha, actually. Something extra for our first day of this campaign."

Cassie nodded and took a sip. It was exactly what she needed to calm down, take in the moment, and center herself before disrobing completely.

"I'm sorry for the way I handled things last week," Cassie said, putting the flowers on a table, then taking another sip of the warm, sweet beverage. "I was having an off day and was exhausted."

"We all have those days," Reid said. "I'm sorry I made it worse. So I brought things to make this day way better."

Cassie felt her heart flutter. She wasn't about to swoon, was she? This was supposed to be the day her unexpected modeling career started. Not the day she was goo-goo-eyed over a very thoughtful man.

"So, we're on our own, but I think that's fine," Cassie explained, deciding to move ahead as professionally as possible. "Kit and Sam should be here eventually. There was a last-minute meeting. But

Sam told me to tell you she's watching us, somehow, so she will know if you mess up." *Ugh, this is the worst. I am the most awkward person in the world.* The invasive thoughts kept coming.

"Sam is scary," he replied, chuckling softly and turning to start setting up his camera and tripod. "It's a little cold outside today, but the sun is bright and high. No clouds. But if you need a break to warm up, just throw a shoe at me or something."

"Throw a shoe?" Cassie had to laugh at something so asinine. "Have you seen these contraptions? I'm locked in. It took me five minutes to buckle these babies. Each." She pointed to the mid-calf platform moto boots in shiny patent leather, with what looked like a million laces and buckles intricately intertwined.

"Are those torture devices?"

"Essentially. But they look pretty sick." Cassie took a moment to twirl around, knowing she was giving Reid a little show. He may have been on notice at the moment, but that wasn't going to stop Cassie from a little bit of taunting.

"And they go with my jacket," he said, taking off the smooth leather and handing it to her. He grabbed a hoodie out of his backpack and headed out to set up the tripod and take test shots.

Cassie held the jacket to her chest, the smooth leather still cool from the chill outside. In true Chicago fashion, after a couple of weeks of winter-like weather, the low fifties popped up in the forecast after the holidays—thank the weather gods, considering Cassie's entire campaign was outdoors. Some people complained that there really wasn't a fall in Chicago, that it goes from blazing hot and humid to frigidly cold. Which was true for the most part, but fall did happen in the city, just two or three months later than expected, and it only lasted for a few days before winter returned.

Cassie stepped behind a screen to get changed. Or rather, get mostly naked. After disrobing in front of the mirror, noticing almost immediately how *everything* was on display through the sheer fabric, Cassie found herself wishing she had a couple of lime-green pasties for a modicum of modesty. The thought reminded her of Friendsgiving night, under the crafty mistletoe, and for a second, she felt calm . . . Until she heard his voice call out, "Ready when you are, boss."

"One sec," she said, wrapping herself in Reid's jacket. It smelled like him—fresh, clean, and masculine—and looked rigid but actually felt buttery soft. She was probably going to have to figure out a way to steal this jacket. She looked in the mirror, did her Wonder Woman power stance, and walked out. "Will I do?"

Of all the lingerie, the "sheer cheeky" portion of Dana's line was the most overt, as overt as one could be when creating lingerie for a variety of women's body types and shapes and sizes and skin colors. Completely see-through, tactilely invigorating, and sexy as hell. Half of Cassie's ass was hanging out, and most of her tits were exposed under that bralette, making her feel risqué and alluring. And she liked it.

Cassie saw Reid swallow and then reach for his own cup of coffee. He vigorously nodded before answering. "You'll more than do. You look like a badass warrior goddess going out for a night of fun."

Cassie felt her pulse quicken. The way Reid looked at her, like he'd never seen anyone else wear lingerie before, made her feel exactly how she wanted to make her clients feel: beautiful *and* powerful. Now she just had to believe that feeling and use it while she modeled. And she hoped, more than anything, that she'd be able to keep it together if Reid frickin' Montgomery spent the rest of the day staring at her like that.

Much like the photo shoot on the BB rooftop, Reid was at a loss for words for how he felt when Cassandra Harris was in front of him. Her Dreamland vision was coming to life, she had everything under control, and she looked smokin' hot while doing so.

And this "cheeky" outfit, as the call sheet put it, would be his undoing.

First, he thought it was her raised eyebrow. Then, her smile did him in. Then, it was her kiss. But now, he was coming apart at Cassie wearing next to nothing in his leather jacket.

"I have an idea," he blurted out, clearing his throat at nearly the same time.

Reid started walking toward the door, while Cassie sauntered over in her sky-high boots. She looked ethereal and dangerous but still playful. Exactly how she showed up in his dreams.

He'd never admit to her that she'd invaded every part of his brain . . . He thought about her while he was editing photos, while he answered inane house questions from his brother, and especially while he was alone, in bed, with no one for company but himself. Their stolen kisses, the almost sex, the night spent talking until the early-morning hours and watching her sleep instead of watching the sunrise . . . Reid had it bad. Real bad.

And this badass warrior goddess getup wasn't helping things.

"I think you should pose with my bike."

His trusty aluminum bicycle was propped up outside, near the brick wall, currently blanketed in direct sunlight. Possibly too bright, but nothing that couldn't be fixed in postproduction. Though he reminded himself that Cassie didn't like to diffuse the integrity of natural sunlight. So, he'd make do with shadows from awnings and neighboring buildings. They'd move as the sun moved, and his bike would be the perfect prop.

"Your bike?" Cassie said, looking skeptical.

"I know what you thought the first time we genuinely interacted," he admitted. "You saw my leather jacket and vintage moto helmet, black jeans, and big boots and expected me to have a Harley. But instead, I had this beautiful, city-friendly, awesome bicycle like some rich hipster who didn't know any better."

"What exactly do you have against hipsters? They're the reason this neighborhood is thriving," Cassie teased, raising that eyebrow, which was almost too much cuteness for Reid to handle. She put her hands on her hips, as though she knew she was torturing him.

"Hipsters aside, this bike is nonchalant enough to be the official ride of the queen of the modern pinups."

"Is that what I am now? A modern-day pinup?"

"Bettie Page and Eartha Kitt would be proud."

An eye roll to define all eye rolls followed that comment, sending shock waves through Reid that he felt from the nape of his neck to the balls . . . of his feet.

"Just get on the bike, Cass," he said, adjusting his camera so it was level with his chest. He knew things would be better if she saw his face to start and not just the mechanism. "Let me see what it looks like . . . If the vision in my head can come true."

"Why, Reid Montgomery, are you admitting to daydreaming about me?" Cassie said playfully and bashfully at the same time.

He knew she was pleased because a rosy hue flushed her décolletage. *Click.* So much for not letting on that he dreamed about her. But she was gorgeous, and he wanted to capture every inch of her.

He held up the camera then and started to move around her as she straddled his bike. Against the burnt-orange bricks, his leather jacket leaped off the facade and into his viewfinder. He knelt down on the rough sidewalk, making the sheer leopard-print cheekies the focal point of the photo. After he took a few shots, he saw Cassie take a deep breath and realized she wasn't comfortable.

"I know," she said before he could say anything to put her at ease. "It's all about the underpants . . . and my butt. So, this is fine, really, it is." But with each passing click of the camera, Cassie hunched inward.

"Cass," he said softly, not looking at his camera's viewfinder. She looked the part, but Reid often had to remind himself that Cassie was not a professional model with years of experience in front of the camera. She was normally the one doing what he was doing, not prancing around in barely there underwear.

"No, it's okay, really," she said again, putting her hand to her mouth, careful not to smear the pink lipstick. She lifted her chin, obscuring the view he had of her eyes, but he knew she was trying to stop tears from falling.

"Cass, think about our first kiss, under the fake mistletoe," Reid said, moving closer, not taking any photos. "The lights, the laughter, the clink of drinks. Think about that. Don't think about how good your butt looks in these panties."

"I hate the word *panties*."

"Cheekies, or whatever, cheeky woman." Reid laughed. "Just think about you and me, kissing under the mistletoe in the safety of the loft, with no one but our nosy friends to notice."

He saw the rise and fall of deep breaths come from Cassie's collarbone, because he knew if he looked anywhere else, he wouldn't be able to focus on helping her through this. After a moment, Cassie closed her eyes, put her hands back on the handlebars of his bike, hitched her foot up into a pedal and said, "Take the shot, Montgomery." It was a challenge and an invitation, a taunt and a seduction. All from the mention of their kiss.

Cassie turned around, let Reid's jacket slide down her shoulders, and arched her back. To save himself—from what, he wasn't exactly sure—Reid lifted his camera up to his face again and quickly moved forward. He took close-ups of her body, unlike any he'd taken of her so far, focusing on the juxtaposition of her smooth brown skin and the weblike netting of the tulle undergarments. The way everything about her was soft and curvy made his mind go crazy with all the things they didn't do that night in her apartment . . . mere floors away.

Seconds, hours, years passed by—she had a way of making him feel like they were transcending time and space. He was consumed by Cassandra Harris, and he could tell she liked the way he was looking at her.

Way to be professional, he thought, smirking to himself. They were fools to think they'd be able to keep up this ruse.

"Reid," Cassie said, putting his jacket all the way back on. "You can't look at me like that."

He licked his lips. "Like what?" he teased, taking another photo when she giggled and readjusted her very tiny bra.

"Like you're hungry," she said, looking up at him through her heavy-lidded eyes.

"Oh, so how you were looking at me during the test shots?"

Without missing a beat, Cassie said, "Exactly."

And with that, Reid set down his camera and walked toward Cassie. She met him stride for stride, but when they were inches apart, a moment of hesitation passed between them. Then the breeze picked up as the sun blazed, and Reid's hands went to

Cassie's waist, while her arms wrapped around his neck. And another searing hot kiss sealed them together.

This kiss was deeper and more desperate, frantic and flirtier than before. Cassie pressed against Reid, like she wanted to capture the light between them and not let one particle escape. Grabbing the hem of his own leather jacket, Reid brought Cassie closer still, and when they parted, they were both gasping for air.

"Cass," he murmured.

"Don't stop, I don't know when the girls will get here," she said, kissing his neck and up his jaw, inching toward his mouth again.

He laughed just as she was about to kiss his lips again, making her stop.

"I asked Sam and Kit to leave us alone for the start of today," he said, smiling into another kiss. He felt her pull away in surprise. "So we could work things out and get comfortable again."

"And look what happened, smart-ass," Cassie countered, attempting to pull away, but Reid held on to the hem of the jacket. She buried her face into his shoulder, trying to hide the laughter bubbling up her throat. He felt her laugh before it escaped her mouth, and when it started, it emanated from her entire body. Cassie playfully smacked his chest and hopped a little on her tiptoes. The happiness he saw in her eyes when she leaned her head back to laugh outright was a joy to behold.

Maybe it was the way he was looking at her, or the way she was looking at him, but Reid knew Cassie saw and felt what he was feeling, too.

"Perhaps it's time for a wardrobe change," she suggested as casually pointed as possible. "Upstairs. In my apartment. Wouldn't want to scandalize the neighbors."

Reid grabbed his camera and tripod and followed Cassie inside.

The elevator took forever to come down to the ground level. Reid was holding Cassie's hand, and the way he looked at her made Cassie's stomach turn over and tie itself in a knot. In a good way, of course.

Just when she was ready to make a mental note to complain to her parents about the wait time on the elevators in their expensively renovated building, Cassie heard the familiar *ding* and the doors opened. Cassie walked in, pressed three, and then moved to a corner. Reid stood in the middle of the elevator, and when the doors closed and Cassie felt the first pull of the elevator lifting, she launched herself at him.

There was no such thing as gravity or decorum. Reid met her intensity and groaned into their kiss, his hands snuggly under the sheer underpants, cupping her bottom and squeezing. A moan escaped Cassie's lips, which also made her giggle.

All too soon, another *ding* alerted them to their arrival on the top floor, and Cassie grabbed Reid's hand and led him to her apartment. She fished a key out of the side of her intricate moto boots, knowing as she bent down, Reid was getting a very well-endowed show. *Let him look,* she thought to herself. He could make the most of it in a minute.

With her door unlocked, she turned around to face him and smiled at him. He smiled back at her, not just a half smirk, but a full-fledged, beautiful smile, like he was already satisfied. She opened the door, pulled him by the belt loop through the threshold, and they stumbled in, kissing and caressing all the way.

Breaking away for a moment, Cassie placed her apartment key

in a small trinket dish on her hallway credenza and took in the bright morning-light view of River North, and then took off Reid's leather jacket, coyly glancing over her shoulder at him. She could hear his breath hitch as she stopped by her sofa, leaning against the back to unzip and unbuckle one moto boot and then the other, letting them each hit the floor with a *thud*. Then she walked with an extra swing in her hips down the hallway, pausing briefly when she realized he was also removing articles of clothing as he followed her.

By the time she reached her bedroom, Reid had removed everything but his formfitting black boxer briefs, and she smiled to show him she liked what she saw. His long, lanky form was lithe and hard, and as she paused in the doorway of her room, she ran her hand over his abs, making him shiver, and goose bumps pebbled her skin in response. Cassie hooked a finger in the waistband of his boxers and pulled him toward her.

They fumbled their way toward her bed, through the maze of shoes and discarded clothes Cassie didn't have the time to worry about now. All that mattered was Reid was there, in her arms, in her home, and nothing else.

"Cass," Reid growled, so deep and full she felt it in her heart. "Should we keep going?"

Cassie kissed his neck, grazing her hands over his chest and up to his face. "Yes, Reid."

With that, they fell backward, cushioned by the many pillows and plush blankets on her bed. Cassie felt every muscle of Reid's body against her own, and she let herself go. Her legs wrapped around his waist, and she arched up to meet his core against hers, feeling the bulge of his erection against her belly. She reached in the bedside table drawer and handed him a condom. As Reid opened the foil package and rolled it down his length, Cassie sat up and tugged at the flimsy bralette she still wore.

"Allow me," he said, now kneeling on the floor next to the bed.

Cassie raised her arms and felt a proud sense of self when she saw the look on Reid's face once he'd taken the bra off her.

"You are so beautiful," he said, and she smiled, feeling the heat rise between them.

Reid gently circled his arms around her, Cassie feeling his movements with every nerve in her body. She shivered as he ran his hands around her middle and up her back, pulling her closer to him in an embrace while kissing her the entire time. She ran her hand up and down his arms, bringing his hands from her back to her front, allowing him to cup her breasts and squeeze the tight buds her nipples had become. He caressed and explored, dipping his head down to kiss her skin and find what made her feel good.

She let out a moan and began panting and let Reid discover what he liked about her body. It was everything.

"You're incredible," he murmured, gazing down at her. He stopped at the sheer leopard-print underpants she still had on. "We should probably remove the rest of the merchandise, right?"

"It'd be for the best," Cassie readily agreed, lifting up so he could easily take the cheekies off. Throwing them to the side, Reid looked at her again, gently caressing her inner thighs and not quite touching where she wanted him most. "Please, Reid, touch me."

The slight pleading in her voice, her fevered breath, and her complete nakedness sent Reid over an edge she didn't anticipate. No sooner than she said "touch me" was Reid's mouth on her, hot and sweet and hungry. A guttural sound erupted from Cassie's throat as he licked and sucked and massaged and touched. Cassie felt her core wind into a ball and slowly, deliciously unwind with each twist of his tongue, each curl of his fingers, and every moan from her own body. Reid seemed to know exactly the right way to kiss, to move, to rub, and it was going to push her over.

Cassie felt the orgasm building inside her, and before she came, she reached down to his face. He stopped, looking up at her and smiling. "I want you," she said. "Inside me. Now."

Smiling more, Reid slid up Cassie's body, and with a swift thrust, filled Cassie in the way she wanted and beyond.

Cassie hadn't felt this way with anyone before—full, satisfied, and overcome with adoration, both for herself and for the man on top of her. They fell into a gentle rhythm, hazy sunlight filtering through curtains, soft moans escaping them both, the sound of their coupling the only thing that mattered.

"Cassie," Reid called out. "You feel amazing. So good."

"Don't stop, Reid," Cassie said, closing her eyes, again feeling her core tighten and bloom.

"Don't stop," she panted out.

Suddenly Cassie felt the blazing sun burst before her eyes, Reid pumping harder and faster than before. She called his name as she came, and moments later, Reid let a deep moan out as he came, too, his forehead against hers, both of them breathing hard. Hands entwined, Reid moved out of her, a sigh exhaled from them both, and then they were kissing again, frantic with need.

"You gotta give me a minute before round two, boss," Reid said, his hand at her cheek and then suddenly at her breast and then at her waist.

"I don't want to wait," Cassie said, writhing against his touch, inching up to move his hand a few inches south. "Touch me. Again."

Reid gladly did as he was told, his hand finding her clit—warm and wet and ready—slowly at first, and then building speed. "Look at me, Cass."

She closed her eyes. With his other hand, he tipped her chin up, hand on her cheek. "Look at me while you come again."

His hand worked feverishly, rubbing just roughly enough to send her over the edge. Her eyes opened, wild and free, "Reid," she gasped, "Reid, I'm . . ."

"I know," he said, his forehead against hers, eyes wide open, watching her pupils dilate and then seeing her eyes close as she whimpered and moaned into oblivion once more.

TEN

Reid felt like he existed somewhere between sleep and dreaming. He had no idea what time it was or how much of the day had passed. Cassie was napping next to him, and in the crimson light that shone through her slightly sheer curtains, he saw freckles dotting her nose and cheeks. Reid wanted to count them and memorize their placement, but instead he hoped for more opportunities to see her in this exact sunlight, so he could learn the contours of her body, every other spot she had a freckle, and what made her cry out. He gently gathered her to his chest and fell asleep.

He soon woke up again, painfully aware of Cassie's absence. He heard movement and turned over to see her sitting at a small vanity, taking down her hair from the intricate goddess style. Her hair fell in perfect ringlets, coiling up like springs when she ran her fingers through each knot. Cassie had touched up her makeup and was wearing a playful pair of sporty boy shorts and a bra, both with what had become the Dreamland signature caution tape straps.

Reid was pleased to see that when she noticed he was awake, her whole face lit up. "Why hello, sleepyhead."

"How long have you been up?"

"Fifteen minutes or so," she replied, turning herself around to face him, but staying at her vanity. "Listen, Reid—"

"Today was incredible, Cassie," he said before she could backtrack on what happened between them.

"It was, really it was. But we have to figure out how to navigate our new dynamic while we're working." She fidgeted in her seat, wringing her hands together and not looking him in the eye. "I don't want to mess this up."

"Which 'this' do you mean—us, or the job?"

Cassie didn't answer right away, and Reid was about to get up and give her a good look at what she'd miss out on before putting on clothes and leaving, when she answered.

"Both, I think."

"Then let's just let things happen," he said, his voice sounded strange and desperate. "Let's agree to be professional on set, when we have a crew, but when it's just us, off duty, let's see where this goes. Because I also don't want to mess 'this' up," he said.

"All right, Montgomery," she said, finally coming back to bed. He pulled her close to him, kissing her neck and then her shoulder, and went to slip down a bra strap when she stopped his hand. "I am dressed for *work*, thank you very much. Not just for you to undress me again. At least not right now. We have work to do."

"Got it, boss." He smiled, kissing her cheek. "Do you know where my underwear ended up?"

"No idea, but there's a variety of brand-new cheekies you could wear instead," she said, comically wagging her eyebrows at him.

"If it turns you on, I'd do it."

Peals of giggles came from Cassie as she continued to get ready. "Maybe later."

Reid smiled and stood up, brazenly letting the covers fall as he started to search around the room for his own underwear. Maybe they were under the bed or under one of Cassie's many, many throw pillows, but he'd have to do without if they had a chance of getting back downstairs both before they lost the sunlight or the rest of the BB team arrived for the final shots of the day. He stole a glance at Cassie, catching her watching him walk around her room naked— her cheeks blushed just as pink as the lipstick she was applying. He felt his own face warm, but he smiled at her and winked.

Locating his jeans just outside the doorway to Cassie's room, Reid put them on and glanced at his phone before looking for his shirt. He had a message from Russ, which he decided to ignore— he'd deal with him later. He also had an email alert from his favorite marketing manager, Rebecca. He walked into Cassie's kitchen and perched against a barstool. And considering his past with Rebecca, Reid didn't want to read this email in front of Cassie.

Skimming through pleasantries and a few details about a day of catalog photos, Reid got to the final line of the email he was dreading.

With the first day of photos for Dreamland under your belt, do you foresee any future pushback with the BB team? Let me know ASAP if there's anything to worry about.

Why the hell were they so quick to assume Cassie would cause a problem? Reid just didn't get it. On set, their flirting aside, Cassie had been professional and ready to do what she had been hired to do—model and art direct. If there was anything of concern, it was that she had shut down when she was uncomfortable . . . which was understandable, considering it was her first major modeling gig. And he had been there to help her through it.

He had helped her through a few other things as well . . . multiple times, in fact.

Feeling smug and incredibly satisfied with the events of the day so far, Reid fired off a vague email to Rebecca. Because he had agreed to be the Luscious Lingerie eyes, he decided to keep things neutral but honest, so his extra "signing bonus" wasn't unwarranted.

First day of Dreamland was fine. CH needed a bit of handholding, but things moved along well. Once we got started, she caught on and led the way. I'll have proofs later this week, per her approval to send to you and the LL team.

"Why so serious?" Cassie asked, bumping him with her hip. She was fully coiffed, primped, and outfitted in caution tape lingerie topped with a mesh boxer's robe; even the sash read "caution." Cassie truly was a knockout.

"Work emails," Reid answered, quickly putting his phone in his back pocket as Cassie nestled herself between his thighs and draped her arms over his shoulders.

"Ready for round two?" she asked, putting her fists up and bobbing back and forth on her feet.

"Wouldn't this be round three or four for you at this point?"

"Round two of photos, of course." Cassie playfully punched his shoulder and laughed. "We should head down; Sam and Kit are on their way."

Reid nodded, grabbing his shirt from her couch where he must have thrown it off earlier. Still no sign of his boxer briefs, but his lack of underpants was the least of his worries.

"Reid just uploaded the shots from yesterday," Dana called from her couch as Cassie walked in. "They look insanely good. You two are a dream team."

Cassie saw the shots immediately after the photo shoot ended; Reid had gone back up to her apartment once they finished shooting, and they had looked at the photos together . . . among other things.

"It's been fun working with him, surprisingly," Cassie said, attempting to be nonchalant as she sat down at the opposite end of the couch. Dana continued to scroll on her laptop.

"This first set of you on the bike with the jacket are fire," Dana said, flipping the laptop around so Cassie could see. "You look like an alien queen ready to ride into trouble."

Cassie felt the blush warm her cheeks, because those early-in-the-day shots made her think about what came after that. And what occurred later that evening. And again that morning.

"Oh my God. The girls were right. You're sleeping with him."

"What did they say?" Cassie said, feeling defensive. She hadn't said anything concrete to anyone, but any time she spent at the studio this week had been an exercise in her abilities to skirt around that specific topic.

"Sam texted me the day of the shoot because Reid asked for it to be a 'closed set.'" She made finger quotes when she said the latter. "She said something in the way he talked about working with you made her think there was more going on between you two. And after the Friendsgiving incident, well, it was inevitable."

Cassie didn't say anything, rolling her eyes and readjusting her position on the couch. She redid the plop of curls on top of her head and avoided eye contact with Dana.

"Come on, Cassie," Dana begged. "I'm hormonal, lonely, going stir-crazy, and I can't drink. Please give me details. I know you want to tell me, your best friend since we were twelve, every single thing."

"I most certainly do not," Cassie countered, throwing a fluffy white pillow in Dana's direction. She grabbed it and placed it behind her, leaning back and waiting for Cassie to start talking. Instead, Cassie just pulled the hood of her oversize cardigan as far down as it could, hiding her giddy face. She peeked back out at Dana, who was beaming.

"That good, eh?"

Cassie sighed and let her head drop on the couch cushion. "Better. I've never felt this way before. And it's not just the sex, it's more than that. He makes me feel . . . everything. Happy, scared, bewildered, flabbergasted, confident, and . . . everything."

"Why, Cassandra Harris, I do think you are smitten," Dana said, grabbing Cassie's hand. "And you're okay, working with him and all?"

"I hope we can make it work, because I don't want to ruin either of these things. The shots look good, and we do the group photo shoot in February. We're going to the Rookery next week for more solo shots—with Sam and Kit because we'll have more props and faster outfit changes," Cassie added the last bit to remind herself that they'd have an audience, albeit a safe audience, but an audience, nonetheless. "There's time between each photo shoot for us to spend together outside of work, which I think is something we need to do. Go on a proper date, get out of this neighborhood."

"Why would you do that? How will I keep tabs on your goings-on?"

"Exactly," Cassie said.

"I'm happy for you, pal. You're killing it as a model and, more important, as art director. You're working with a great photographer, you're leading our team to awesomeness, *and* you're having orgasms. Who says we can't have it all?"

Later on, Cassie walked home, breathing in fresh air and taking her time so she could settle in with her thoughts. Reid Montgomery—bad-boy pinup photographer, genuinely nice guy, supremely sexy, and great lay—was important to her. And she liked having someone to think about, wonder about, and hope about. Thinking about the way he had looked at her when he thought she was still asleep after their first time, wondering what else he liked to do in and out of bed, hoping he'd text or call her soon . . . all things she hadn't had with another person in a long time. It made her happy.

She felt her phone buzz and had to admit she was a tiny bit disappointed when it wasn't Reid.

> Headed to Bugles in 15, want to meet up?

A text from Sam, accompanied by a selfie of her flicking off the camera while Kit grinned in the background.

CASSIE

> Just left Dana's, heading home, but may come out later. OK if I invite Reid?

SAM

I just texted him and he said to ask
you. You two are gross.

Cassie smiled as she reached her apartment building and decided to take the stairs. She had rounded the corner to her floor and
was reaching for the stairwell door when it opened.

"Mom? What are you doing here?"

"Visiting my daughter on a nice winter day is so horrible?" Her
mom, Glenda, walked back into the hallway to Cassie's floor and
gave her daughter a hug.

"I was just getting back from the studio and Dana's. What's going on?"

"Well, I wasn't too far away, checking in on the new gallery
space opening in a couple of months, and thought I'd stop by. But
I was especially surprised when I opened up Insta-book—"

"Instagram, Mom."

Her mother raised an eyebrow at her, and Cassie had one of
those *I'm turning into my mother* moments.

"Whatever, dear. But imagine my dismay, and your father's as
well, when this is what our daughter—our sweet, demure, professional daughter—is currently doing." Handing over her phone,
Cassie looked down and saw half of her ass in a repost by the Luscious Lingerie Instagram account. "So you're modeling lingerie now?
I thought that was Dana's job."

"Mom, I can explain. Dana is pregnant and couldn't do the job
we envisioned. I stepped in to help out."

Her mother looked at her over the ridge of her glasses. "You
volunteered to take off all of your clothes?"

"Well, Dana suggested I do it, and honestly I'm really glad she did. I'm still art directing the campaign, there's a really talented photographer involved, and this is going to be good for business and my own career."

Cassie could feel her shoulders rising, and her voice was getting pitchy. She looked at her mom, and aside from feeling slightly perturbed about her daughter scantily clad on the internet, Glenda didn't look upset, just surprised.

"Also, did you hear what I said? Dana is pregnant!"

"Oh, honey, I knew that already. I sent a gift and everything. I saw Riki at Mariano's a month ago." Cassie knew her mom liked to stop by her favorite market whenever she was in the city and had time to hit the salad bar. "I'm not even mad about the photos. What I am mad about is that you didn't tell me or your dad that your campaign shoot was starting this week. Or that you were starring in it. Why didn't you mention it at brunch in the last few weeks?"

"It's taken me a while to get used to the idea. But you should see the clothes, Mom. They're really unique, nice quality, empowering, and they fit a variety of sizes. The company is awesome and has been lovely to work with, too." In the hall toward her room, Cassie wheeled over a clothing rack of lingerie to show her mom. "Next week we're getting stuff for the big group shots. My apartment and the studio will be covered in lace and spandex."

Cassie could feel her mother studying her, and she hoped it was because she was thriving and having fun with her work, not because she was wearing underwear in a professional setting.

"These are cute," Glenda said with a smirk, holding up a black pair of shorts Cassie didn't recognize. "But they don't really fit in with the rest of the collection."

Oh God oh God oh God Reid's boxer briefs.

Somehow, they ended up on the bottom of the rack of clothing, and now her mother was holding them. *This is so weird*, Cassie thought.

"Well, those aren't, those are my, they don't . . ." Cassie sputtered, looking for an explanation, but took a deep breath, squared her shoulders, and calmly took them from her mom. "Those belong to someone else."

"I gathered as much, Cassandra," Glenda said, smiling. "You've had a look about you for a while, and I knew things were going well at work, but I've guessed there was something else. It's nice to see you happy."

"Thanks, Mom." That went better than expected.

"You should invite this person to brunch this weekend. Your father and I are very curious."

There it was. A nice little bombshell of a suggestion that was anything but. "I'll see if he's free."

"Does *he* have a name?"

"Reid, Mom, okay? That's all you're getting from me for now." Cassie smiled sweetly and then narrowed her eyes at her mom. "So what's this gallery you mentioned?"

"That's really what I wanted to talk to you about," Glenda replied, scooting up into one of the barstools by Cassie's kitchen island. "It's a new space in Wicker Park. A gallery for now, but it could be a meeting or event space, too. Multifunction, nonresidential. I was wondering if you could reach out to some artists for a soft open in two months or so . . . Maybe even show something yourself?"

Cassie gave her a curt smile and said, "I'll reach out to some local friends and a few people in Milwaukee and Madison, too."

"Cassandra," her mom said. "Why not show your skills? I know you love this boudoir stuff and working with Dana and now apparently modeling, but you're talented in your own right. Don't forget that."

"I know, Mom, and I like using my talent to make people feel beautiful. Myself included." As soon as she said that out loud, Cassie realized it was true. She was known for making her clients feel at ease and unique because of her even-keeled demeanor and out-of-the-box ideas for locations and props. And having Reid to put her at ease when she was uncomfortable with her own photo shoots, but still under her art direction, made Cassie feel in charge and empowered.

Cassie's phone buzzed with a text message right as her mom's did, too. Reid was asking if she was heading to Bugles or staying in, with a winking emoji. Cassie tried to stop the smile from taking over her face.

"Well, your father is wondering where I am, and I see you are preoccupied," Glenda said, gathering her jacket. "I'll see you and this Reid on Sunday. I've already made a reservation at Simone's again, so I'll just update it to four."

"Bye, Mom," Cassie said, giving her mom a tight squeeze and walking her to the door. "I'll think about the gallery and get you a list of potential names before Sunday."

"Cassie," Reid breathed out. Was this real life? Could he even form words? Instead of meeting up with everyone at Bugles, Cassie asked him to come over and no sooner than he was through the door had she dragged him to her room, pulled off his pants—though carefully placed his boxers on her side table—sat him down, and was giving him the best blow job of his life. Her hands worked in unison with her mouth, warm and soft, moving up and down at the right rhythm . . .

"Cass, wait, I'm going to—" but it was too late. He came, hard and fast and he closed his eyes in satisfaction. When he opened them, Cassie was looking up at him and smiling, with an edge.

"What's going on? That was great, really it was, but something's up."

"My mother found your boxer briefs when she came by earlier."

Reid felt his eyes widen. "Sorry about that."

"It was good, in a way. I hadn't really told my parents I was seeing anyone, so that gave it away."

"Good," he said, pulling his underwear back on and then bringing Cassie closer, her lush thighs straddling his lap from under her very demure black dress, buttoned all the way up. He reached for the top button, but she grabbed his hand and kissed it.

"I'm glad you think so, because now that they know I'm seeing someone, they invited you to Sunday brunch this weekend."

Before he knew what was happening, Reid was laughing. Uncontrollably. And Cassie's confused face made him laugh more. She playfully pushed him, and he fell back on her cushy bed.

"What is so funny?" she asked, smacking his chest and starting to get up. His hands went to her waist to keep her on top of him. Rolling her eyes and then smoothing her dress around her in a perfect circle, she let out a tiny sigh and waited for an answer.

"Did you bring me over here and give me possibly the best blow job of all time just to ask me to go out to brunch with your parents?"

"Would it be terrible if I said yes?"

"Cassie, I'm not complaining at all about what just happened, but please don't feel like you have to butter me up to do things like meet your parents. I'd love to meet your parents."

"Really?"

He understood where she was coming from; he wasn't close to his parents, so why would he want to meet hers? But he'd always liked meeting the families of the people he cared about and was always pleasantly surprised when they were nothing like his.

"Yes. You've made them sound pretty great, and like I told you before, I want to make this work, and—"

"Shut up, Reid," Cassie said seriously.

"Why?"

"Because I'm going to take my dress off and then I'm going to kiss you, and then I'm probably going to give you another beej before we—"

"Did you just say beej?"

Cassie stopped unbuttoning her very prim and proper black dress, revealing a very improper lacy bra. "Do you want another one or not?"

"Yes, please."

Later, while Cassie was in the kitchen making a cup of tea and Reid was leaning on the island, he said something he'd been thinking about for a while. "I want to take you out on a date."

"Right now?" she said, sipping her hot beverage.

"No, Cass, but I want to take you out, have a full day with you. Maybe Friday?"

She pulled out her phone to check her calendar. "That works. I have two boudoir sessions on Saturday, so I was just planning on catching up on contracts and some editing during the day on Friday."

"I'll come by the studio in the afternoon to pick you up," he said, smiling.

"You look very pleased with yourself," she said, pushing a mug of tea toward him. "Should I be worried? And what should I wear?"

"Clothing is always optional when it comes to you, but at least wear comfortable shoes to walk around in."

"I'll keep that in mind. Are you going to tell me what we'll be doing?"

"Bring your most trusted camera, and we'll go from there," he replied, formulating a plan for the perfect date with Cassie.

ELEVEN

—

Remind me who's coming in tomorrow?" Cassie asked Sam on Friday after lunch.

"First, it's a new client, wedding gift for her husband-to-be. She dropped off her stuff this morning before you got in. Should be simple," Sam replied. "But then you have a couples session with the Masons."

Cassie groaned and pouted. The Masons were perhaps their most loyal clients, but they always got a little too fresh with each other during their sessions. They had been coming in every few months for the last two years and never seemed to catch on that no one actually wanted to see them grinding on each other. Sure, the very nature of boudoir photography was to look and feel sexy, but not necessarily put on a show for the photographer.

"Did you say the Masons?" Kit chimed in. "Do you think he'll make me put 'guyliner' on him again?"

"Probably, they put 'emo music video' down for their style request. But they're bringing their own clothes," Sam said as the buzzer rang.

Cassie jumped a little, felt her cheeks warm before she could say it was Reid.

"Reid, be a darling and hold these," Kit said as he walked in a few minutes later. She handed him six riding crops and blindfolds. "Now where did I put that whip?"

"What did you just involve me in?"

"Didn't you read the call sheet for the final group session?" Sam said.

Cassie smirked at how punchy she was about her schedules.

"The swimwear shoot next month? Cassie will be in the black latex suit, Kit and I will be in silver bikinis, and everyone else will be in silver or white lace lingerie. Cassie will be our dominatrix queen, supervising a really weird orgy."

"I still think a heavily pregnant Dana would make for a better dominatrix queen than me," Cassie said, taking the riding crops from Reid and putting them on a shelf. She kissed his cheek.

"Get a room," Sam said to them as she gathered her things. "See you both on Monday."

"Kit, are you okay to lock up?"

"Of course, mes chers, just getting organized for tomorrow and then I'll be off," Kit said, smiling brightly at them both. "What are you two up to this afternoon? Bit brisk out, no?"

"Yes, what are we doing today?" Cassie asked, elbowing Reid in his side. "Wait, what are you doing with that blindfold?"

"Nothing, nothing at all," he said, not so slyly putting it in his back pocket, sheepishly grinning at Kit. "We'll return it on Monday."

"All right, and now we're going." Cassie pushed Reid toward the door. "Bye, Kit."

Kit waved them off, pulling the door shut as they descended the stairs. As he walked, Cassie watched his hips move in his jeans and liked how he glanced back at her every now and then. But mostly she just looked at his butt because it was really cute.

They walked outside, steeled themselves against the cold temps, and fell into step together as they walked.

"Now will you tell me where we're going?"

"To an L stop," Reid replied, mouth forming that slightly sideways smirk. The same smirk she was starting to crave seeing every single day.

Cassie hated being that girl who fell hard and fast for a guy, especially once they started sleeping together on a regular basis, but she had never felt so at ease with someone like Reid so quickly. She had gotten to know him better and shared things with him that she'd told only to her best friends. She felt like she could trust him, and that made being intimate with him more meaningful. Sometimes she wished he'd open up a bit more to her about things outside of work, but then she'd remind herself he had a less than ideal upbringing, and hopefully he'd tell her more when he was fully ready.

Making their way up the stairs to wait for the train, they huddled in the vestibule that did little to stop the harsh wind blowing that day. Reid stood facing Cassie, trying to block the wind.

See? He's thoughtful and protective and just plain wonderful, she told herself. *And you're falling fast for him.*

There was no point in trying to deny it, especially to herself. She was falling for Reid, and she was going to let it happen. It felt right and fun and sweet. Cassie wanted to continue to feel this way.

"This weather has thrown a curveball in my plan," Reid said, burying his hands in her pockets and pulling her closer to him. "Are your pockets lined with fleece?"

"Are yours not?" Cassie retorted. "You need a proper winter parka, not just your leather jacket, silly."

"I'm wearing a sweater under it," he insisted. "I'll be fine. And now I can put my hands in your pockets for warmth and do this." He kissed her, his nose cold against hers, his mouth warm.

"So what was your plan?" Cassie asked after the kiss ended.

"I wanted to just wander around the city and take photos with you. Mostly of you, but I know you're over being in front of the camera, so I thought we could have a muse day."

"I like being in front of the camera when you're behind it," Cassie said. "Amuse day?"

"A. Muse. Day," he explained. "Where you search for your muse. We've both been busy, but the last thing I want to do is get stuck in a routine rut. Every couple of months, I pick a neighborhood and wander and just take photos of what looks cool. No setting up a shot, no outside parameters. Just me, my camera, and the moment."

"That sounds very nice, but this wind is going to literally take my nose with it the next time it gusts," Cassie said, turning to Reid when the wind did blow again, though it wasn't as gusty as it had been on their walk over. "What's the plan now?"

"I'm going to take you to a place that I adore, and I think it will be exactly what you need."

"Back to your apartment?" Cassie had yet to go there yet; Reid was always at her place.

"Maybe later," he said, breaking away as the train arrived. Once they were on and seated, he continued. "If you're willing, I want to take you somewhere to hopefully inspire some ideas for your side project."

The last time either of them had brought up Iconic Lights, Cassie had accused him of stealing her idea. In the heat of the moment, she failed to realize that he was really offering to help her sort out her ideas about the concepts she wanted to include, and trying to find out if there were any specific details that made a big difference to the integrity of what she was going to portray. Now, she was ready to keep talking to him about it.

"And where would that be?"

"Salvage One," he replied. "The vintage shop and rental place."

"Oh, I know it well," Cassie said, smiling. "I've done a couple of sessions there. I haven't spent too much time in the store, though."

Reid looked smug with himself as the train lurched toward its destination. And Cassie had to admit it was a thoughtful date idea.

It was a short walk to the shop, and because it was a cold afternoon in January, it wasn't very busy. They were greeted by a woman who offered to hang up their coats, and Reid explained the goal of coming there: to find inspiration. She smiled and wished them luck.

Cassie loved antique shops like this—full of hidden gems from the past. The recent interest in mid-century modern decor and furniture was great because that style was now readily available, but nothing compared to the real deal. The low couches, sleek angled chairs, and retro atomic patterns always appealed to Cassie, and she was thrilled to see so much of it in the store.

"Cassie, look up," Reid said, gazing at the ceiling. A mint-condition Sputnik-style chandelier was overhead, brass fixtures gleaming. Instead of the common white-coated bulbs, this one had clear light bulbs, so Cassie could see the filament. It wasn't turned on, so the natural light shone through the glass and twinkled off the bright brass and metal coils, casting beautiful shadows.

Thank goodness for high-zoom technology because Cassie was entranced. She wanted to capture as many angles as possible of the chandelier and the way the brass burned in the sunlight that had suddenly burst through the cloudy Chicago afternoon sky.

Cassie took photos with her trusty 35mm Fujifilm SLR camera for who knows how long. Everywhere she turned in Salvage One, there was unique glasswork sparkling in the light, dark shadows cast across gilded mirrors, and windows hazed with age, but it was exactly what Cassie was looking for when it came to her own side project.

Reid quietly followed her around the shop, making sure to stay out of the way. She appreciated his company and the thought that went into this proper date. Cassie looked back at him at one point, while he stood between two massive wooden bookshelves. He took a step forward, and Cassie put up her hand.

"Don't move," she said.

He stilled, only slightly moving his eyes to notice what Cassie noticed. She knew it was making him uncomfortable, but he humored her and let her shoot.

"You should consider a career in modeling, Mr. Montgomery," Cassie said, inching closer to him. The light was coming in from behind her, flooding his face in warm light. To some photographers, he'd be considered washed out, but she saw how it would illuminate his honey-green eyes, showcase the stubble on his jawline, the shadows framing his face just so—deepening the crease of his clavicle, which she recently learned was a very ticklish spot for him—his unkempt hair spiking into the darkness surrounding him. He was a bright spot in the shadows, both in the photos she was taking and in her life.

Cassie stopped looking through the viewfinder of her camera and looked at him. She knew she was staring, but it didn't matter. He didn't seem to mind, as he met her gaze and didn't break it.

"What is it?" he gently asked.

"Nothing," Cassie replied, smiling back at him. "Just looking at you."

He smiled back and took her hand.

"This is just what I needed," Cassie said, leaning against Reid as they continued to peruse. "I feel refreshed and really good. You know, my mom suggested that maybe I show something at the gallery she's opening soon. Maybe I will."

"I think that'd be really cool, something new," he agreed.

They spent a while longer looking around, Cassie deciding to buy a milk glass trifle dish for Kit's upcoming work anniversary, and then they braved the cold once again. Cassie didn't mind the weather anymore; she had a warm feeling all her own.

After a delicious early dinner at the Publican, Reid and Cassie continued their trek around Chicago, walking around some more before getting on the bus that would take them to River North.

Spending the afternoon with Cassie, taking photos, exploring a different neighborhood, and being near each other was better than he expected. They didn't feel the added pressure to act professionally like at work, and they didn't need to force a label on whatever this was. They could simply be together. Cassie was different from any woman he'd ever known—he trusted her, was impressed by her talent and determination, and she made him feel strong and confident and silly and shy all at the same time.

"Where to next?" Cassie asked, bumping into Reid's side, bringing him back from his thoughts. "Now can we go back to your apartment?"

"I had a couple more stops planned," Reid explained, laughing. "But you really want to see my apartment, and I'm not one to deny a lady's request."

"Why don't you tell me about what else you had planned," Cassie said, taking his hand.

"Well, first, I planned on doing this," he said, suddenly stopping and kissing her cheek and down her neck, slipping his hand under her bright yellow scarf. His cool hand met the warmth of her neck, making her gasp.

"Is that all?" she breathed, turning her head so their lips were almost touching, but not quite. Reid moved his head down and kissed her deeply, in the middle of the sidewalk. They were near the bus stop, and the evening commuter traffic had picked up. Annoyed passersby walked around them, but Reid didn't care. He wanted to kiss Cassie.

"Then what?" Cassie asked, breathing deeply as her deep brown eyes looked up at him.

"Then I thought we could go to the Drifter for the burlesque show and have dessert," he suggested, leading her toward the bus vestibule.

Cassie's laughter rang out from behind him. He thought the speakeasy vibe of the Drifter would be right up her alley. "What's so funny?"

"That sounds lovely, really it does, but," Cassie began, her laughter overtaking her once again, "Kit and Sam both dance in that show. And while I don't think they'd mind, I don't want you to get too turned on by them when I'm in the room."

Reid felt his mouth drop open and then close again. He had no idea Kit and Sam danced burlesque. Sure, he'd seen local baristas and the guy who worked at his favorite record shop at the Drifter's show, but never anyone he actually knew and had conversations with on a regular basis.

"They just started, actually. They took a class for fun, kept up with it, and started working on a show together. Now they want to start performing more," Cassie said, noticing what Reid assumed was a puzzled look on his face. "So, you probably haven't seen them, unless you're taking that dance class, too."

"Maybe I am," Reid said. "And as much as I enjoy Kit and Sam, I'd rather be around them when they're actually wearing clothes."

"Correct answer, though you will be seeing them scantily clad in bathing suits soon," Cassie replied as they got on the bus and found a seat together. "They mentioned going to Bugles after the show, but that won't be until much, much later. And we can always get dessert there."

The lurch of the bus turning caused Cassie to lean on Reid. Once the bus evened out, Cassie stayed leaning on him, and Reid was getting used to the feel of her snuggled against him.

"Then we have some time for other things," Reid whispered, and he watched her eyebrow raise and a mischievous smile curl her lips.

"Or we could stay in entirely," she said, taking his hand in hers. "Let's play it by ear."

Deciding to take their chances in the blustery weather and walk from River North to the Gold Coast rather than transfer to yet another bus, Reid was practically running to his apartment when they finally reached his neighborhood. With the way Cassie kept looking up at him through heavy-lidded eyes, Reid was more than ready to spend some quality alone time with her.

"I didn't realize you lived nearby," Cassie said as he stopped outside his building. It was a newer high-rise, full of studios and apartments of different sizes. Some of the floors were still being worked on, but Reid didn't mind the noise of construction. "I remember when they started working on this building last year."

"Yeah, I was one of the first people to move in." Reid unlocked the door and nodded at the doorman. They headed toward the elevator, which was luckily waiting on the first floor.

"For some reason I imagined you in an older building," Cassie said.

"What, like yours?"

She shrugged. "Maybe."

Up on the fifteenth floor, Reid led her down the hall to his corner apartment. He paid exponentially more for being in the corner, but there was a sense of privacy he really enjoyed. And it had a stunning view.

He opened the door for Cassie and let her in first. Luckily, he'd had the sense to clean up earlier that day. It may not have the vintage feel Cassie anticipated, but it was his little home and he liked it.

And seeing Cassie in it felt right.

Of course, Cassie immediately gravitated toward his huge windows, where the entire neighborhood was lit up below them. She peeled off her jacket and scarf and stood in front of the sliding glass doors that led to a balcony.

"Reid, this view is gorgeous," she said, wrapping her arms around herself.

He wasn't looking out the windows but at her. He came up behind her and breathed her in. "You are gorgeous."

Cassie turned around and immediately put her mouth on his. She laced her fingers around his neck as he snaked his arms around her, pulling her close, deepening their kiss. He backed up to where his couch was, bringing her down with him.

The day they had spent in such close proximity but not privately left them both desperate for the other—even with clothes on, the heat between them was almost unbearable. Cassie writhed on top of Reid, sending his body into overdrive.

"Sit up, Cassie," he urged. Looking up at her, lips swollen from his kiss, she was perfect, and she was his. She was wearing a rather sweet-looking cardigan with lace running along the buttons, which he ran his fingers over before he started at the bottom button and worked his way up. Each button revealed more of a simple little white tank top. On anyone else it would have been any other normal garment, but on Cassie, it was hotter than most of the lingerie he'd already seen her in.

Reid slid the cardigan down over Cassie's arms and brought her back to him to continue kissing her. Her skin looked bronzed in the dim light of the room from his small lamp and the lights from the city view behind them. She was soft and lush, trembling in his arms, ready for more.

Reid shifted underneath her, so she was still in his lap and he was sitting up. Cassie reached for his shirt, but he stopped her. Gently he pushed her back on the couch, and he unzipped her jeans, sliding them off her legs. He ran his hands back up the length of her legs, pausing before touching just beside where he knew she ached for him, and her hips reached up to meet his hand.

"What do you want, Cassie?" he asked, running a finger along the inner edge of her underpants. "Tell me."

"You, Reid," she said, her voice deep and dusky. "I want you."

At that, something loosened inside of Reid that he hadn't realized he was holding back until that moment. He yanked off her underpants, which made Cassie gasp with delight, and kissed his way up her legs, playfully biting at her thighs, and then, with a teasing lick at her center, he all but devoured her.

Reid moved on instinct alone, feeling when Cassie shuddered with pleasure from licking, sucking, and touching. The sounds she made came from deep within her, and he knew he'd never tire from hearing them. He slipped a finger inside her, curling it around and pulsing in and out, and just when he felt her begin to clench around him, Cassie stopped him and started to pull him up.

Reid shook his head, keeping his hand on her. "I planned this day for you, and it included this, too."

Cassie smiled and leaned back, raising her hips, brazenly pushing her sex against his hand, grinding. Reid felt her tense around his finger, and he slipped in another, working them together harder and faster. He knew she liked it because of the sexy little sounds and sighs of pleasures she made. Suddenly, she called out his name and stilled his hand with her own.

Reid smiled—he loved watching her do that. This time when he felt her pull him up toward her, a growl escaped from the back of his own throat. He discarded his clothes, took a condom from his jeans pocket—his earlier wishful thinking coming to fruition—and was inside her in record speed.

She was still wearing that simple, sexy white tank top that he pulled down along with the cup of her bra to expose one beautiful breast, which he kneaded and teased, causing another moan to come from Cassie's mouth. Reid felt the pressure building in his body and knew his own release was near, but he slowed down, moved deeper, and kissed Cassie. She started moving faster against him, crying out his name, tightening and releasing around him at the same time. His thrusts picked up in speed, riding out her orgasm as his own started.

"Cass," he whispered through heavy breaths. "That was incredible." His hand was still on her breast, their foreheads touching, their breaths steadying together. He slid out of her with a sigh, discarded the condom, and reached for the blanket draped over an armchair. Reid brought Cassie toward him, and they snuggled under the warmth.

"I'm going to have to let you take me on dates more often," Cassie said, reaching up and tracing his jawline with her hand. "This has been an awesome day."

"I'm glad you had fun," he said, kissing her forehead. "I'd like to take you on more dates . . . On an exclusive basis."

Reid smiled as he watched Cassie start to grin.

She bit her bottom lip and then said, "Why, Reid Montgomery, did you just ask me to be your girlfriend?"

"In so many words," he said, bringing a hand to her face. "Is that cool?"

Cassie nodded, cradling the hand that was caressing her cheek. "I'd really like that a lot." Then she started to giggle. And those giggles turned into a full-on chuckle.

"As much as I love your laughter, this isn't exactly the reaction I expected," Reid said, getting playfully defensive.

Cassie calmed herself. "It's refreshing to have a label, and it's just nice, and cute, and you're cute and very sexy and . . . I'm happy. You make me happy." She nestled into Reid's chest and he tightened his embrace around her.

TWELVE

*W*ell, *this is awkward.*

Reid got to Simone's early so he could check in with James and make sure he knew to make things extra special for Cassie and her parents, Vincent and Glenda. But much to his surprise, they were already inside waiting at the bar before the restaurant had even opened at 10:00 a.m. for brunch service.

"Reid, my man," James called out warmly when he noticed him walking to the bar. "Cassie's parents are here already and are delightful."

Reid and James clasped hands in greeting, and Reid noticed James's grip was tighter than normal. Cassie's parents must have been a bit much for him to handle first thing on a Sunday morning.

"Reid Montgomery?" Vincent Harris said, standing up as Reid walked over. They shook hands, and Reid noticed the look that passed between Vincent and his wife. "We're glad to meet you finally. Cassie has told us a lot about you."

"I've heard a lot about you both, Mr. and Mrs. Harris," Reid said.

"Please, call us Vincent and Glenda," Glenda replied, standing up and giving Reid a quick but warm hug. "Our daughter will laugh that we got here so early. We're always interested in seeing properties in the neighborhood near our buildings. Simone's has become quite the staple in River North. James was here early and kind enough to let us in. He told us you know each other from grad school."

From there, the conversation settled into pleasantries about college and Reid's start in professional photography. Reid skimmed over the details on his family but didn't shy away from explaining he had a younger brother. "Russell likes to travel, so when I do hear from him, he's always somewhere random, like the middle of the Ozarks or up in Wyoming. Last month, he was in Colorado working at a ski resort, but he recently came back home and is in the southern suburbs." Before he knew what he was doing, Reid was telling Cassie's parents something he realized in that moment that he had yet to fully explain to Cassie. Russ had been keeping up his end of the bargain to find a job—working at a convenience store he could walk to—and doing repair work on the house, preparing it for sale in the coming months. Reid hoped this stretch of good behavior from his brother would turn into something more permanent. He always thought Russ meant well, but he would do anything he could to try to cut corners. Hopefully, this plan to be an actual positive influence in Russ's life would pay off . . . Reid felt the strain on his savings account after paying Russ's debts and buying the house he didn't want anything to do with anymore. But upon completion of the final Dreamland photo shoot, he'd get the rest of his payment from LL, and he could start beefing his savings back up . . .

Before Reid could continue spilling his guts about his brother, James brought over a tray of mimosas.

"On the house," he said, while Vincent and Glenda expressed their thanks.

Reid checked his phone, hoping for a message from Cassie. But when he checked the time, he noted that it was still fifteen minutes before their actual brunch reservation. Cassie was probably just now leaving her apartment to walk there.

Rambling aside, Reid liked Cassie's parents. They were easy to talk to, had interesting opinions, and enjoyed learning about new people.

"Glenda, Cassie was telling me about the new gallery opening," Reid said after they all tried their mimosas. "That'll be great in Wicker Park."

"Oh, I agree, Reid," Glenda said, turning toward him excitedly. "Cassie just sent me a list of artists to look through. If only I could convince my daughter to actually show something there." Glenda looked at Reid with an eyebrow raised. Now he knew where Cassie got it.

"I think she is," Reid said, immediately regretting it. Maybe Cassie had told him about wanting to show Iconic Lights in confidence. "I mean, she mentioned you asking her to put something in the gallery."

"We know Cassie loves her boudoir business and now the ad campaign and all that," said Vincent. "But she's really an accomplished photographer. She could and should be doing serious things."

Reid wasn't quite sure how to take Vincent's comments. He hoped Vincent didn't mean to undermine the work that both he and Cassie had been doing for most of their adult lives, but something about the way he said the word *serious* rubbed Reid the wrong way. He nodded and took another drink.

Glenda asked James about his process for opening a restaurant, and Reid sat back and listened, though he was still thinking things over. Just as he was about to check his phone again, Cassie arrived.

Reid was sure he'd never get used to seeing Cassie walk toward him, knowing eventually she'd come sit right next to him. He'd spent the last two days replaying the conversation in his head about what they were officially, and it always made him smile. Her dark brown hair wasn't in the tight coils he'd grown accustomed to but in looser waves that he wanted to run his fingers through. Her cheeks were still flushed from the cold, and as she pulled her gloves off her hands, Cassie looked around the restaurant and met his eyes and smiled.

That smile quickly became a look of surprise when Cassie noticed who was already sitting with Reid at the bar.

"And here I thought I was on time and a few minutes early," she said, giving both of her parents a hug.

"Oh, Cassandra, you know being on time is late in our family," Glenda said, squeezing her daughter's arm.

Cassie looked at her wristwatch. "Technically I'm still early by three minutes. When did you all get here?"

Glenda relayed the morning's events to Cassie, who rolled her eyes in a very daughter-like fashion, apologizing to James for her parents' imposition.

And through it all, she held Reid's hand, like it was a completely normal thing to do. Because now it was.

The restaurant host let them know their table was ready. "Anything you need, let me know," James said as he headed back behind the bar.

"I like him," Vincent said. "Maybe I should get into the restaurant business, too."

"Dad, you have enough going on," Cassie said, looking at her menu. "Let's get through the gallery opening first."

"Speaking of which," Glenda said. "Reid here tells us you may have something to show at the gallery."

Reid could feel Cassie's glare before he looked up from the menu. And when he did, he saw it was the exact look she had given him back when he decided to watch her work at the Lucious Lingerie meeting. She was not amused and her red mouth was slightly pursed to the side and her head was tilted just *so*. "Did he?"

If Reid had been standing, he would have been on his knees in that instant.

Cassie, Vincent, and Glenda all looked expectantly at him. "Cassie just mentioned something about showing at the gallery," Reid finally said, cautiously slow.

"It's not set in stone or anything, but I am working on something. For myself," Cassie said.

"Cassie dear, we didn't say anything else, but we are happy to know that you're doing something serious," Glenda said.

"Everything I do I take very seriously. I own a business, I'm respected, and I'm leading the art direction on a major national ad campaign."

"An ad campaign in which you won't be wearing clothing," Vincent said.

Cassie let a moment pass before continuing. "You've never said anything about Dana's modeling before, and you think of her as a second daughter. I like what I'm doing, and the photos look really good. I feel great about them, and I'm not going to let you belittle it like you do even when I'm the one taking the pictures." She said everything quietly while staring at the menu but made sure her parents heard her words. Reid knew Cassie wanted her mom and dad to respect what she did, but above all, she wanted them to be proud of her. It was a foreign concept to him because of his tenuous relationship with his family. But that didn't mean he couldn't relate to Cassie or want her to feel supported.

"We're keeping the photos very tasteful and fresh," Reid said. "They're really beautiful and showcase Cassie in the best way possible."

An uncomfortable silence fell upon the table. Their server came by to take their food orders, and even she noticed something was off.

"You're the photographer?" Vincent finally said after ordering an omelet.

"Yes, he's the photographer," Cassie answered, setting her glass down a little harder than anticipated.

Reid wasn't exactly sure what was going on, but something deeper was passing between Cassie, her parents, and himself.

"Do you always take pictures like the ones we saw online?" Glenda asked.

"Not exclusively, but I do a lot of work with Luscious Lingerie," Reid answered to more raised eyebrows. "The company that is putting out Dana's line."

"I see," replied Glenda. "Well, that's certainly interesting."

"Cassie's running the show. The concept, the direction, wardrobe, model selection—"

"Well, aside from myself," Cassie said with a sarcastic smile.

"I'm just pushing a shutter button. She's the boss," Reid said, taking her hand.

"A boss you're now seeing on a personal level," Vincent said.

"Dad, please."

"I'm just getting things straight, Cassandra," Vincent said in a tone that Reid was sure Cassie knew to take seriously. He felt an urge to sit up straight. "This is the man who's been ostensibly steal-ing work from you for years, who almost took the campaign away from you, and now you're dating?"

"Vincent, enough," Glenda said, calmly putting her hand on her husband's. "Let's just move on."

Without menus to peruse, the silence between all of them was overwhelming. In his own mind, Reid realized that this was yet another reason why Cassie was so hesitant about modeling instead of photographing and art directing. Her parents had supported her through everything, and they wanted nothing more than to see her succeed—something he now wanted as well. But his part in LL's weird spying tactics was adding to what had been keeping Cassie from reaching her full potential all these years . . . people who thought they knew better and could take advantage of her hard work. Reid's feelings for Cassie went beyond lust; he really cared about her and wanted her to do well. And he had to decide how he could do that without jeopardizing everything.

After their food finally arrived and everyone dug into their waffles and omelets, the conversation cautiously shifted to their meals and other mundane updates about the past week. Cassie wasn't exactly surprised that her parents fell into their usual routine of questioning what she had chosen as a career in her life. And it wasn't that they necessarily maligned that she chose to be a photographer, it was that they didn't think what she was doing with her boudoir business and supporting Dana's modeling was lucrative enough for their daughter.

What was surprising, however, was that Reid had taken it upon himself to tell them she was planning to show something at the gallery opening when she was still mulling it over. It was the second time he had brought something up without really thinking about how she might react beforehand. Cassie truly enjoyed the time she spent with Reid, but she didn't want him making small talk with her parents over the things she told him in confidence, lying in bed together.

She took a moment and studied Reid, who was sitting next to her. He kept his focus on his food but nodded accordingly at whatever it was that her parents were chatting about. They were experts at diverting conversation away from full confrontation. Cassie's parents always said what they needed to say to express their disapproval and then moved on. Cassie always felt like she was the one contemplating every single thing they said and spending hours afterward agonizing over what she could have said or done differently.

But this was the thing about her current situation—Cassie liked what she was doing. She loved the uncertain hours and clientele she met through Buxom Boudoir. She had a core group of friends that she not only liked as people but also as coworkers. And surprisingly, perhaps most of all to herself, Cassie liked modeling lingerie. Never in a million years did she think she was going to do something like this, but modeling in the way she envisioned—the way she planned to showcase her best friend's hard work and empower her—was satisfying in a way that she didn't expect.

And then there was Reid. Unexpected but also satisfying, surprising, and exciting. Little miscommunications aside, Cassie was falling for Reid. Even though she was annoyed with him, she let a little sigh escape when he pushed his sweater sleeves up to reveal his strong forearms and again when he reached for her hand as they stood up to get their jackets and leave.

James came by when they were heading out and shook hands

with Vincent again, who gave him his business card and a promise to get in touch for a meeting. At the front of the restaurant, Glenda gave her daughter a reassuring hug, asking her to call her to talk later that night. Cassie nodded and turned to her dad.

"Cassie, I just want what's best for you," Vincent said quietly as they hugged as well.

"I know, but you have to let me do things my own way."

Their embrace ended, and they looked at each other for a moment.

"Well, Reid," Glenda interjected, breaking the heavy silence that had settled on the group again. "I suspect we'll see you again soon." With that, she gave him a hug that Cassie knew was her mother's way of making a peace offering. Her father, on the other hand, nodded once, shook Reid's hand, and then headed toward the door.

Outside the couples parted ways, thankfully going in opposite directions.

"Can I walk you home?" Reid asked.

"Sure," Cassie quickly answered before she changed her mind.

They walked hand in hand, maneuvering through the brunch crowds in the neighborhood, picking up their pace when a crisp wind came in off the river.

"You know," Cassie said. "They mean well. It's just me and them, really."

"You've told them about me, about before," Reid said, looking ahead and not at her. "When you weren't getting jobs because I was getting them."

"It was a pretty consistent occasion," Cassie said. "Which I know you didn't have much control over, but it was understandably annoying when it happened all the time."

"I get it; it's fine, just . . . weird that your dad would remember something like that."

Cassie smiled. "I think he was more perturbed by the fact that you've been the one taking the pictures of me in little to no clothing."

"And now we're dating."

"And now we're dating," she repeated, smiling.

Cool it, hormones. Cassie said to herself as she felt her heart flutter when he said they were dating. *You're supposed to be mad at him for a little longer. Or something.* Even her conscience was betraying her.

"What are you thinking about?"

"About how hard it is to stay mad at someone whose eyes are as green as yours."

Reid stopped in the middle of the sidewalk. They were less than a block away from her apartment, but it didn't matter. She was staring into said green eyes, and she was this close to swooning.

"You're mad at me?"

"Come on, Reid. Iconic Lights, yet again."

A frown furrowed Reid's brow. "I know, it just came out. Your mom is actually really intimidating—I told her about my brother out of nowhere, too," he said, pulling her close and tipping her chin up.

"Your brother?"

Reid took a deep breath before explaining but didn't let her move away. "Yeah, my younger brother, Russ. He's back in town and making my life difficult."

"I had no idea, Reid. Is he okay?"

"I think so. At least he is now," Reid said. "But we don't need to talk about him; that's beside the point. I'm sorry. I know it's not my place to talk about your projects, but I think they are all so cool—boudoir photos, lights, and little to no clothing."

Before she knew it, Cassie was up on her tiptoes, Reid was leaning down, and they were sharing a sweet, tender kiss in the middle of the sidewalk, forcing people to move around them. Hearing something so personal from Reid about his family really meant a lot to her.

"Take me home, Reid," Cassie said breathlessly when their kiss ended.

"Okay, boss."

THIRTEEN

To: Cassie, Kit, Sam
Subject: SOS SAVE ME FROM BOREDOM

Riki will make drinks. Bring treats and more drinks,
including at least one that I can have, too. Tomorrow
around luncheon. xoxoxoxoxooooooo

PS YOU MUST COME ON PAIN OF DEATH. DON'T
MESS WITH MY HORMONES.

Cassie walked through Bugles, nodding at the bouncer as she
sauntered in and saw Kit ahead of her. She picked up the pace
and tapped her on the shoulder.

"Cassandra love, where have you been these last few get-
togethers?" Kit exclaimed, setting down her Trader Joe's bags to
give Cassie a hug. For the past week, Cassie would leave work the
minute she could to spend time with Reid, be it at a photo shoot or
just hanging out with him and continuing to "explore their relation-

ship," which apparently was what people in their thirties called "having copious amounts of sex."

"Oh, well, you know . . . Reid and I are an official 'thing' now, so probably with him," Cassie said, feeling her cheeks warm.

"Really? That's amazing! We've all been wondering when it would finally take hold."

Cassie felt her eyebrow raise into her hairline. "Oh really? You've been talking about us?"

"Well, you know we can't help but gossip," Kit replied. "Plus, it's high time one of us single ladies paired off. I'm happy for you, my friend. He's a good man."

Cassie felt a smile spread across her face. It was one thing to feel happy in a relationship, but it was an entirely other thing when her friends approved of the guy.

"What are you two losers talking about?" Sam's even-toned, always-sarcastic voice called out to them. Cassie was happy to see that she was smiling. She gave Sam a hug, and though Sam acted like she hated it, she squeezed Cassie back.

As they walked up the stairs to Dana and Riki's apartment behind Bugles, Cassie paused and turned around.

"Look, I'm sorry I've been absent aside from work stuff the last month or so. This thing with Reid, well, we're still navigating what it all means and—"

"It's fine—you're getting laid, we aren't, it's cool," Sam said, smacking Cassie on the butt as she continued past her.

"Speak for yourself, little lady," Kit said, also walking by and winking at Cassie as she did.

Cassie adjusted her scarf and tucked a loose curl up into her messy bun before declaring, "I love you both so much."

"But not as much as what you're getting from Reid."

Cassie didn't need to see Sam's face to know she was rolling her eyes while she said that.

"Don't say too much, Cassie, you know that Dana will want full, explicit, detailed . . . details," Kit said, knocking on the apartment door.

"Welcome, my friends," Riki greeted them all. Cassie realized she really had been gone too long, because Riki's normally jet-black, blunt-bobbed hair was now cut into a side fade with long pieces on top dyed silver.

Giving Riki a long hug after Kit and Sam were inside, Cassie ran her hands through Riki's newly shorn tresses. "Number one, this look is amazing, and I'm obsessed. Number two, how are you doing in all of this? Bed rest is hard on the mama, but the caretaker takes on a lot, too."

Riki looked at Cassie with reserved eyes and squeezed her hand. "It's definitely a lot, but I'm okay. You know how Dana can be when she's restless. But I think this afternoon with the girls will be greatly appreciated. I will appreciate it, too."

Cassie smiled at Riki, linked arms with her, and walked into the main living space of the apartment. Riki had transformed their normally cluttered space into a den of love, light, and relaxation. Their couch was pulled out into a sleeper sofa bed, covered with extra pillows and blankets. Dana was cloaked in a luxurious silk robe, and her elevated feet were encased in obscenely fuzzy socks. Kit and Sam had already made their way to the small dining room, which housed a bar cart set out with a fabulous cocktail prepared by Riki. Before getting her drink, Cassie crawled up the sofa mattress and settled in for a snuggle with her best friend.

"I'm so glad you're here," Dana said, cradling Cassie in a warm and undeniably maternal embrace.

"Me too," Cassie said. "I'm sorry I've been a little boy-crazy the last few weeks."

Dana laughed, Sam scowled, and Kit sighed.

Cassie smiled to herself. There really wasn't anything like the comradery of a great group of girlfriends. Yes, the time she had been spending with Reid was awesomely awesome, but she missed her time with her friends.

"Can you all please tell me when I'm being a lovesick, annoying person next time? I miss this," Cassie said, finally coming up from Dana's embrace.

"I'll take any reason to tell you you're acting dumb," Sam said. The whole room just gaped at her. "What? Being silly over a boy is stupid."

"Just you wait, missy," Dana called out. "Someone is out there right now, waiting for you to crush their heart and come back for more."

"That person doesn't exist," Sam replied, with a slick flick of her wavy hair. Her dark brown eyes surveyed the room, daring anyone to contradict her.

"I didn't think it would happen for me, either," Cassie softly admitted, taking a sparkling beverage from Riki and then reaching into her grocery bag for sparkling apple cider for Dana. "But then out of nowhere, there was Reid."

"'Tell me more, tell me more . . .'" Kit sang out, making them all laugh. "But really, darling, you seem very happy."

Cassie moved from the sofa bed to an armchair and grabbed a handful of snack mix Riki had graciously put out. "I am happy, in a way I didn't really know I wanted to be. And yes," she admitted, "the sex is phenomenal. But I'm also open to sharing more with him, you know? It's different from anything else I've ever felt."

Cassie saw a look pass between Dana and Riki that showed they understood. She looked at her best friend and her wife, expecting their child in the coming months, ready to take on parenthood and whatever else came after that. Cassie wasn't necessarily ready for that step herself, but she thought Reid could possibly be a part of her future plans, whatever those might be. And that was comforting. And terrifying. And wonderful.

"Tell me all about the photo shoots," Dana said suddenly. "Did you get the swimwear samples yet? I need to know what they look like. I have a vision in my head, and if they don't match it, I'll throw a fit."

Their conversation changed over to strictly fashion and photo shoots, and while Cassie was a part of the conversation, she let her friends take the lead—she was content sipping a cocktail, curled up and cozy, listening to her best friends and thinking about her man.

For the third time in the last two days, Reid was avoiding his brother's phone call. He knew it was probably some trouble with the house, and trouble meant shilling out more money to Russ; something that hadn't ever really changed for most of their lives.

Growing up, Reid hated the fact that they all had *R* names: his father, Robert; his mother, Rose; then Reid himself; and finally Russ. There wasn't any meaning behind it, just the fact that in some fleeting moment, they decided—or rather, their lack of discretion decided—that they should start a family.

Things kept running hot and cold for Reid when it came to Russ. Sometimes he felt a real sense of caring for him and everything he was going through. But Reid also felt like Russ had always taken advantage of what Reid was able to handle when it came to bailing him out of a bind. He had grappled with these same feelings growing up, and his solution back then had been to leave and let Russ fend for himself. But this time, he knew he had to—he wanted to—do the right thing for someone in his family.

Russ had called him early that morning. Reid was awake and about to get in the shower when he saw Russ's name show up on caller ID. But he didn't answer, and instead he got in the shower, where his mind wandered to the sounds Cassie made the night before in his bed, and his hand strayed down, down, down, just like Cassie's had . . .

He had to turn the water to cold before he could get out, because there was no way he could go more than a few minutes without thinking about her skin under his hands, the way he felt when he was inside her, and how they lazily laid together after. Whether they were wrapped in the hazy maroon of Cassie's bedroom or the blackout gray of his own, Reid would rather think about his girlfriend instead of his annoying younger brother, who was asking for too much from Reid before he ultimately left—at least that's what Reid expected Russ to eventually do, in any case.

His disastrous meeting with Cassie's parents notwithstanding, Reid was still invested in a real relationship with Cassie. Sure, he'd agreed to be someone's boyfriend before, but this time it was different. It felt final, in a way, and he liked that. Cassie was perfect for him: gorgeous, smart, kind, and sexy as hell. He couldn't get enough of her, and he wanted it to stay that way.

So as he was simultaneously avoiding his brother and attempting to do some editing work for a different client, Reid was less than enthused when he saw an email come in, just days before the big finale group shot: Luscious Lingerie was sending some of their marketing and sales teams, including executives, in to observe the final photo shoot in the Fern Room at the Garfield Park Conservatory. The entire BB team had been jokingly calling this final shoot "the orgy." It would feature Cassie in a black latex swimsuit, cut and fitted perfectly to her ample, soft curves, wearing a short lace cape, thigh-high lace-up boots, a black lace masquerade mask, and holding a riding crop, while everyone else in the shot would be wearing different pieces of the Dreamland collection in white and silver. There were a lot of moving parts . . . Sam and Kit were also going to model, and Cassie was going to be the star, commandeering a group lovefest of lace, caution tape, and not much else.

And when Reid saw that none other than Rebecca Barstow was going to be at the shoot, he knew it would be trouble. He knew in his heart he'd have to tell Cassie at some point that he had been paid a bonus to keep the campaign "in line" with LL's usual look. But he also genuinely understood Cassie's vision for the final photos and wanted to be true to her as much as—if not more than—he wanted a big paycheck. He'd suggested different shots, moved set pieces around from time to time, but he really had been letting Cassie take the lead. Now that he and Cassie were involved, however, things were only going to get muddled further. Would Cassie think of his suggestions thus far as collaborating, or merely a tactic to implement LL's usual style into her shoot? Reid wasn't sure he wanted to know the answer to that question.

Oh, and then there was his history with Rebecca to contend with, too. They had always kept things casual and never really interacted outside of his work for LL, but sex had definitely happened after some of those past campaigns.

But not this time, because he was with Cassie. And Cassie deserved to know how things had gone down between him and Rebecca in the past. But knowing how Cassie worked and operated on the day of photo shoots, he didn't want to stress her out. So, he wouldn't mention Rebecca until the shoot was over. But he wasn't confident that Rebecca wouldn't want to fall into their usual pattern.

Reid heard a knock on his door and knew that it was James— the doorman of his high-rise knew James was coming and had permission to just let him up. Reid opened the door, the two friends greeted each other, and Reid offered James a beer as they walked into his kitchen.

"What's in the bag?" Reid asked, hoping James had brought food from the restaurant.

"New winter ratatouille recipe we're going to try, starting next week. Something warm and heavy for the coldest temps. I need opinions. I was hoping Cassie would be here for another viewpoint."

Reid shook his head. "She has an early photo shoot this afternoon and then tomorrow has an early final fitting for the big finale photo shoot, so she said she was just laying low."

"Things going well with you two?" James inquired, navigating through Reid's kitchen with ease.

Before Reid could answer, his phone buzzed on the countertop . . . again. This time it was a text message.

RUSS

Can you answer your phone? I need to talk.

Reid set his phone down, but not before James could peek at the sender.

"Russ is giving you shit again?"

"I have no idea what my brother wants right this second, but I'm not in the mood to deal with one of his messes right now," Reid said, flipping his phone over so he couldn't see the next text message light up his screen. "He probably wants me to support some dumb get-rich-quick scheme he's trying, or he's found something majorly wrong with the house in Tinley . . . You know how he can be."

"Wait—Russ is here?"

Reid realized what a crappy friend he'd been lately. Between Dreamland, spending time with Cassie, and signing away his life when it came to the house in his name, Reid had been slightly busy.

"Yeah, he's back in our old house. We—I should say *I*—bought it," Reid said, a little prouder than he meant. "To get our parents out of our lives forever. It's extreme."

"To say the least," James said. "But how does Russ fit into everything?"

Reid launched into an explanation of what had been going on with Russ for the last few months, leaving James's mouth agape.

"Not much has changed for Russ," James said, "but he is your brother. Maybe give him a break and at least see what he has to say. Make sure he didn't set something on fire."

Reid had thought about doing as much, but every time he went out on a limb for anyone in his family, he felt like he was ultimately taken for granted.

"He says he's trying to do things right this time. But I'll talk to him later," Reid replied, watching James navigate through his kitchen with ease. "So, I just found out Rebecca's going to be at the photo shoot this week."

"*Rebecca* Rebecca? When was the last time you . . . hung out with her?"

"A few months ago, right before things started with Cassie, actually."

"Shit. Have you said anything?"

"No, I don't want to bring things up to Cassie before the shoot; she gets so stressed. And I don't want to reach out to Rebecca because I'm worried she'll take things the wrong way and think I'm either trying to make her jealous or making excuses to not sleep with her." Plus, she'd expect some sort of dirt on Cassie, and he, quite frankly, didn't have anything to report.

"Come on, man; give her more credit than that. Rebecca's a cool chick, and I doubt you're the only person she spends extra time with after photo shoots." Avoiding eye contact, James quickly turned around to check on the food warming up on the stove.

"Dude . . . you and Rebecca?"

"It was a while ago," James said over his shoulder.

Reid just shook his head and laughed. James had a way of knowing everyone who's anyone in Chicago, so he wasn't exactly surprised by this connection.

"What's going on with you and Kit?" Reid asked, trying to avoid talking about himself anymore.

James shrugged as he handed a steaming and fragrant bowl of vegetables. "I was hoping you might have an answer about that, actually."

"What did you do? This is amazing by the way," Reid said biting into a parsnip.

"I didn't *do* anything. Kit said she was too busy with work to do anything, including keeping it casual. She hasn't responded to me for the last week."

Reid wasn't completely privy to the Buxom Boudoir schedule, but he did know they were all working overtime this week and next because of the LL stuff.

"Well, I haven't heard or overheard anything from any of them," Reid said, continuing to eat.

After a few moments of only the sounds of forks scraping bowls, James finally said, "First, you should text Cassie."

"Why?"

"She's who matters most, right?"

"Yeah."

"Then text her first. You'll feel better."

"And say what?" Reid said, taking a long swig of beer. "Hey, I used to sleep with the person who can make or break this campaign? Oh, and my sucky baby brother who mooches all of my money has moved back home, convinced me to buy the house we used to live in, and lives there now?"

"I was thinking something along the lines of 'I miss you; can I visit you at work today? I'll bring some amazing ratatouille from my best friend, James, who puts up with my melodramatic crap?' Then tell her about your past with Rebecca in person, but assure her things are completely done between you two."

Reid glared at James, knowing he was right. "Okay, then what?"

"Text Rebecca and let her know ahead of the photo shoot that you want things to be professional between you two. Short and direct, but not mean, because, well, she's the boss."

"Cassie's the boss. But Rebecca could talk to her own boss, who is the actual boss." And Reid knew Rebecca could skew things to Cassie's disadvantage. Or perhaps to his detriment, and he'd be out of a guaranteed paycheck.

James just rolled his eyes.

"All right, I get it, I can do these things," Reid agreed. "Thanks for bringing clarity to the situa—"

"Then call your brother. Make sure he isn't dying or being threatened. Find out if he's safe, and if it's within reason, help him. You'll hate yourself if something is going on that could have been easily avoided if you answered your phone." James paused, taking a swing of beer before continuing. "If you think Russ is serious about starting over, give him his number and I'll see if I can get him a job as a busboy or food runner. Maybe find him a mentor or something like that."

James may have been a terribly charming, borderline bro-ish guy, but this day, he was actually giving good advice. Reid finished his beer, picked up his phone, and got to work.

"Thank you. I think he's a good kid for the most part. Or at least, he means well," said Reid.

"But, most important, you have to be up front with Cassie and tell her about Rebecca over this damn delicious food. She knows you well enough now to realize that you're not going to do anything stupid to hurt her career. And after all is said and done, when you're the hero in all of this, text me so I can gloat about how right I was about everything," James said as he picked up his own phone and keys. "You're welcome."

"Thanks, Jimmy boy," Reid said as James walked toward the door, flicking him off. Reid had purposely left out the details about his additional covert involvement with the Dreamland campaign. On the one hand, it was easy money because Rebecca had just asked for reports of anything to be worried about. And as far as Reid was concerned, there wasn't anything to be concerned over at this point. But the implication was there—a big-name company who could move Cassie's career forward wanted someone to keep watch on her and her work in case any unforeseen problems arose. Reid didn't feel great about it, but it was going to make his hopefully brief stint with homeownership easier to manage.

Reid had done what James suggested—he texted Cassie, offering to visit her at work that evening so he could catch the end of a couples photo shoot. Cassie agreed to his visit, but only after she received approval from her clients that another photographer would be on set to observe her work. Then he texted Rebecca about keeping things professional, to which he received an almost immediate thumbs-up emoji response. Rebecca was a straightforward woman and knowing she had hooked up with James and hadn't come running to him crying about it made him see her in a different light . . . one that meant she was made of tough stuff.

But when his phone started ringing a few minutes later, he was surprised to see that Rebecca was calling him.

"Bec, to what do I owe the pleasure?" he said, and immediately regretted it. Too schmoozy and not at all the tone he was trying to keep with her.

"Reid, would you like it if I just started calling you some sort of nickname and never stopped after being asked more than once?"

"That's the beauty of my name, though, Bec," Reid retorted. "It's already short. Monosyllabic. There's no need to give me a nickname."

"You're insufferable, you know that?" Rebecca said, the familiar sound of clacking on a keyboard in the background. "I've been meaning to call you and check in since you haven't had much to report on our little Dreamland situation."

Reid took a deep breath—this was not a conversation he wanted to have this day of all days. He'd been searching for a way to tell Rebecca that her behind-the-scenes spying plan was really unnecessary, but now he just needed to say it. Cassie was the right person for the job. If she could have photographed herself, she should have done so because this project was made for her, and she was the driving force behind all of it. From day one, Reid should have seen this was the case and bowed out, but that was before he had gotten to know Cassie. Now it was personal, there was no way to avoid it anymore. And he wanted Cassie to have control.

"There's nothing to report. Cassie is doing a formidable job. A better job than I would have done in charge of this campaign, actually. You should give the job to her officially."

"That's not going to happen, Reid," Rebecca said. "The reason this entire shoot has moved forward at this pace is because of your involvement with it."

"And that's fine, Rebecca, as long as I'm only the photographer. What are they going to do? Stop production?"

The silence on Rebecca's end gave Reid hope they would move forward without any issue. As it should have been from the start. With the way he felt about Cassie now, and the way things were falling into place for her professionally, Reid was going to do what he could to make sure things worked out to Cassie's advantage. But could he do that and still make the money he needed for the house? Maybe that didn't matter anymore, when it came to doing what was right.

"You'll keep me up to speed if there are any issues?"

"Aside from the fact that Cassie was blindsided and asked to model in the campaign she was guaranteed the lead on, and, might I add, is doing so like she's been in front of the camera for years, there are no issues, Rebecca."

Rebecca didn't have much to say after that, and the call ended without any other pushback.

Next came the part he was dreading most, which was saying a

lot considering he had just texted his current girlfriend to meet up so he could potentially ruin everything and spoken to his former booty-call-turned-colleague in quick succession. Calling Russ would be awkward, and he'd probably lose his mind with both frustration and curiosity. When Reid had told Russ he would help him pay to fix up the house, he hadn't really thought about what it meant for the future. Once Cassie knew about Russ in greater detail, she'd probably want to meet him and know more about their childhood . . . And what Russ had been doing so far from home for so long . . . and what had brought him back so suddenly.

Would Cassie be bothered by this? Reid didn't have time to think of that because before he could chicken out for the umpteenth time, he hit his brother's contact info and waited.

"Hey, big brother," Russ said into the other end of the receiver. "How are you?"

"What's going on, Russ?"

"I think we have an issue with the house."

Reid rolled his eyes and held the phone with an ironclad grip.

"What is it, Russ?'

"It could be nothing, but it is an older house, so we should be safe rather than sorry, right?"

"Will you just get to the point?"

"Look, I actually have experience in this because I worked with a specialist and this clearly is the same thing—"

"Russell," Reid interrupted. "What is wrong with the house?"

"Asbestos," Russ said.

Well, shit.

"Are you safe, Russ? It's not a hazard for you to be there, right?"

"No, I'm good. I didn't touch it, I just saw it when I was up in the attic over the garage. I called a guy and got a consult. I used my last paycheck from the convenience store to pay him, so I'll need some help with next month's mortgage and utilities."

"That's fine," Reid said. He'd make sure Russ was covered for this unexpected expense. And he was impressed that Russ took this initiative to get things rolling. He caught what could have been a major setback down the road. "Have you said anything to Dad?"

"Hell no . . . but Mom showed up, so I told her everything." Russ's extreme soft spot for their mother always found him somehow.

"Is she still there?" Reid felt a strange tug at his chest when he asked this. Rose Montgomery hadn't been home for more than a few days here and there in recent years. But she was apparently willing to make the trek back home to see the baby of the family.

"She's doing her usual thing . . . moving from place to place. She's only stayed in the house one night but complained that I started working on repairs too early for her. I have no clue where she's been, but her car is here, really beat-up and awful-looking."

"I'll come by on Sunday and see you both, okay? Try to convince her to stick around for more than a few minutes," Reid said. "If anyone can change her mind into staying, it's you."

"Okay, Reid."

The last thing Reid wanted to do was see their mother. But he knew he'd have to face his family at some point, and seeing to it sooner rather than later would be best for all of them. But now . . . now, he just wanted to see Cassie.

FOURTEEN

The Masons were back yet again, and Cassie was at her wit's end with the two of them. After they didn't love the photos from the emo-music-video-inspired shoot from last month, they decided to go full-on "punk rock tinged with goth" this month. Kit had done her best guyliner work on Mr. Mason and spiked Mrs. Mason's waist-length curls as best she could until they just decided to go for a "wet" look. For everything.

Green Day blasted so loudly from the speakers in the studio, because of course they'd requested *Dookie* as their mood music, that Cassie didn't know the buzzer had rung or that Kit had let Reid in until she saw him in her peripheral vision while she continued to take photos of the Masons in various poses. She looked over her shoulder at Reid, whose eyes had widened at the display before him.

Mr. Mason was wearing a black tutu held up with suspenders over black cargo shorts, while Mrs. Mason wore a shrunken white T-shirt with visible pit stains and a black lace thong. They had provided their own drop cloth, with indecipherable graffiti in neon colors. And they were dry humping each other while Cassie took photos.

Cassie had explained to Reid the nature of these clients, and while they often went just over the line, they were loyal, paid on time, and sang her praises all over the place. They were uninhibited, a little raunchy, and clearly having a good time together. Their carefree attitudes and vibrant personalities, Cassie had to admit, were kind of fun to photograph.

Cassie noticed Reid set down a bag of the promised ratatouille from Simone's, and her stomach growled in response. Reid hung back, while Kit gathered up her stuff and blew Cassie a kiss as she walked out the door.

"Ms. Cassie," Mr. Mason called from the set. "You should join us one of these times. We saw your photos online."

"Oh, yes please," Mrs. Mason agreed. "You looked like a queen. You'd bring a certain regal panache to our photos."

"Well, I have a great photographer," Cassie said, winking at Reid. "But I'm only modeling because Dana is preggo."

"Nonetheless," Mr. Mason continued. "Don't you want to join in the fun?" The Masons started making out with added gusto, and Mrs. Mason's hand started to go underneath her husband's tutu when a loud cough came from behind Cassie.

She shot a glare back at Reid, who frowned at her and the question posed by her clients. She gave him a silent reprimand with a raised eyebrow.

Cassie knew the Masons were being ridiculous and downright inappropriate, but she had it under control. She continued to take photos for the final ten minutes of their hour. When Cassie put down her camera and called time, the Masons immediately snapped out of the sensual spell of being photographed in sexy poses together, gathering their regular clothes and packing up all the random props they brought. Mr. Mason excused himself, thankfully, to change out of his tutu in the bathroom. As Mrs. Mason put on sweatpants and pulled her hair into a bun, she noticed Reid.

"Are you a model? Because Cassie's the very best. You're in good hands."

"She's definitely the best," he said, grinning at Cassie.

Cassie smiled back at Reid, but then walked toward her client as she gathered her things. She enjoyed getting a compliment from a devoted patron, but she had to put her foot down. "Kelly, we've talked about the on-set antics, more than once. And as much as I love seeing my favorite clients completely at ease in front of the camera, I can't in good conscience keep working with you both if you keep crossing that line."

Mrs. Mason sheepishly looked from Reid to Cassie and tucked her hair behind her ears. "I know, Cassie, I'm sorry. We just get so relaxed working with you."

Cassie nodded, giving her a small smile. "Please have another chat with him, all right? I love that you're comfortable, and I know these photos have become an important part of expressing your . . . affection. But I also need to be able to work freely and to my best ability. You know if Dana had been here, she would have stopped the shoot immediately. I don't want to have to do that in the future."

Kelly Mason nodded in agreement and started to say something when her husband's booming voice came back into the room.

"We're going to Bugles this evening, for the burlesque show," Mr. Mason said, now wearing a bland beige polo shirt and khakis. "Will we see you there?"

"Not tonight, I'm afraid, but you'll see Sam and Kit," Cassie answered over their feigned protests and whining. "I have a lot of work to catch up on. Modeling is taking up all of my free time." Cassie gave a little side glance to Reid, who inched closer to her. The Masons were smart enough to notice and hurried themselves out of the studio.

Cassie started to pack up a gray drop cloth she had draped over a chaise longue when Reid took the cloth from her, balled it up and threw it behind him, pulling Cassie down into his lap as he sat down.

"Reid, I want to clean up so we can get out of he—"

Before she could finish, Reid kissed her deeply. She sank into his embrace, wrapped her arms around his neck, and kissed him back, forgetting about the drop cloth and cleaning up her stuff.

Later, with his forehead against hers, Reid took in a deep breath. "It's been a long day," he murmured. "And I've been waiting to do that for all of it."

"Happy to oblige, Montgomery," Cassie said, pulling back to look at Reid's face. Though he looked serious, the expression was no less handsome than the smirk that had attracted her to him in the first place. She loved looking at him, was always trying to find a reason to take his photo, and wanted to just spend time with him for no reason at all. When he texted her earlier, telling her he wanted to visit her while she worked, she smiled for ten minutes straight, which both Kit and Sam made fun of her for. The fact that he brought her delicious food and kissed her with wild abandon were both added benefits.

"I'm proud of how you handled that situation earlier with your frisky clients," he said, still staying serious, but his eyes brightening. In the late-afternoon sunshine streaming through the loft windows behind him, he looked ethereal. "I thought I was going to have to tell that guy off, but you knew exactly how to speak to them. I'm sorry it's happened to you more than once."

Cassie was unexpectedly overwhelmed by Reid's expression of pride in her work ethic, and knew she was smiling a little too widely. "Like you've never been propositioned by your models before. Or anyone else involved with a photo shoot you've been on."

"Not quite so blatantly," he replied. "You were calm but still direct. You've explained to me how you stay even-keeled for a reason, and today I saw why. You're a true professional running a successful business, and it shows."

Cassie placed her head into the crook of his neck. They both took deep breaths, almost in unison, as she relaxed into his arms again. "I'm nervous about next week. Are you?"

"Not nervous, but maybe worked up? It's always a lot to handle when the LL execs are there. Which I did want to talk to you about," Reid said, running a finger along the V-neck of her sweater, which Cassie caught in her hand and batted away.

"What about Luscious Lingerie? They've been bugging us for a couple of months now about coming to a shoot. They should just linger in the background, right?"

Cassie was nestled on Reid's chest, and she felt the deep breath he took before he started. "I've been working with LL for a couple of years at this point, and I've gotten to know Rebecca pretty well. She started around the time I began my work with them."

"Okay, so?"

"Yeah, so . . . Bec and I have a history."

Cassie sat up, feeling her skin warm, and not because she was close to Reid's body heat. She knew what he implied by mentioning this. It seemed there actually was some truth to Reid Montgomery's bad-boy rockabilly persona.

"You and . . . Bec," she replied, making that hard *c* extra sharp. She looked him in the eye.

"Yes, a history that's history," he said. "Nothing current. In fact, I texted her earlier to let her know nothing was happening any longer."

Cassie was satisfied with this response, and it seemed like the forward-thinking thing to do, but she still felt like there was more going on than he was telling her. "Okay."

"Cass, you can see the text if you want—she's cool, it's fine. I just didn't want you to not know about it."

"I appreciate that, Reid, and no, I don't need to see the text, I believe you." She moved to get up and start putting stuff away, but Reid didn't let her get farther than the edge of the chaise. Cassie pursed her lips and attempted to move again, but Reid pulled her back to him, and she let him.

They held each other for a while, not moving, not questioning, not thinking. They simply sat together, entwined and calm.

"I thought it would be better to tell you ahead of the shoot," Reid finally said, toying again with the seam of her shirt.

"I hate to admit I feel a bit jealous, but I'm glad you said something, to both of us. Does she know that it's because of me?"

"No," he replied. "And only because she and I never really had an exclusive thing going on. And I have it on good authority that I wasn't the only person she liked to see on a nonexclusive basis, so . . ."

"Oh, Reid," Cassie groaned. "Don't slut-shame the woman you previously deemed worthy of sleeping with because you weren't the only one." Did every awkward conversation they had have to be a teachable moment?

"I didn't mean it that way," he said a little too quickly. "Honestly, we were never an item, and we never saw each other unless it was after a photo shoot."

"Yeah, says the principal photographer for the company that she's the lead marketing manager for," Cassie said, raising an eyebrow and rolling her eyes. It was an instinctual reaction, but hopefully her point was made to him. "Reid, it is fine. Really. But just so you know, I'm there to impress her next week, not you. So don't mess things up because you're nervous about having your current girlfriend and your former fuck buddy in the same room."

While her words had been bold and direct, Cassie had been looking at her shoes the entire time. But after a quick glance at Reid now that she had said her piece, Cassie knew her point had been made. A moment later, Reid's eyes darkened to a deep jade green, he bit his lip, and then he promptly did the same to hers.

This woman would never fail to impress him. Admittedly, being put in his place had never been one of Reid's favorite things, but everything Cassie said to him made sense, and he heard it clearly from her. Well, once his brain caught up to the words she was saying, because he was usually distracted by how pretty her mouth was, or the way her hips flared out just *so*, begging him to lose self-control. And every shirt, every damn shirt she owned, was either a V-neck that was teasing him or a button-down waiting to be undone.

He wanted to tell her everything right then—about what had been going on behind the scenes at Luscious Lingerie and how he figured out pretty quick that she and the Buxom Boudoir team were the right choice to be in charge of the Dreamland campaign. About his brother, his shitty parents, and how he and Russ were working toward getting on with their lives, without having to worry about Robert and Rose anymore.

And about how he felt about her. How that was the only thing that kept him grounded and focused. How it made him want to move forward, strive to be better, and do everything with her by his side.

Cassie felt perfect underneath him; at some point they'd moved away from the chaise longue and on to the couch near the front of the studio. The mottled evening sunlight filtered in through the giant windows, and Reid gazed down at Cassie as she pulled him toward her, and he sank into another perfect kiss.

He let the morning melt away into something more meaningful with Cassie. Instead of thinking about work, his family, and the house quickly becoming a money pit, Reid focused fully on his gorgeous girlfriend and how *she* made him feel.

His hand raked across her soft skin, caressing her neck, palming her breasts. He reveled in her response to his touch, the sighs that escaped from deep within. She sat up once again to deepen their kiss and reached for the hem of his shirt when he felt himself still her hands.

"Hey," she said softly, her hand going to his cheek. Cassie rubbed her thumb along his stubbled jawline, and Reid leaned into it and shuddered from the sensation. "You okay?"

He let out a deep breath, taking her hand into his. "It's been a day," he said, and launched into a long explanation about what had been going on with Russ and the house. "So, he's . . . here. He's been here. And I wonder if I've been a terrible brother to him all these years because he so desperately wants our parents to pay attention to him, and what that has done to him. I've always ignored calls and texts from Russ, but now, part of me really wants him to stick around. And still, another part of me . . ."

"Is pissed off," Cassie finished for him. "And you should be. He spent years using you for money when he was in a bind, and now he's here, wanting to start over and disrupting everything. Your dad sounds like a piece of work, and I don't blame you at all for taking desperate measures to get him out of your life for good. And your mother, well, she didn't reach out at all, did she?" Cassie shifted and sat up to face Reid. "I know I don't know much about siblings or having unreliable parents, but all of that sounds so painful, Reid. And I'm here to listen if you need me to."

He felt that pang in his chest again. Hearing Cassie support him, no questions asked, was a relief and also a vise around his heart. Cassie busied herself tracing his hands, intertwining their fingers, leaning against him again. Reid knew that this wasn't the ideal time, but with the way the day had gone so far and how desperately he found himself wanting to tell her things he normally kept to himself, Reid was deep in his feelings and knew he couldn't keep them in any longer. He wanted to say something that meant something—something he knew would change everything . . . for the better.

"Cass," he said, playing with her hand as she did his.

"Hmmm?"

"I love you."

Her hand stilled but stayed in his. Reid could feel her stiffen, but she didn't move away. Cassie sat up out of the easy lean she had positioned herself in so she could look him in the face. She didn't say anything back, but she was smiling. Reid noticed the way the few freckles that dotted her nose and cheeks stood out when her face flushed.

"Reid, I—"

He interrupted her before she could say it back—or not—by kissing the very tip of her nose and engulfing her into a huge hug, then covering her mouth with his. Reid hadn't planned on telling her this, but his emotions got the best of him, which was new territory. He was there, she was there, and it just felt right. The idea of hearing those three words back almost scared him more than not hearing them, so he decided to let his declaration be it for the time being. Neither of them spoke for some time, and when they finally stopped making out like teenagers, the sun had set, the streetlights had turned on, and Reid insisted on warming up the ratatouille he had brought over. He'd deal with everything else later.

FIFTEEN

Cassie had a little more pep in her step. And because she was feeling so peppy, she decided it was time for a good old-fashioned darkroom day with everyone's favorite sourpuss.

Sam met her at the darkroom co-op Cassie belonged to, in her typical all-black ensemble; but this time, Cassie noted, her Dr. Martens were glittery, and she was wearing an intricately crocheted, bright red scarf.

"Sammy, show a little restraint, all this color!" Cassie exclaimed as she walked up to Sam waiting outside for her. It was cold out, but the sun was bright, and there wasn't much wind.

Sam rolled her eyes, giving Cassie's leopard-print headscarf, olive-green parka, and platform saddle shoes the once-over.

"I'm going to borrow those shoes for my next burlesque show," she said, pushing her sunglasses up and giving Cassie an air-kiss and fluttery hug. She opened the door for Cassie and followed her inside. It was the middle of the day, so aside from the attendant checking people in, no one was there, and it was blissfully quiet. Cassie readied her materials, and Sam checked the chemicals before turning off the bright lights, and the dim red bulbs flipped on.

Cassie hummed to herself as she put the negative in the view-finder and briefly exposed the image. After she left the studio and Reid the day before, she had stopped by the darkroom to develop her film the old-fashioned way. She wanted complete control over the way the light's exposure came through when it came to her side project. Sam was working on her own stuff, usually random objects she found as she traipsed through the city.

"Pipe down," Sam said, standing across from Cassie at the first tray of chemicals. They waited for their images to show up, Sam gently tipping the tray to ensure an even exposure. "What are you so perky about today?"

"Nothing," Cassie immediately responded, but she knew that the muted red lights of the darkroom couldn't hide her happiness. "Reid said those three words yesterday."

Sam looked at Cassie for a beat before saying, "Really? It took him this long?"

Cassie frowned, taking tongs and moving her photo from one tray to the next. Of course, it was the photo of Reid she had taken during their vintage shopping date. She smiled, admiring not just how handsome he was, but also her own composition of the photo. No one would have known they had been in a store, the way he emerged from the shadows.

"What makes you think it took him so long?"

"He's been head over heels for you since the minute he started hanging around. Those early photo shoots and all the days you two spent together 'location scouting'? He's had it bad for months."

Cassie continued to move her photo along, dipping it into a water bath and then hanging it to dry, before starting over again at the viewfinder.

"So, what did you say after he told you?" Sam asked, joining

Cassie at a nearby work space. Cassie stood near her and saw a brief glimpse of Kit's face as Sam started her own process over again.

"Well, that's the thing," Cassie said, and it had been the thing she'd pondered about ever since. "It was like he didn't want me to say anything back, whether I would have said it back or not. Before I could even mutter out a 'thank you' or something embarrassing, he had gotten our dinner ready, and we talked about other things." She left out the making out because she knew Sam would tell her they were disgusting weirdos.

"What *would* you have said?" Sam asked. "Do you think you're ready for that step?"

"I think so," Cassie said, doing her best to convince them both.

Sam held up a finger and slipped through the small revolving door that kept harsh light out of the darkroom. She returned a moment later and held up a shiny silver flask. She took a deep swig. "Take a drink," she ordered Cassie, and Cassie followed the instruction.

The whiskey rolled down her throat, leaving a heated trail that she hoped would change into courage of some sort.

"Okay, tell me what your hang-up is."

Cassie had to give it to Sam . . . Though she didn't always feel quite as close to her as she did to Dana and Kit, Cassie was always surprised by the things she observed and the insight she could offer. If only Cassie had been so pulled together when she was in her twenties.

"Well, we always seem to be having these big important discussions about how different things have been for us in life. How hard I've had to work for my career and he just coasts by. How he can get away with certain behaviors and I have to keep everything together to make sure no one is offended by my feelings. Even yesterday, before his declaration, he was just reassuring me that a past relationship was completely over and it wouldn't change how things are between us." Cassie worked as she talked. Her Sputnik chandelier photos turned out phenomenally, as she expected.

"It's exhausting, having to be the moral compass of the group," Sam said, taking a quick nip from her flask and offering it to Cassie. She waved it off.

"And more so when it's your boyfriend," Cassie agreed. "But he really opened up to me yesterday, in a way that was different. It was meaningful and interesting . . . about his family and things like that. It was almost like the overwhelming emotion he has tied up with all of that stuff fed into him telling me he loved me."

Sam was back at the viewfinder, and before she turned back around, she said, "I don't doubt that he's wild about you, Cassie, and I think he could love you. It's been a few months; you've spent a ton of time with him in your underwear, and not just for fun. Emotions and hormones are running hot. But you should figure out pretty quick if you're ready to say it back to him, because he strikes me as a calm and down-to-earth guy who has a lot of feelings."

See, she was insightful.

"Sammy, thank you," Cassie replied, nudging Sam with her shoulder as they stood admiring their work hanging to dry.

"And you better make sure we get that blindfold he stole last week back. We need it for the final shoot. And for the love of all that is good in the world, please make sure it's clean."

The house in Tinley Park looked almost exactly as Reid remembered it, except the trees were taller, and the vacant lot that used to be behind it was now a strip mall with a convenience store, a couple of fast-food restaurants, and a little bookstore.

He remembered the big picture window in the front and knew his mom could probably see him from her chair set back a ways, but he'd still have to knock on the door. He half expected to see Russ leaning over the back of the couch against the window, just like he did when he was waiting for Reid to get off work or come by for a holiday when they were younger.

Reid raised his hand to knock, but Russ opened the door. "Reid, hey," he said, giving him one of those awkward guy hugs that started as a handshake and then morphed into an embrace.

"Good to see you, Russ," he said. And it was. His brother looked older but otherwise the same. They shared many of the same features, like their dark hair and lanky build, but while Reid's eyes were hazel-green like their dad's, Russ had dark brown eyes like their mother's. "Where's Mom?"

Reid walked through the threshold, and the house looked and smelled the same. He expected to see their mother sitting in the recliner that was older than Reid, which had been her spot when she was around.

But she wasn't there.

"She left, Reid. She said she didn't have a reason to stay anymore, since we own the house now. Well, *you* own the house now."

Jesus, that stung. Reid wasn't surprised that she left, but he thought maybe she'd want to see him for a minute or two before taking off again.

"Did she say where she's going?"

"She planned to meet up with a friend in Michigan or something, then she was heading west. You know how she is," Russ said.

Reid nodded and looked around. Russ had been busy—he'd pulled up the old carpet that was hiding hardwood, and the floorboards had been repaired in a few spots that would eventually need to be painted white. "Do you know when the asbestos crew is coming?"

"Later in the week. I switched my schedule around to make sure I'd be here for that, so you don't have to worry about it. I figured you'd be busy with something in the city."

Reid looked at his brother, realizing Russ was different than he had assumed. Whatever he had been through had changed him. He was really trying to make changes in his life. And Reid had spent so much time avoiding him and placating him with money, when maybe what Russ had needed was a brother.

"I'm sorry, Russ," Reid said. "I have had a lot going on, but it's not fair. I shouldn't have ignored your calls. Maybe it's too little too late, but I'm here now. What can I do?"

"Thanks, Reid," Russ said, rubbing his jaw and looking anywhere aside from Reid's face. Reid watched his brother take a deep breath and consider his fresh start, away from the random jobs, their terrible parents, and money trouble. "I thought I'd love being back here, but now I'm just stuck. I'm taking classes at the community college and trying to get something under my belt finally so I can get out of here, away from everything. Away from them. Like you did. I don't know what's next, but I want it to be better."

His brother was trying to make things work, and because Russ had always idolized and wanted attention from their parents, Reid had ignored him. They talked more, eventually moving into the kitchen, where Russ had already painted the walls a nice neutral gray. Russ seemed to have a knack for seeing an opportunity to make something better. The more they talked, the more Reid realized he had an idea about how to really help his brother.

"Things look really good, Russ," Reid said, going to the fridge and grabbing a couple of bottles of water, then tossing one to his brother.

"As the new guy, I work weird hours at the convenience store and my classes are all online," Russ said. "I watch a lot of HGTV for background noise and get a lot of inspiration."

They both laughed at that, and Reid let Russ tell him more ideas he had to improve on the house before they put it on the market.

"Russ, I'm glad you're here. Thank you for dealing with all of this. You've been out here doing the work, and I'm just signing checks," Reid said, hoping he was convincing his brother to keep doing what he was doing.

"Hey, you know your friend James? Do you think he'd ever have something for me to do at his restaurant?" Russ asked.

Reid was surprised by the initiative Russ was taking, but he liked it. "Yeah, actually. He mentioned something along those lines the other day. But he's running a successful business, Russ. You have to be serious, even if it's just running food or doing grunt work."

"I got it, Reid."

Reid could tell Russ didn't like that he implied he wasn't going to do good work or automatically flake. Being a reliable older brother continued to confuse him, but he still wanted to try to work on this new relationship.

"So, uh, are you interested in the restaurant business? As a career or something?"

Russ folded his arms across his chest. "Yeah, maybe. I mean, I've thought about it. Of all the random things I've done, being in a kitchen or behind the bar is the most interesting to me."

"That's great, Russy boy," Reid said, throwing out the nickname he called him growing up.

"I looked up Simone's, and it's been on a bunch of 'best of' lists. Did you know James was named a 'Chicagoan to Watch' last year?"

Russ perked up in a way that showed Reid he was genuinely interested in working with James.

"Yeah, I took the photos of him and most of the other people featured on that list," Reid said curtly. He didn't know why, but for some reason, he was a little jealous by how much Russ looked up to James in that moment. "I was even thinking maybe you could come to a photo shoot some time, be my assistant."

"Oh, yeah, okay. Definitely. That'd be cool, too."

Reid had no idea where this random idea came from, but he thought maybe if Russ saw how interesting his life was, Russ would be impressed by him, too.

"I'd pay you, of course."

"No, you don't have to," Russ said quickly, shifting on his feet.

Reid needed a crash course on big-brother etiquette. "I'll also get you in contact with James."

"Awesome, that would be really great."

Cassie was waiting for Reid at her apartment. On the phone earlier, he said he'd gone to see with his brother and that he had a lot to tell her. He sounded stressed, which was saying a lot because he was usually so collected.

She was also stressed, and not because of the photo shoot in two days. Cassie had stressed herself out further by checking in with her parents and social-media stalking Rebecca Barstow.

First of all, Rebecca was a knockout. Long chestnut hair, bright blue eyes, flawless olive skin, and a killer smile. Second, she was a great Instagram follow. She shared hilarious memes, weird videos, and her photos were nice but not manufactured. Third, Cassie had done all of this while she was on the phone with her mother, who kept repeating everything Cassie said to her dad even though Cassie was on speakerphone, and her dad had just grunted in response.

"So your final photo shoot is in a couple of days. Are you nervous?"

"A little. There are a lot of moving parts because it's a huge group shot with a ton of models, a lot of the Luscious Lingerie execs are going to be there, and I have to give up a bit of control because I'm the centerpiece of the entire orgy."

"Sounds like you do have it under control, though. Right, Vincent?"

"Sure, if running around half-naked is something you want to control."

"Dad, what is that supposed mean?" Cassie laughed. In their usual fashion, her parents had come around to this current situation, just as they had when she decided to go to college for photography (the compromise there came with a double major in business) and when she started Buxom Boudoir (that time on her own terms). She understood where her dad was coming from, seeing his one and only daughter in next to nothing . . . though she hoped he wasn't looking *too* closely.

"Well, your last set looked amazing," her mother said, "and I'm looking forward to this one. Orgy and all."

"Add the word *orgy* to the list of words you never want your mother to say out loud," Cassie said. "Well, I better go. Reid will be here soon."

There was an extended pause from her parents' end. "How is Reid?" her mother asked.

"He's fine. Excited for Tuesday's shoot." And they left it at that. Cassie had to trust that they'd come around to Reid. Maybe after the campaign ran, they'd be able to look at Reid as her boyfriend who was also a photographer, and not the photographer taking photos of her in lingerie.

Getting off the phone with her parents, Cassie pulled out a variety of snacks in case Reid was hungry. She smiled to herself when she heard her buzzer go off, and she waited by the door for Reid to come up. Cassie hadn't seen him in a few days, and aside from a smattering of texts from him about meeting up with his brother, she wasn't aware of what else he had going on.

When he came out of the elevator and walked toward her, she knew something was off. Cassie held the door open and stepped aside so he could walk in. Before she could close the door all the way, his mouth was on hers, his hands snaked up her neck and into her curls. She felt his neediness through his kiss—he needed to feel something other than what he had been dealing with . . . he needed her.

Cassie peeled off his jacket, grazing her hands under the hem of his shirt and making his breath hitch. His hands immediately went to work on the buttons of her shirt, and she helped him along by pulling her top over her head, tossing it with his jacket. She backed him up against the island in her kitchen, and Reid swiftly spun her around and lifted her up onto the countertop, a move she hoped he never stopped making. Cassie wrapped her arms around his neck, her legs around his waist, and continued kissing him, sinking her fingers into his dark hair.

He broke away first, taking in a deep breath and putting his forehead on hers.

"Cass."

"Reid."

He smiled. "I needed that."

"I could tell, Montgomery," she said, leaning back a little to look at his gorgeous face. She liked having him there, nestled between her thighs, but she also liked being taller than him for once. "To what do I owe the pleasure?"

"I don't know. I saw you standing there waiting for me, and I just had to kiss you like *that*."

Cassie raked a hand through his hair and searched his face. "How did today go?"

He explained the complicated nature of things with his brother, and Cassie felt for him, and for Russ, too. She didn't know what it was like to have a sibling, but she was well aware of what it was like to be confused by a family member's actions or reactions.

"He's a good guy, Cass. I was stupid to let him fend for himself all of these years. And I feel bad that he's realizing our parents leave a lot to be desired. Eventually, our mom just left, and he had to tell me that after dealing with her BS for the last couple of days . . . I should have been there for him."

"Hey, look at me," she insisted. "You're a good guy, too, Reid. So maybe you've cruised through certain aspects, including building a genuine relationship with your brother. But that doesn't mean I love you any less."

The words just tumbled out of her mouth before she could stop them. She stilled, watching Reid's face brighten.

"Cassie, you don't have—"

"I know I don't have to say anything. I want to say it to you," she said. "I love you, too, Reid."

He let out a sigh. "Today was a hard day."

"I know." She tenderly put a hand to his cheek.

"You made it better. Thank you for listening. I'm completely out of my depth with this family stuff," Reid said, glancing to the display of snacks next. "Wait, and food for me, too? You're the best."

"I was thinking maybe we could postpone the snacks until later?" Cassie couldn't hide the need that tinged her voice to a lower register. She tightened her legs around Reid, turning his head away from the snacks, and lowered her mouth onto his. His hands caressed her thighs, pulling her to him, leaving her teetering on the edge of the kitchen island as he inched closer to the spot where she wanted him so badly.

Telling Reid she loved him was no small feat for Cassie. She had spent time ruminating on what his declaration meant to her, and quickly realized this man was the one for her. He supported her, wanted to be better, and had become better during the months they had known each other. He was kind to her friends, dealt with her overbearing parents, and, best of all, Reid loved her, too. Said it first, even, and used every opportunity to show his care and attention and *love*. And it meant so much.

Now it was her turn to show Reid how much he meant to her.

Deepening her kiss, sliding her tongue over his lips, Cassie let her hands wander down to his belt buckle and jeans, and Reid slipped the tank top she still wore over her head. He stepped back to finish taking off his pants, while Cassie hopped down to take off her leggings.

"I kind of liked you up there, above me." He laughed.

"We can re-create something similar in my room," she replied, glancing over her shoulder as she walked down her hallway, undoing her bra and throwing it at him. The sound that came from Reid aroused Cassie more as she confidently strutted and let him watch her do so.

Cassie's room was dimly lit, with only the light from her bedside lamp that cast long shadows across her walls. She stood still, waiting for Reid to touch her, but she could only hear his breathing from behind her. His breath breezed at her neck, causing goose bumps to form across her entire body. She leaned into him, feeling his chest against her back. Reaching behind, Cassie lifted Reid's hands to her breasts, pressing his palms to her already puckered nipples, and guiding them in their caress. A deep moan came from her as shivers ran up and down her entire body. She felt powerful and vulnerable at the same time, and she wanted to share it all with Reid.

He nuzzled her neck, kissing his way from the sensitive spot below her earlobe and down her shoulder. Slowly he kissed his way around across her collarbone, hands following the trail his mouth left.

"Reid," she rasped.

"Yes, Cass?" he said between kisses.

His eyes darkened as Cassie hooked her fingers in his boxers to pull them down, his impressive length springing out with gusto. She then slowly, almost too slowly for herself, pulled her own underpants down, savoring the look of pure lust in Reid's eyes. She playfully, but forcefully, pushed him down to sit on her bed, and then to back up against the headboard.

"Cass, you're driving me crazy," he growled, reaching for her hip and squeezing. "What are you doing?"

"Setting the scene exactly how I want it," she replied, smiling at the husky tone of her voice, straddling over his thighs. Cassie took him in her hand, pumped one, two, three times, quickly put a condom on him, and then rubbed his head against her entrance. Delirious with pleasure, she finally gave in to what they both wanted.

Inch by glorious, sinful inch, Cassie lowered herself onto Reid, stopping just before she had taken him to the hilt. "Tell me again," she demanded.

Reid's face grew serious, but there was something else there, something more. He pulled her closer to him, which brought Cassie down the last inch. She thought she was going to come right then and there, full and satisfied, and—

"I love you."

With that declaration, Cassie started to move. Slowly at first, but as both of their moans and cries grew louder and stronger, she moved faster and faster, and Reid met her rhythm perfectly. Bracing herself with a hand on the headboard, Cassie dug her nails into Reid's shoulder as she let herself go.

Her orgasm rolled out from her center, her core turning molten and emanating through her body. She seized up, and, just when she thought she was done, Reid reached down and pressed against her clit, and Cassie unraveled as she came again.

"I love you, too, Reid."

He smiled back at her. "I could watch you do that forever."

"Let's start with all night."

SIXTEEN

—————

The buzzing of Reid's phone woke him up. It took him a minute, but he realized Cassie was in the shower from the dull din of running water against the tub. He was exhausted and thoroughly satisfied from staying up all night with the woman he loved.

He let the phone go to voice mail, found his boxers, and walked into the kitchen. The sunlight was bright and filled the room, shining and warming what would probably be a chilly February day. He pulled two mugs from the cabinet, started the coffee maker, and opened the fridge door to see what he could scrounge up for breakfast. His pondering was thwarted, however, by the sound of his phone vibrating back in Cassie's room. Reid groaned, but jogged back to the room to grab it again, in case it was urgent. He saw that is was Russ.

"Hey, what's up?"

"Sorry for the early call, Reid," Russ said, sounding out of breath. "I heard from the inspector about the asbestos, and he said he can come earlier in the week to look around to give us a quote."

"Cool, so everything's in place?"

"Yeah, he actually wants to come tomorrow instead. I thought you might want to be here, just so you know the deal with everything."

"Shit, Russ," Reid said, clapping a hand to his forehead. "I have a photo shoot tomorrow. One that can't be rescheduled."

"Maybe later in the day? I can see what he can do."

"That'll work. This is a big group shoot, and it will take most of the morning and early afternoon, so the later the better," Reid replied. They both hesitated before speaking. "Do you want to come to the shoot? Be my assistant for the day? Then we can head back to the house together for the asbestos guy."

"Hot models in their underwear? Hell yes, Reid."

"It's not like that, Russ. It's still a job, and believe me, by the end of it, you'll be over seeing people half-naked."

"I've seen the lead model on Instagram. She's superhot, so—"

"She's also my girlfriend, so you'll cool it."

"Whoa, what? Really?" Russ started nervously laughing. "I had no idea. Congrats, man."

"Yeah, thanks," Reid said. "Look, I gotta go, my girlfriend just got out of the shower."

"Jesus, Reid, I get it. Bye."

Cassie sauntered over to him in a fuzzy robe and laughed, sitting on Reid's lap. "And to whom exactly were you explaining my current state of undress?"

"My brother, actually." He felt a grin creep up the corners of his mouth. "Apparently he follows you on Instagram and thinks you're, and I quote, 'superhot.'"

"I seem to have a way with Montgomery men," Cassie said, pinching Reid's cheek. She continued to her vanity and busied herself with finishing getting ready. He went back to the kitchen, poured coffee in two mugs, and cracked a few eggs to scramble. Reid wondered if now was the right time to fully explain what was going on with LL's execs, his initial involvement in the campaign, and how he'd tried to smooth things over and assure Rebecca that this campaign was under the best art direction possible from Cassandra Harris.

Just as he was plating the eggs, Cassie wandered into the kitchen and sat at the island. Reid turned around to present the eggs and toast and a few strawberries when he saw her face. It was downtrodden and defeated, not something he expected to see after the night they'd had together.

"Cass? What is it?"

She held up her phone. Putting down the food, lest he drop it on the floor, he looked . . . at the weather app?

"Thunderstorms. Tomorrow."

The final shoot was relying on bright skies to fill the Fern Room of the Garfield Park Observatory with sunshine. The joys of Chicago weather, yet again.

"Cass, I can bring lighting equipment, not a problem."

She shook her head and then shrugged her shoulders. "I know I should be adaptable, but I really just wanted everything to go perfectly. For the LL execs to see my vision completely, for every single thing to go off without a hitch. This is going to be the real launch of my career."

Reid nodded, hoping she took it to be reassuring and not just to placate her. He understood her concerns; it was hard to relinquish control over something painstakingly thought over. He wasn't used to relying on cooperative weather for as much natural light as possible for everything he shot, though. And in the pit of his stomach, Reid felt guilt over the executives being there who wanted to take away her control completely, and the hand he had in that. But he knew with this slight setback in Cassie's meticulous plans, now was not the time to reveal yet another blow to her.

"Hey, it's February in Chicago. It's a miracle we have the light we have today. Tomorrow could easily be the same, and we won't know until then. Every other thing that is under your control is completely in hand, isn't it?"

"Yes." She pouted, holding her coffee mug with both hands and peering down into it.

"For now, eat up," Reid said pushing her plate toward her. "Then we can figure out a game plan for thunderstorms."

Cassie gave him a small smile and started pushing her eggs around her plate before finally taking a bite. "What did your brother need?" she asked a minute later.

"Oh, nothing really. I invited him to the shoot to be my assistant for the day," he replied. "I should have asked you first, I can call him back if—"

"No, it's fine. I'd like to meet him. As long as he isn't too intimidated when I'm in a black latex bathing suit with a riding crop and whip in hand."

Reid laughed and put an arm around Cassie. She leaned into him from her barstool and stole a strawberry from his plate. He liked to think he had something to do with calming her down and lifting her spirits after the disappointing weather report. Maybe it was trivial in the long run, but Reid loved being able to make Cassie smile no matter what. It made him happy to provide for someone other than just himself after all these years. He realized he was also doing the same thing for Russ. Cassie was changing his outlook.

"It's completely unfair," Dana said, looking at Cassie's test picture from a fitting with Kit for the final looks. "I'm here, gigantic and full of another human being, while you get to have a fake orgy with a ton of gorgeous people, all while looking like a knockout yourself, and I can't even be there to root you on."

Cassie laughed and handed her friend a pistachio macaron with an apologetic smile. "A sweet for my sweet?"

Dana took the confection and ate it with a pout.

"It's supposed to rain, you know," Cassie said. "I'm upset about that. But Reid said he'll come equipped with the right kind of lighting to simulate the sun. I'm skeptical, but we'll see."

"I'm going to say something, but I want you to know it's probably hormones, and I'm sentimental mush over everything right now," Dana said, tears already starting to puddle in her eyes. "I'm really proud of you. I know I tell everyone I discovered you and knew you had it in you all along, but really, I pulled you out of your comfort zone, completely sabotaged your vision, and risked your career, and I'm sorry. But also, you're welcome."

Cassie was crying, too, thinking about everything Dana said, and enveloped her best friend in a hug before she could say more.

"I never would have done any of this if it weren't for you pushing me to do the best I can. Your tactics were a little extreme," Cassie said, softly patting Dana's pregnant belly, "but I'm glad I'm doing this. And I'm glad you're here to cheer me on from afar. This whole experience has changed my life for the better. So, thanks . . . and also you're welcome, because I look damn good in your lingerie."

They both cackled and began poring over the photos again. Dana suggested exaggerated poses for the next day, and Cassie took notes. In one of the pics, Sam had secretly stolen a shot of Cassie and Reid. Cassie gazed down at the photo, smiling at the two of them. Cassie was looking at Reid's camera, scrolling through shots no doubt, and Reid had his hand around Cassie's waist, resting in a gentle hold on the curve of her butt. Looking at the slightly blurry finish of the instant photo, Cassie could practically feel the weight of his hand on her body because it felt so right having him close to her. They looked good together, even if he was fully clothed and she was in a practically painted-on bathing suit.

"Good grief, girl. You've got it bad," Dana said, bringing Cassie out of her daydream.

"I guess I should thank you for him, too. If it hadn't been for that day you suggested I model in the campaign . . ."

"What can I say? I'm here for you, in more ways than one."

"And I'm here for you, D, these last eight weeks," Cassie reminded her. Riki had kept Dana on strict bed rest, stricter than what her doctor had recommended, and Dana had surprisingly gone along with it.

"When the big day does finally arrive, I want you and Riki to be there with me," Dana said, her face suddenly serious. "I don't know how I'll do this otherwise. I know it's natural, and my body will know what to do, but I'm still terrified."

"I shouldn't say this, but I'm scared about it, too," Cassie said, knowing she could be honest with her best friend. "But I do know one thing—you're going to fight to do whatever needs to be done for this baby girl. And I can't wait to meet her."

They were both crying again. And hugging. And laughing. They were still wrapped in each other's arms half an hour later when Riki came to the apartment to change before the evening dinner rush started.

SEVENTEEN

Reid shuddered as he saw the bright flash of lightning and heard the almost immediate clap of thunder crash through the sky. The rain was a steady flow, and everyone who walked in that morning—models, hair and makeup assistants, and LL execs—shook off excess water. Sam had figured out a way to condense the outfits so one long hanging rack could be utilized as a way to hang coats. The frantic rhythm of a busy shoot gave Reid a jolt of energy, even as he poured his second cup of coffee.

He loved this part of the job, all the different people coming together to make something beautiful. It didn't matter if it was an editorial fashion shoot or an ad campaign—or in this case, a little of both—for a few hours, there was a sense of community and pride in the work being collectively done.

He glimpsed Cassie when she walked in, but she was immediately hustled off to hair and makeup. It was funny to see Kit and Sam also in tall folding chairs nearby, getting coiffed and painted up. Normally they were the ones setting the scene, but that day, they were a part of it. Kit was chatting with the hairstylist working on Cassie's very long, very sleek ponytail that was currently on a mannequin head.

Reid took his coffee, looking for Cassie but finding his brother instead. He had convinced Russ to come along, and Reid could tell he was a little overwhelmed by it all.

"You're in charge of all of this?"

"I told you, I'm just the photographer. Cassie is the one running the show," he reminded him. "Did you bring in those lights like I asked?" Russ had agreed to be his assistant for the day. It wasn't much, but Reid hoped giving him menial tasks for a few hours could give him some insight into what he did and what Russ could do someday. Maybe he wouldn't be a photographer, but Reid wanted to show him that there were other forms of gainful employment besides the corporate jobs Russ thought he wanted to avoid. Reid watched his brother as he unloaded equipment, set up tripods and other stands, and moved chairs around, and he noticed how Russ observed everything going on around him. He was engaged in the busy environment, and Reid hoped his brother was continuing to make plans for his future beyond finishing community college. The fact that he was actively interested in working with James at Simone's was promising and showed how much of an effort Russ was making.

Reid was brought out of his thoughts by a quick punch on his shoulder and laughter.

"Hey, Reid. How's it going?" Rebecca Barstow, marketing manager extraordinaire, said, squeezing his shoulder. "This is quite the production. The execs are impressed." She lifted her chin in the direction of a few people standing near the entrance of the observatory, wearing suits.

"It's good to see you, Rebecca," Reid replied. "This is definitely a bigger-scale operation. The rest of the photo shoots have essentially been Cassie, a couple of people from her team, and me. Good day to have the bigwigs on set."

"They like what they've seen so far, Montgomery. And considering you never really had to bring up anything of concern, things must have gone well. It's your signature style but softened."

"That's all Cassie," Reid said. "She's running the show, I'm just following orders. You didn't have anything to worry about with her."

"She's really beautiful and has some really nice ideas for sets and composition," Rebecca agreed. "A lot of what's getting approved will make my job so much easier."

After this overly cordial exchange, they both looked at their phones for a few minutes. Reid answered a few logistical questions for the extra crew on set that day, giving pointers on where they should position crates for different model heights and how heavy the eyeliner should be on some of the extras.

"When do we get to see Cassie?" Rebecca asked, watching a few of the other models walk by in robes. "Her modeling has really taken things to the next level."

Reid noticed the very specific way Rebecca complimented Cassie on being a model. And he, again, reminded her that this was entirely Cassie's vision. "I'm just doing what Cassie, the art director, wants done. I wouldn't have come up with any of the Dreamland concepts on my own."

"Yeah, but you made them your own," Rebecca countered. "The moto jacket and bike shots are pure Montgomery. The low angles, the pinup poses, the oversaturated light. And judging by what you brought today, the green ferns are going to look great juxtaposed with the black latex and silver lame everyone will be in."

Before Reid could come back with another reminder, the woman of the hour walked toward him. He knew his mouth was agape—Cassie was breathtaking. Her black, one-shouldered bathing suit was high-cut, giving her legs for days, and the latex looked painted on her body, outlining every single lush curve he'd spent the last few months exploring, both professionally and intimately. Her hair was slicked back out of her face into a high ponytail accentuated with long extensions that flowed down to her hips. Her face was fresh and simply adorned with makeup, aside from the jet-black lipstick, outlined to perfection and showcasing her beautiful lips. She also wore thigh-high black leather lace-up boots that made her several inches taller and all the more powerful.

"Holy crap," Rebecca said under her breath. "She's a smoke show in person."

Reid walked over to Cassie, meeting her worried gaze with a reassuring smile. "You look incredible."

"Thank you," Cassie said. "There are more corporate people here than I expected. Not to mention the rain, and three models haven't shown up, and I don't think I'll be able to get out of this getup if I have to pee, and I really, really want you to kiss me right now, but I can't mess up my makeup."

Reid itched to give her a hug or a kiss but decided to keep things professional in the middle of the busy set and in front of the executives. "You're going to do exactly what you planned to do," he said quietly. "Also, these boots are sexy as hell."

He watched Cassie's eyes dip down to his mouth and the look she gave him when she glanced back up to his eyes was primal. "I'll try my best to keep them."

"Cassie Harris?" a voice called out. "Nice to see you again!"

Rebecca had gone full sycophantic marketer, a transition that she could turn on and off in a snap. Reid also knew that Cassie would hate this overly hyped, too-nice persona. It was why she let Kit and Sam do most of the social media for Buxom Boudoir.

"Rebecca Barstow, how lovely," she said, matching Rebecca's tone. Reid was surprised. "It's nice to talk to you in person and not over email."

"This is amazing," Rebecca said, motioning behind her to the set, and then again at Cassie. "You look just as stunning as the plans explained. I can't wait to see this guy work his magic with the camera."

If Reid had been dealing with any other people in the world, this conversation would have sounded convoluted and forced. But as he stood between Rebecca and Cassie, he saw that they were just two professionals trying to get to know each other and feel each other out in regard to this project. They both had the same goal, and when it came to getting this campaign and lingerie line up and running, each woman's success would only benefit the other. He also felt they could be friends as well, which was both nice and terrifying at the same time, considering they had probably figured out what had been and what was going on between them.

"I'm going to have to steal those boots from you," Rebecca said, laughing. "Are they yours or part of the shoot?"

"They actually belong to Dana, who is bummed she couldn't come," Cassie explained, her face turning serious. "Her doctors are watching her blood pressure really closely and trying to keep the baby in as long as possible. She's not quite eight months."

"My sister was on bed rest for her first kid, and it was no joke," Rebecca said in empathy. "This has been awesome, Cassie. Good luck today, and let's set up a time to hang out after work one night."

"I'd like that," Cassie said, watching Rebecca walk back toward the execs who were now perusing the photo shoot set nearby. "Well, she's actually pretty awesome."

"Yes, I agree," Reid said as even-keeled as possible.

A smile spread across Cassie's face, like she knew how awkward he felt.

"Feeling better?"

"Slightly," Cassie said, gazing around her. "I just wish the clouds would clear for a few minutes."

"Uh, Reid? Where do you want these— Whoa," Russ said, looking up from the bags he was carrying, which he almost dropped when he saw Cassie. "It's you."

"It is me," Cassie responded. "Russell, right?"

"Yeah, Russ," he said, handing Reid the bags and outstretching a hand toward her. "Nice to meet you. My brother is lucky. I mean, you know, to work with you and everyone here, and . . ."

Reid rolled his eyes at his brother's bumbling. "He's right, I am lucky. Russ, take these over to the tripods you set up earlier."

"Maybe when I'm not cosplaying as a nightmare queen we can actually talk," Cassie called after him. They both watched as he walked away and nearly dropped the bags again when he noticed Sam and Kit walking toward him in skimpy silver bikinis. He could have sworn he saw Russ wink at Sam, and based on the scowl Sam gave him as she walked on, Reid was positive he was right.

"Did you see that?" Cassie said, squeezing Reid's bicep. "He has no idea what he's in for."

They shared another laugh, and Reid wished he had his camera on him right then and there. Cassie looked unbelievably gorgeous, severe in just the right way, but juxtaposed with her smiling face and laughter-brightened eyes, he wanted to capture this moment forever. But he also knew it'd be an image he'd never forget.

"Cass," he breathed.

"Reid," she replied. "I have to go, we're starting in a few minutes." Cassie quickly squeezed his hand, and she sauntered off.

"See you in a few," he called after her.

Setting down his lukewarm cup of coffee and grabbing a water from the snack table, Reid weaved his way through models and stylists, careful to avoid shimmery makeup and lace rompers on his way back to Rebecca and the LL execs, who were gathered in front of a privacy partition. He knew he'd have to make an appearance in front of them at some point.

"Reid Montgomery, just the man we were talking about," Rebecca said. "All good things, I assure you."

"Naturally," he said, turning on the charm these executive types always seemed to enjoy. "Glad to have you all here today."

"Like I was telling you earlier, we love the work you've been doing with Cassie, and today is a clear culmination in your vision," Rebecca stated.

"We feel your signature style is all over this campaign, Reid," a man added. His name was something like Ted or Tom. "We know how much this means to Cassandra's and Dana's work so far, and Rebecca tells us that you're sticking up for her in a way. But we'd all feel better about giving you the art director credit on this campaign. Our buyers know you and your work with us. Plus, you'd get a pay increase."

"Not if it means Cassie's being demoted," Reid said immediately. "This is her project with Dana, and if it hadn't been for Dana's family situation, I wouldn't be involved."

Rebecca silently pleaded with Reid, opening her eyes wide to indicate he should just go along with what they said. Something told him she never relayed his message about Cassie's direction for this campaign. "She won't be demoted, correct, Tim? The work she has done supports the compensation we agreed to. And this is just a title change, like we'd been planning all along, right, Reid? You have been keeping an eye on everything she's been doing all these months, and it's clear that you've added a few of your own touches to the final direction."

"True, but I'm still not comfortable with this 'title change,' as you put it."

"Reid, this is the type of shoot that puts a new model with creative ambitions in front of people willing to give her a chance to do more than pose," Tim said.

"But she's not just a model," he said, rubbing the back of his neck. This conversation was not going the way he thought it would after he had explained to Rebecca that Cassie was doing a job that exceeded expectations and that she was more than deserving of top billing.

"Would a fifty percent pay increase for you make a difference?" Tim asked, with assured nods from the rest of the executive team.

That stopped Reid cold. That much money would make things with the house and his brother so much easier. But could he accept this and be able to look Cassie in the eye? After all the things she told him she'd gone through just to get to this point? After all the photo shoots they'd both wanted to work on when he was always chosen over her? After all they had shared together?

"We'll discuss this more later," Rebecca said, breaking the tension. "I think you're needed on set, Montgomery." His pause had been long enough that everyone around him had assumed he agreed. And he couldn't bring himself to deny it.

Reid turned around and almost ran into Russ. "Ready?" he asked.

"Not sure. Are you?" Russ's voice had an edge to it, and he was looking at his feet.

"What's up, Russ?"

Russ shrugged. "Just tell me where you want me to go. I'm your assistant for the day."

Reid studied his brother. They may not have been close, but Reid could tell something was bothering him. But he didn't have time to suss out everything that was bothering Russ at the moment. First, he had to take career-defining photos of his beautiful girlfriend.

Cassie felt a sheen of sweat spread over her entire body. She took deep breaths, trying to steady her heart rate and bring forth a sense of calm over herself. Or at least the appearance of calm, because right then and there, she was livid.

A few minutes earlier, she could've sworn she was having a panic attack. Her breathing was shallow and rapid, and she couldn't help but pace back and forth, but then again, she was also having very clear thoughts. Clear thoughts about punching Reid in the face.

He didn't realize that the spot where he met with the Luscious Lingerie corporate reps was next to where she was getting ready. He didn't realize she could hear every word they were saying from behind the privacy screen, how they lifted him up and relegated her to just having some ideas and being a model. He didn't realize that she could hear his silence when they offered him more money. That he didn't take the opportunity not to do exactly what she had been telling him had happened to her for years.

He had been spying on her for months. Making sure things went according to LL's plans. Everything he had suggested, had told her to consider doing, hadn't been in her best interest. It had been in his.

And now she had to take sexy pictures in front of a room full of people.

Kit came behind the partition, her lithe body on full display in a simple silver string bikini, with milkmaid braids twisted around her head into a crown. "I found the lace mask and the cape, so let's just— What is it?"

Cassie knew from Kit's face she must look as angry as she felt. "Did I mess up my makeup?"

"No, sweet love, but what is wrong?"

"Nothing I can tell you about here," Cassie responded, sitting in a chair. "Let's put the mask on."

"Cassie, Reid's brother, Russ or whatever, has boundary issues. He won't stop staring at me and following me around. I mean, at a distance." Sam joined them, wearing a white mesh romper over a sporty silver bikini and very dramatic black eye makeup. "Wait, what's going on? You look really—"

"Angry," Cassie finished. "I'm angry. But I will deal with it later. I've got an orgy to lead."

Stalking past Reid without so much as a glance, Cassie was ready to channel all of her frustration and anger into this photo shoot. She just had to get through these group shots and she could be done. Done with modeling for the time being, done with corporate expectations, done with . . . well, she wasn't sure she was done with Reid, but from what she'd overheard, the money was enough for him to put her aside and let his name be plastered on her work.

Should she have seen this coming? How much time had she

spent feeling disappointed after losing campaign after campaign to him? The final day of photography, and here it was again—disappointment. It never really left her alone, did it?

Cassie had finally felt like she'd found someone to truly open up to and trust. More than her parents, more than any of her friends, she had trusted Reid.

Sam gave her a concerned look, and Cassie was reminded of the day in the darkroom and the advice she gave her. She wasn't the only one who thought Reid was a good person, the *right* person for her . . .

So why this sudden change? Why this reversion to his past be-haviors of only doing what made sense for him and him alone?

Nothing made sense. Not Reid, not modeling, not this photo shoot. Cassie felt like all the joy had been sucked out of her.

And now she had to put on a show.

Reid stood next to her as she surveyed the scene. Before he could do anything aside from inhale, Cassie tied the short lace cape around her shoulders and moved away, taking his chance to speak to her. She rearranged a few people, made sure Kit and Sam were closer to the middle of the photo near her, and she found her place.

"Sam, do you mind?"

Sam lifted her fingers to her mouth and let out a high-pitched whistle. The room fell silent.

"Let's begin everyone. Reid, whenever you're ready."

Cassie didn't register that Reid was speaking. She could barely look in his direction. He moved people around slightly, inching them in different directions after taking a few test shots. Suddenly, the silence in the room surrounded Cassie, and everyone was look-ing at her.

"Sorry, are we ready?" she said.

"Are you ready, Cass?" he asked, quietly and concerned.

"As I'll ever be."

She placed a hand on her hip and jutted out her foot with a loud, satisfying stomp. It was a basic pose, but with the sea of pretty people with gorgeous bodies of all shapes, sizes, and colors at her feet, Cassie knew it was a powerful picture. She just hoped the LL execs saw it that way too, and that Reid realized who he was messing with.

The friendly sound of a shutter clicking from a camera put Cassie in a trance. She moved slightly, giving Reid time to take shots and move around. She smiled, then scowled, then gave a demure glance up. She bent her arm, sucked in her waist, pushed it out. She marched from side to side, pulling her knee to her chest for a few frames in a row.

"Good, keep doing that," Reid urged. She stomped and raised her knee higher. "Kick out, too."

They fell into a simple rhythm, feeding off each other's energy. Every now and then, Kit or Sam would cheer out, and soon the other models who were also in the background of the shot joined in.

"Let's take five," Cassie suggested after a while. "When we come back, we'll add props, take out a few models, add them in, and see how it goes. And I want a few of just me and the BB ladies . . . Got it?"

"Sure thing," Reid said. "You heard the boss, take five."

Cassie marched past Reid and headed toward the area where she had been earlier. Just before going behind the screen, she looked at Reid over her shoulder and knew he understood. She saw him look at her and then at the group of people simultaneously making and breaking her future standing right in front of where they had met before. He scratched his jaw, rough with scruff, and Cassie felt a tingle in her own palm because she knew exactly what that felt like, in her hand, against her cheek, along her inner thighs . . . But that didn't change the utter betrayal she also felt, boiling under her skin, waiting to burst forth. And she was ready to let it.

Shit.

Shit. Shit. Shit.

Reid knew Cassie had overheard him with everyone from LL. But he also knew that Cassie was going to do whatever she could to make this day a success. After the shoot, he'd tell her everything— about how things initially started with Luscious Lingerie, everything with Russ and their unreliable parents, the house, and how it all had come to a head . . . It wasn't enough, he knew that, but it was the truth, and that's what Cassie deserved.

The models followed Cassie's lead and got back into their positions, this time armed with various props. Cassie wielded a whip, and Kit and Sam both held riding crops. Cassie's black lipstick, refreshed and reglossed, popped against her brown skin. The lush green ferns were the perfect backdrop, and the cloudy weather muddled the light, even with the spotlights Reid brought. It was diffused over the scene, giving it a whimsical and hazy quality.

He took a deep breath before putting his camera up to his face. Reid decided to work off the tripod to keep a steady hand, but he picked it up and moved through the set to get close to the merchandise, knowing it was what LL would want him to do.

"What about the wide shots of the whole scene?" Cassie said, still posing, her face still in character. "So the entire line is represented."

"Just taking some close-ups for variety. I'll move back out in a minute."

Cassie's eyebrow raised, and her expression changed from demure to disheartened.

Reid took a few steps back, gesturing to Russ to bring over his taller tripod. "Cassie, flick the whip some; Kit and Sam come in closer." They followed his direction, but Cassie's face didn't change. And he knew he was the cause of it. She kept looking over his shoulder, where the LL execs and Rebecca were standing. He then felt a tap on his shoulder.

"Reid, the peanut gallery is wondering if we can soften things a bit," Rebecca said. "It's looking a bit aggressive and not like a dream."

"Aggressive?" Cassie called. Kit and Sam looked at her, worried. "Too aggressive? *I'm* too aggressive? Even though I'm the one in charge, right? I'm the one who gave such great ideas? That's how you put it, right, Rebecca?"

Rebecca didn't respond and avoided Cassie's eye. The entire room went still.

"If I look too aggressive it's because I decided to look that way, and that's how the photos are going to be right now. And as for it not being like a dream," Cassie inhaled deeply. "Maybe it's because this scene is a nightmare."

Rebecca looked at Reid and back at Cassie, and nodded, realizing she was out of her depth. Reid saw her start talking down the execs, who did not look pleased.

"Cass, please, don't—"

"Don't what, Reid? Don't act like I'm squeezed into a latex bathing suit, which, by the way, I look fucking amazing in? Don't let my emotions get the best of me? If anyone has issues with what's happening right now, they can come talk to me, okay?" Cassie coiled the whip and then let it unravel. "Or maybe, people should talk to you, Reid. Since *you're* the one in charge and directing all this." She gestured behind her, the black whip flailing as she motioned.

"Cass, I didn't mean for—"

"I don't need to hear it, Reid. Just push the shutter."

Somehow, after her outburst, Cassie reined it in, went back to smiling and batting her eyes, and finished the photo shoot. As she wiped off her makeup and shimmied out of the bathing suit, Cassie used every fiber of her being not to cry, because she knew if she started, she wouldn't stop.

Kit and Sam offered to stay with her once things wrapped, but Cassie assured them they didn't have to do that. She wanted nothing more than to be alone.

"Don't tell Dana every single thing," Cassie said to them. "I know she'll want all the details. I'll fill her in tomorrow." Maybe by then she'd have a better idea about what was actually going on.

Cassie gathered the rest of her things, grabbing the various tote bags and backpacks she'd brought that day.

"Cassie!" she heard Rebecca call. "Wait a sec." Cassie braced herself for the fallout she expected after what had happened in the middle of the shoot.

"Rebecca, hi," she said, trying not to sound annoyed, adjusting one of her many shoulder bags. She hoped Rebecca wasn't coming over to convince her to talk to the LL executives. The last thing

Cassie felt like doing was apologizing for what had happened or acting like everything was fine. She just wanted to leave before anyone tried to bring it up.

"Let me help you," Rebecca said, taking a bag before Cassie could insist she was fine. "Are you going outside?"

"Just to the entrance to wait for my ride."

"Yeah, me, too. Look, about earlier," she began. "I don't want to make excuses, and based on the way things panned out, I take it you heard about the art director change."

Cassie gave the smallest of nods to acknowledge that statement. "From what you made it sound like, it was never mine from the start. Just something to placate me, to get the job done."

"It's hard, the situation you ended up in, and you did an incredible job overall, but what the execs wanted, and what they're used to seeing, was Reid's handiwork. I hate it because I've watched you this entire time and I know how much you did oversee this from the start. Reid told me that several times."

"Great job sticking up for me, then," Cassie said, and immediately regretted it. "Sorry, I—"

"No, I get it. It sucks. And I did, after watching you work on the rooftop that day, I insisted that it was time for us to let in some new blood when it came to our campaigns and the direction going forward for special collections. I tried, but they wanted Reid," Rebecca explained. "But they did say they'd be willing to work with you again because the end result of Dreamland was so positive."

"With or without a babysitter?"

Cassie saw Rebecca's eyes widen, piecing together that Cassie had overheard the conversation earlier. "Without, and I'll insist on that."

"Okay . . . And as a model or an art director? Because this modeling thing definitely wasn't my plan from the start. You know that. I'm a photographer first and foremost."

"I don't know," Rebecca said.

Cassie wondered if Rebecca saw her complicit role in all of this. Some of it had to do with trying to do her job, but most of it was her working against Cassie, no matter how much she said she liked the work that had been done. "I'll see what I can do."

They left things at that, and Cassie stayed by the door with all her bags in tow. She relished the moment of solitude. She checked her phone and saw her rideshare was still five minutes away.

"Cass, wait up," Reid said, seemingly unconcerned. Was he honestly walking toward her like nothing had happened? Even if he was trying to play things off like they were no big deal, Cassie wasn't going to spend any more time with him than the time she had while waiting for her car to show up. She could barely stand the sight of him.

Putting her bags on the ground, Cassie busied herself with stuffing errant hairs under her trusty red bandanna. She had tied it up hastily to get out of the conservatory, but she wished she'd taken an extra minute to secure it.

"Look, Reid, I heard what you, Rebecca, and the LL team were talking about."

"I gathered as much," Reid muttered. His arms were folded across his chest, and Cassie could tell he was clenching his jaw.

Oh, so you're mad? Cassie didn't have time for this mess.

"And you're just taking the art director credit? After everything? What happened?"

"I'm not taking anything. I told them to give it to you. They made the change on their own."

Cassie felt the air leave her lungs, and she took in a gulp of air. She tilted her head back, as though she could will the tears back into their sockets instead of letting them stream down her face.

"What, um . . . what happened, Reid?" Cassie heard her voice crack as she asked her question. "And please don't lie to me. Rebecca already filled me in that this was the plan from the beginning, including you watching me for them. And you knew about it."

"I don't know how to explain it," Reid said, shuffling on his feet, and pushing up his sleeves. He had to look so handsome in a moment when she despised him. "Rebecca came out of nowhere and said the higher-ups wanted someone to make sure things went how they wanted. She wanted to work with you but was getting pressure from her bosses, so I think it was out of her hands."

"No. What happened, Reid?" Cassie paused to give them both a second to gather their thoughts. She had a feeling something else was going on and he just wasn't telling her, and it was like he was trying to place the blame somewhere else. "What's so different from earlier in the week and now? Everything you said to me, everything I said to you, didn't mean anything, did it?"

Reid let out a deep sigh, then answered. "Of course it meant something, Cass. I just . . . we got together and then all of these things just came up, and I opened up to you completely, and now we're here."

Cassie felt like she was falling. An abrupt, chilling sensation that could only end with a crash.

"Where are we, Reid? Because right now, I feel like you're in a position to make a lot of money and get credit for the work I did. You just pushed a button."

"Cassie, I talked you down from so many ledges during this process. I did what I could to make you comfortable and make sure your first time in charge went well. Okay, fine, I was willing to go along with their bullshit brand management, but you can't say I didn't help out when it came to brainstorming, especially the day in front of your apartment."

They studied each other's faces, remembering that day in the bright sunlight and what happened between them. The desperation they felt to be together that first time. Cassie wondered if she'd ever feel that same unbridled passion for someone again.

"All my life," Reid continued. "I've been able to move through it with ease. I'm not saying it's fair or it's right, but it's the way I've lived, and I was fine with it. Then I met you and . . ."

"And what?"

He hesitated. "And I let you in, and now I don't know what to do. Maybe it's too much, Cass."

There was the crash. All of his life he'd coasted through, and apparently loving her was too much for his mediocre existence that he was "fine with."

"I don't know what to think about that," Cassie said. "I know I've never felt the way I feel about you with anyone else. You're right, you have helped me with work and with my own confidence. You helped me see that I can be passionate and I should be proud of who I am, my body, my profession. I'm proud of the work we did and the relationship that grew between us."

"Cass, you don't have to say anything, it's me and I—"

She held up a hand to stop him from stopping her. "I'm proud of all the things we did together. But if you can't admit that the paycheck was too much to turn down, then maybe all of this ends now."

The look Reid gave Cassie nearly broke her right then and there, but she wouldn't—couldn't—let him see her cry. Thankfully her ride arrived and her driver got out to help her with her bags. Before she climbed in the car, Cassie looked at Reid one more time. He was watching her, his expression worried. She felt a sob fill her throat, and she quickly sat down and shut the door, closing her eyes, finally letting the tears she had been holding in fall.

EIGHTEEN

———

One Month Later

told you you'd be a star!" Dana squealed from the tablet screen. The first of the final shots with the Dreamland logo and Luscious Lingerie marketing copy had gone up on social media, and Cassie was on her way to becoming a body-positivity icon. "You're viral! You were on *Windy City Weekend*, which, let me tell you, is a big deal to those of us stuck at home during the day."

"You're almost there, our dearest mama-to-be," Kit said. Dana insisted being on FaceTime when she called to check in during office hours, something she had done throughout her bed rest. Some days she was there for hours before anyone remembered to end the call. It was like having her there in the studio, cackling at a cat video or brainstorming out loud.

"I don't know if I'd say viral," Cassie replied without looking up from the set of photos she was editing before sending them to the printer. "But my in-box is almost at capacity. People want to send me free stuff to wear and post about on my social media, but the only photos I really post are for work."

"Cut the 'humble' crap, Cassie," Sam said. "LL posted to their

Twitter that preorders are the highest they've ever been for any of their custom lines. Your ass is selling the merch. And it looks damn good on the side of a bus."

A rather sweet photo of Cassie at the Humboldt Park pergolas with shadows running across her body in a somewhat demure nightgown, muddy combat boots, and smeared makeup had been recently approved to go on a few city buses that summer and would be seen on the CTA bus routes after the official launch party of Dreamland over Memorial Day weekend.

Reid smeared the makeup on my face himself that day. With his hand, but then with his mouth when Kit and Sam were pretending not to look. He held me close between shots to keep me warm, too.

Thoughts like this popped up in Cassie's mind throughout her days and invaded her dreams at night. No matter how hard she tried, Reid was present in some way. The only way she could successfully distract herself from thinking about him and what he was doing and where he was and who he was with was by focusing on work.

And that she did extremely well.

Cassie booked more clients, edited and fine-tuned photos, and delivered digital albums, almost all within twenty-four hours depending on what time she got started. She went to the BB studio early, stayed late, and then took work home with her. Kit or Sam would offer to pick up lunch, but Cassie would open the fridge and showcase the week of planned meals she had made over the weekend and brought in with her on Mondays so she wouldn't have to think about it; she could just warm up whatever she brought and get back to work.

Her work had once again become her solace.

Cassie knew to fend off the worried glances in thinking she was spreading herself too thin or the "just checking in" texts from Dana and Riki. She made social appearances, too—a happy hour at Bugles here, one of Kit and Sam's burlesque performances there, and a girls' night in at Dana's apartment, too. But she was cautious with herself, only going out on off-peak nights, when she felt like she might not accidentally see Reid. She did see James one night but left before he could catch her eye. She figured if James was out, then so were Reid or his brother, Russ, whom she heard from her friends was sticking around. She just wasn't ready yet.

Maybe this is what Reid meant by "being fine" with how his life had been. She wasn't totally unhappy, but she also wasn't the same person she had been a few months ago. Cassie knew she had to navigate this on her own, figure out what her new baseline was, and what that would mean going forward. Reid Montgomery wasn't easily forgotten.

But neither was she.

One night, after a grueling schedule of four boudoir sessions, two completed edits, and one angry phone call to the printer, Cassie was looking forward to going home, having a large glass of wine, mixing M&Ms into popcorn, and rereading an old romance novel. She rounded the corner to her home when she heard a familiar, breathy voice call out her name.

"Cassie, my love, what a coincidence. We were just walking this way," Kit said, Sam next to her.

"You both live in different neighborhoods and nowhere near me."

"Correct. So why on earth would we follow you?" Sam said, holding up a very nice bottle of whiskey.

"We were sent by your fairy godmother," Kit said, brandishing a bottle of sparkling rosé.

Cassie laughed at how perfectly their libation choices suited their distinct personalities. "I see Dana sent me an angel and a devil, but I suspect both of you are up to no good."

Up in Cassie's apartment, everyone with a beverage in hand and a variety of snacks, Cassie got down to business. "All right, out with it. Get on with your intervention."

A knowing glance passed between Sam and Kit. "We told Dana you'd know what was going on," Sam said. "But we're worried about you. You seem . . . okay."

"And that's a bad thing?"

"No, never, not at all," replied Kit. "We just want to make sure you're processing everything with the LL stuff, and with Reid, too."

Cassie couldn't stay too mad at her friends. They were clearly nervous about bringing any of it up. Sam was already on her second tumbler of whiskey, and Cassie and Kit were going to finish this bottle of rosé easily and probably split something from Cassie's wine stash as well.

"I appreciate you two coming to check on me, and Dana's concern from afar, but really, I'm coping. I have bad days sometimes, but work has saved me. And I'm not just working on stuff for BB, either."

"Do go on," Kit said. "This is the most you've spoken in weeks."

"I'm working on a show for my mom's new arts and event space, the Glen Gallery. I've been helping her find other artists and photographers to feature, and I've also been printing my own work to show, too." Cassie took her phone from her sweater pocket and showed them the draft of an e-vite to the grand opening of Iconic Lights.

Cassie had braved the elements of February in Chicago—the actual worst of the winter months—to continue traipsing around the city to find places where the light hit just right. Streetlamps casting shadows on lonely park benches early in the morning, the afternoon sun bursting through trees in a park, the dust in the air after she made her bed, made hazier by the sheer curtain behind her drapes. Shadows crossed textures, light created layers, and the everyday became extraordinary through her lens. Cassie let herself create, without an agenda or a professional endgame. Her goal was to showcase photographs she was proud of through a carefully curated show—something she was going to see through completely on her own from start to finish.

"Whoa, Cassie, this is major," Sam said, scrolling though the details. "And you've been thinking about this for a while. Congrats on putting it all together."

"Thanks, Sammy," Cassie replied, feeling her cheeks warm. She gave them details about some of the other artists who were showing as well, but Cassie's project was going to be the main event.

"Don't take this the wrong way, but are you going to invite Reid?" Kit asked, immediately glugging down more wine.

"I think I have to; he's in a couple of the photos." It would only be fair.

"Have you talked to him at all since the final shoot?" Sam asked.

"Not really. He texted me when the first shots went up to say congrats and well done. He asked how I was doing, and I said I was fine," Cassie answered, reaching for a chocolate-covered pretzel stick. "I asked him how he was doing, and he also said he was fine. That was last week. And I think we both are fine. If you see him out, you can be friendly. I'm okay with that."

"That's all . . . fine," Kit said, doing her best to sound supportive. "I'm just glad to hear that you have plans for the future."

"I know LL has been trying to reach out to you," Sam blurted, covering her mouth like it was a mistake. "They emailed our 'general info' email account. Have you talked to Rebecca?"

"I have," Cassie said.

Kit nodded eagerly, blue eyes wide with attention. Sam cocked her head to the side, waiting for more information.

"My outburst actually did more good than harm. The execs were impressed with my 'passion' and wanted to talk more. Though I did mention to Rebecca I took major issue with her use of the word *aggressive* during her feedback."

Apparently, in this instance, being an angry Black woman led to treatment that wasn't dismissive or unfair. And Cassie was ready to take things head-on.

"Do the execs want to talk to you as a model or an art director?"

"Both, and possibly as a collection creator."

"Get out, Cassie! What lovely news after all of this," Kit exclaimed.

Sam kept a straight face and asked, "Are you sure you even want to work with them again? After the way things panned out the first time?"

Cassie thought for a moment, then drained her glass of rosé and moved into the kitchen to open a new bottle of wine. "No, I'm not sure, Sammy-Sam. Thank you for reminding me, because the call did sound too good to be true. But once this campaign goes live, my ass, and my *work*, are going to bring in more offers than any of us are ready for. And I'm looking forward to it."

"You deserve it all and more. To our fearless leader," Sam offered as a toast. She held up her glass, and they all clinked their drinks together.

Reid felt like something was missing. It wasn't too hard to fall back into his old routines, even with his brother currently sleeping on his couch while the asbestos removal took place at the house in Tinley Park, working as his assistant on photo shoots, and picking up busing shifts at Simone's courtesy of James. While his relationship with his brother was developing, Reid still felt emptiness like a pit in his stomach.

He missed Cassie.

What had Reid been thinking that rainy afternoon after the final Dreamland photo shoot? What he said to her wasn't a total lie—he was overwhelmed by the emotions and the relationships he'd developed as he got to know Cassie. He and James had been friends, but now he thought of him as his best friend. He liked hanging out with Kit, Sam, Dana, and Riki at the Buxom Boudoir studio or at Bugles. But most of all, Reid had found someone who both challenged and encouraged him, who made him feel on top of the world and also put him in his place when necessary. Reid had found Cassie, and now she was gone. He didn't know why he didn't tell her about his insistent but futile attempts to stick up for her with Rebecca, but at this point, he did know it was too little too late.

Over the course of the last month, however, Reid had found himself heading to Bugles, hoping that she'd be there by chance. He had seen Riki, of course, who seemed to regard him with caution but wasn't hostile. James took him to a bar across the city, and it wasn't until it was underway that he realized he had been wrangled into attending a burlesque show starring Kit and Sam. Admittedly, it was a sexy show laced with their distinct personalities and a touch of humor. He stayed out and had a couple of drinks with them after they were fully clothed, and it was pleasant. He enjoyed seeing them all again and finding out how they were doing. Kit was overly nice, and Sam was her usual sarcastic self, but they didn't make him feel unwelcome. He knew that Cassie must have told them it was all right to be nice to him, otherwise the full wrath of the Buxom Boudoir team would have been thrown his way. Reid refrained from asking too many questions about Cassie, though she did come up in conversation from time to time. He was careful not to overstay his welcome because the last thing Reid wanted was to make anyone feel uncomfortable about where their loyalties lay—he knew the answer was with Cassie. Still, Reid liked having a tight-knit friend group. But he also was painfully aware of the one person who wasn't there beside him.

Then, out of the blue, he saw an invite in his email in-box to the Glen Gallery, and Reid was surprised to see it was from Glenda Harris. He was floored—and proud—however, when he saw the featured artist was none other than Cassandra Harris. Reid was happy that she had added him to the guest list, but now he was suddenly nervous.

After double-checking that James was also going to be there, Reid RSVP'd yes and decided to bring his brother along. He knew Russ wanted to see Sam again, and this gave him a great opportunity to actually interact with her. Plus, it would be nice for them both to get away from their work and to see friends around some great local art.

And it would be nice to see Cassie again. Even his brain was betraying him.

Reid spent longer than usual getting ready and dressed up a bit. Russ decided to change when he saw Reid in a button-down shirt and dress pants. Reid let him borrow a sweater when Russ declared he had nothing to wear.

Though the gallery was a short train ride from Reid's apartment, winter was still blustering on in mid-March, so the commute was unpleasant. But whenever they went anywhere, Reid had been taking Russ via public transportation so he would learn the lay of the city. Russ had spent more time away from Chicago than he had been in it, even living in such close proximity when they were young. Plus, by the time Russ would have wanted to go into the city more with his brother as a teenager, Reid was an adult and had his career to focus on. The simple act of teaching his brother how to use the L and CTA buses confidently in Chicago had become a new way to bond.

Weather aside, the gallery opening was in full swing. Bright light poured out of the large windows, and near the front desk was a standing rack for coats, as well as a spread of hors d'oeuvres and different drinks. Grabbing a beer for himself, Reid started to walk through the space.

Glenda had done an impressive job on her gallery. Any structural updates maintained the integrity of the building. Exposed brick and polished concrete floors complemented the light gray walls and visible ductwork in the tall ceilings. New light fixtures hung down, spotlighting artwork without overpowering the features of the photographs, paintings, and sculptures. Turning a corner of a wall he realized could be moved to change the layout of the room, Reid saw a group of familiar faces.

"Reid, darling Reid, how lovely to see you," Kit exclaimed, giving him a side hug. "Your brother and Sam are in a dark corner somewhere. Isn't this glorious? I'm so glad you're here." Without missing a beat, Kit began a conversation with someone passing by. Reid thought he recognized a client or two from Buxom Boudoir, but he wasn't sure.

"Reid, good to see you here," James said, shaking Reid's hand. "It's been a while."

"Yeah, I've been busy," he said. He had made the time soon after the final photo shoot to make appearances, but in the last week or so, he'd hung back from social outings. He had returned to his loner ways, focused on work, and he was sure his idea to come to the gallery and see Cassie again had something to do with that retreat, after he found himself missing his friend group—a group that he wouldn't have had without initially meeting her. "I'm glad I was invited tonight."

"Cassie's really making her mark. This show is incredible. I've never looked at lights like this before."

James was right—Cassie's Iconic Lights series showcased her unique vision of what light could be. The way shadows changed in a single frame and oversaturation could be sinister. "She's really special."

"That's for sure. You should look around, I can tell you want to," James said as Kit put her arm through his and they walked off to mingle. Apparently, things had started up again between them recently, though Reid wasn't sure how long this casual fling would last.

Reid continued to walk around, stopping at each of the walls that featured different artists, all curated by Cassie. He noticed work by a mixed-media artist he hadn't seen in years and was pleased to see the care with which Cassie had put together this show.

Continuing to peruse the art, Reid froze when he recognized the same Sputnik chandelier he and Cassie saw at Salvage One a couple of months earlier. She had been fascinated with the shape of the bulbs, the way the light passed through the filaments, and how it looked unlit. He appreciated the way she cropped the photo, emphasizing the way light filtered through, imperfect perfection detectable in the decades-old glass. He remembered how close he felt to her that day, everything opening up between them like they had no other way of existing in those moments.

Then he saw her—across the room, surrounded by a throng of people offering congratulations and asking her about working together or setting up informational meetings. She was beaming, skin glowing under the soft lights, her gorgeous body lovingly draped in a dark green sweater dress that enhanced every curve he had memorized, stopping right at the top of the very same thigh-high boots she had worn during the last photo shoot.

He was staring, and he didn't really mind if anyone noticed. He hoped she'd look his way, just to see her face-to-face for a moment, but she was in the midst of a conversation with two eager women, pointing at a photo he couldn't see from where he was standing. He moved in that direction.

He wasn't prepared for the way his chest tightened at the look of genuine happiness that filled Cassie's face when she saw him across the room. She ran a hand through her hair, which was loose and softly curled, different from her usual messy bun or trusty red bandanna, but no less beautiful. Flicking her hair over a shoulder, Cassie waved at him and smiled.

He waved back, then nervously rolled his sleeves up his forearms. He didn't know what to do just then. Should he continue to make his way over toward her? Or try to play it cool and walk around the gallery? He looked at artwork for a moment but decided to make his way toward Cassie.

As he got closer, Reid saw that she had a smile on her face while she talked to the crowd around her, laughing from time to time when she greeted someone new. Reid loved seeing her so relaxed and in control—she seemed at ease and in her element.

Noticing how many people were around Cassie, Reid decided against cutting into her moment. He walked by the group, wishing

Cassie would look over at him, but she didn't. So he kept walking and was soon face-to-face with himself.

As if it wasn't already wild enough that he was there, Reid Montgomery had the audacity to look damn good at the opening of her mother's gallery, and her Iconic Lights show. He always looked good, as far as Cassie was concerned.

Not that she was complaining. Reid had put forth an effort to look extra handsome—the navy-blue shirt brought out the russet undertones in his dark brown hair, offset by slim-fitting gray dress pants that made his ass look great . . . She knew everyone in that gallery would be checking him out before too long. Cassie tried really hard to be nonchalant, but seeing Reid there made her stomach flip and flutter, and she was so happy he came. She was still upset with him and knew that if they did have the opportunity to talk about things beyond the usual pleasantries, they had a lot to work out. But for now, Cassie was going to let the evening progress, and if that meant being cordial with Reid, then she would let that happen.

She kept stealing glances at him, waiting for him to get closer so she could try to break away from the stream of people talking to her. It was hard work, contributing to the conversations in front of her and subtly keeping tabs on the man who had broken her heart a month ago. But for now, Cassie basked in the glow of the success of her show—quite a few pieces had already been bought, both her own and the work of her fellow artists—and that she had enticed Reid enough to come out.

"Cassie, love, look over there," Kit said, giggling as she brought

Cassie another glass of champagne. Cassie had barely touched the first glass Kit had brought her, but she was thankful for this second glass now that she knew Reid was there. "Do you see them? Our Sam and Russell? How quaint."

Cassie smiled at the two of them. Russ appeared to be doing well, living through repairs on the house in the suburbs and now working with James in some capacity. Sam wasn't quite smiling, but she wasn't frowning, either, which said a lot. Recently promoted to office manager of Buxom Boudoir, Sam was taking initiative at work and otherwise. Cassie was happy for the youngest member of the BB team and knew Sam was happy to find someone to connect with, even if he happened to be the brother of Cassie's ex.

Referring to Reid as her ex, albeit in her private thoughts, was hard. She had spent so much time hoping that he would call or text or show up at the studio or her apartment like something out of a movie, but no such luck. Cassie had let herself wallow for a few days, and then became the workaholic who got her to this point— sending out her updated portfolio for prospective ad campaigns, taking lingerie modeling by storm, hosting her own art show, and watching her business grow exponentially.

And all because she let a cute guy take some photos of her.

Okay, so that wasn't entirely right, but it was part of it. And Cassie would never forget it. Still, she was proud of herself and wanted to keep moving forward and creating new things, and Reid wasn't necessarily in that same direction.

"Here she is, the star of the evening," Cassie's father, Vincent, said, wrapping his daughter in a bear hug. Her mother soon followed suit. "We're so proud of you and this work."

"My gallery opening could not have been in better hands,"

Glenda said, giving her daughter's shoulder a squeeze. "Everything looks amazing, the mix of artists and art forms is perfectly eclectic, and your work is front and center. I love it all."

"Thank you," Cassie said with relief. For so long she had to prove herself to everyone, including her parents, and to now have their approval, she felt somewhat at ease. "Business is booming, the Dreamland campaign is about to go national, and I'm glad to have this show underway so I can figure out what's next."

Cassie noticed a curt nod from her father as he exchanged a glance with her mom.

"We are proud of your work ethic and how you strive to be the best at it all," Vincent started to explain, but Cassie stopped him.

"Dad, Mom, I love you both very much, and there's no way I'd be here today without all the support you've given me my entire life . . . but I'm not striving to be the best. I am the best. I'm continuing to explore my creativity and make art on my terms. Sometimes, it's a photo of vintage lights and an elevated concept for a series"—she waved toward the Sputnik chandelier photo, which took up almost an entire wall—"sometimes, it's taking pictures of people at their most vulnerable and most powerful. And sometimes, it's having someone take pictures of me in my underwear. I know you don't always regard what I do as serious and you want me to do more, but I'm not going to separate my passion and my business. I'm going to fight and work really hard, like I already have been, to do both on my terms."

Saying all of this felt like a weight lifted from Cassie's shoulders. She had said her piece, and no matter what, she knew she meant it. She stood tall in her boots and waited for their response.

Glenda looked at her husband and smiled proudly, and then

turned that smile to Cassie. "What more could we ask for? We're happy for you," and Cassie was engulfed in a double hug from her parents.

Reid stared at the photo of himself. He barely remembered Cassie taking it, but the more he thought about that day, he recalled those moments in the shadows when she made him stand between two towering bookshelves and he became the model and muse for her.

A tap on his shoulder brought him out of the memory.

"Hi."

"Hey, Cass," he said. Unsure about going in for a hug, Reid decided to clink his beer bottle with her glass of champagne. "Congratulations on all of this."

"Thank you," she said, taking a sip. "I'm glad you're here."

"I'm glad you invited me." Reid toyed with the label on the beer he held, watching Cassie play with one of her curls. When Reid's eyes finally met hers, he felt such a ridiculous urge to wrap her in his arms, he nearly dropped his drink. "So, uh, what's new?"

Kill me now, Reid thought. This was not how he thought this was going to go. Not that he had a plan. And Cassie did approach him, after all. Not that that mattered, either, because at this point, Reid would do anything just to breathe the same air as her.

"Um, well, all of this, I guess," Cassie said, looking around the room. "And work, of course. Since the photos went up—"

"You looked amazing," Reid blurted out. "I mean, you look amazing now, too, but in the ads with the logo and all that."

Someone please put me out of my misery, he silently begged the universe.

"Yeah, well," Cassie said after he interrupted her, which he realized after the fact. "Since the photos went up and had a great response, BB has been busy."

"That's awesome, Cassie," Reid said. What else could he say?

"So, what do you have going—"

"I didn't mean for anything to—"

They both started talking at the same time, pausing when they both started laughing a bit at how awkward they were making this interaction.

"Look, I'm sorry I didn't call after the shoot," Reid began. He had so much to say, and he knew if he started, he wouldn't stop until he had her forgiveness. "I should have told you about needing the money to help Russ, and I'm not trying to make excuses. I knew about everything with LL and Rebecca, but I thought I had—"

"Reid, we don't have to do this here," she interrupted gently. "I'm sure you have your reasons behind it all." Cassie began walking, but not away from him. It was slow enough that he understood she wanted him to walk with her.

"I want to explain."

"I know."

They stopped in front of a clay sculpture of a crude light bulb, still in its dark terra-cotta color. Reid could see how Cassie would love that it was dark and rudimentary, while her light photographs were concise and polished.

"Cass," Reid said, putting a hand on her elbow as they stopped in front of a painting in a corner. The lights weren't as dim, the scent of Thanksgiving dinner wasn't wafting through the air, nor were there makeshift bunches of mistletoe dangling from above them, but the same swoony feeling crept over him, much like it did the night of Friendsgiving, the night of their first kiss. He set his beer down on a small table with other empty drinks. "I fucked up. Bad. And you deserve better than me and my shitty judgment. I'm proud of you and what we had. I'm proud of everything you brought to my life, including opening myself up to new relationships with friends and with Russ."

"Reid, we shouldn't do this now."

"I know, and it doesn't excuse the things I said after the photo shoot. I just need you to know I'm sorry, and . . ."

Cassie took a step closer to him, finishing her champagne as she did. Setting it down next to his discarded beer bottle, she took yet another step closer. Reid could see the freckles he loved tracing across her nose and cheeks, could feel the softness of her breath, which he could tell had picked up because the swell of her chest strained against her formfitting green dress.

"And what?" she said softly, tucking her hair behind her ear.

"And you look incredible tonight, your artwork is amazing, and you should get me in touch with your agent, because they are doing great work on your behalf." They both laughed at this, knowing it was Cassie herself.

"Don't you know, Montgomery? I have an 'in' at this gallery."

"Not a chance. I'm pretty sure you got here on your own," he said. Reid was about to do something rash, like take her hand or attempt to stick his tongue in her mouth, but Cassie was distracted by her phone.

"Cass, can we maybe go somewhere . . . Cassie? What is it?" Reid watched Cassie's eyes widen in fear at the message and frantically search the crowd. She was looking for someone.

"I'm sorry, Reid, I need to find— Sam!" Reid followed Cassie's concerned gaze and saw Sam and Kit with their heads together, faces frowning at their phones. Sam looked up, her confused expression quickly changing to fear. Kit was already wiping tears from her cheeks.

"Cassie, what can I do?" he asked, taking her hand for comfort.

Cassie looked up from her phone, brow furrowed and tears threatening to fall. "It's Riki. Dana's in labor. She's having the baby right now, and they can't stop it. I have to . . . I have to—"

"You have to go."

"I want to talk, soon, okay?" Cassie held Reid's hand, and his gaze, for an intense brief moment, and then she was gone.

NINETEEN

R eid, calm down," Russ said to his brother, who hadn't stopped pacing the apartment since they got back from the gallery. "It's her first pregnancy; it'll probably take forever."

Reid stopped mid-stride and stared at his brother. "I'm not going to ask why you know that."

"I watch a lot of *Grey's Anatomy* reruns during the day," Russ replied, looking pleased with himself. "Cassie would have let you know if something went wrong."

"What makes you so sure?"

"She watched you all night and smiled a lot while she did," Russ said.

"How would you know? You were too busy canoodling with Sam."

"Who says 'canoodling'? You are so old. Anyway, I saw her. She couldn't keep her eyes off you all night." Russ had taken off the sweater Reid lent him and was now in a T-shirt that was at least a size too small, and Reid was pretty sure Russ had stolen a pair of old sweatpants from the back of his closet. Still, within a matter of months, Reid was now glad to have Russ around and could appreciate the man Russ was on his way to becoming. "What I really want to know is how are you going to get her back?"

Reid, who had started pacing again, stopped dead in his tracks. "What are you talking about?"

"I overheard everything at the photo shoot, Reid," Russ said. "What you said to the executives and then what you said to Cassie. Why didn't you tell her the truth?"

Reid moved to sit down on the couch his brother was currently lounging on. He swatted Russ's feet off the end he wanted to occupy. They overlooked the bright lights of Chicago, and Reid took it all in for a moment, his thoughts, of course, wandering to how wonderful Cassie had looked standing in front of that window not so long ago.

"If I took the pay raise, we'd be set with the house. Enough to cover the asbestos removal and any other repair work. We could probably hire someone so you can focus on school and your other jobs."

"Reid, I appreciate that, I really do. But you didn't have to do that for me," Russ said, pulling at a frayed seam on his tee shirt. "I know one thing from moving from job to job—there's always another one waiting to be found. I would have figured it out."

"You want me to void those checks I signed already?" Reid threatened. "You ungrateful little prick."

Russ knew he was joking, or at least the dopey grin on his face said so. "No, I mean it, thank you. For all of your help when I was truly desperate over the years, for everything with the house, for letting me crash there, and for helping me find my footing while I take classes. I may sign up for in-person classes next semester."

"Well, look at you. A real college coed," Reid said, throwing a fake punch Russ's way after he finally finished his litany of thanks. "But I am glad to give you this opportunity."

"Was it worth it? To take that away from Cassie?"

Reid thought for a moment. "Probably not. But being with Cassie helped me figure out what I was missing in my life overall. Connections with people who I care about."

"Stop, big brother, you're gonna make me cry," Russ said, pretending to wipe a tear from his eye.

"Well, look what it got me . . . A freeloading creep who steals my clothes."

"Shut up, you're being stupid," Russ said, flicking Reid off. "And you need to figure out how you're going to get her back."

Somewhere over the years on his own, Russ had become wise. "You're right, Russ. But if I'm stupid, then so are you, college courses notwithstanding. What's the deal with you and Sam?"

Russ's dopey grin formed yet again, and a slight blush crept over his cheeks. "I've been up-front with her since the moment I saw her in that bathing suit and combat boot outfit at the photo shoot. Why does she always look like she wants to stab something?"

"Because she literally always wants to stab something."

"Awesome."

Reid's phone vibrated, with Russ's soon chiming in with a text message alert. They both smiled.

DANA

Have you checked your mail today?

CASSIE

Just got home and didn't check.

DANA

IT'S HERE!

Cassie squinted at the blurry image Dana had sent her. A bunch of black and green blobs with curly fonts that looked similar the Luscious Lingerie logo . . .

"No way," Cassie said out loud to no one, and she ran down the three flights of stairs rather than taking the elevator. She almost barreled into the neighbor who lived directly below her coming out of the stairwell. After exchanging pleasantries and holding the door open for her, Cassie quickened her pace to the mailboxes.

In front of the elevator, waiting for it to arrive, Cassie finally held a bright green envelope, closed with a wax seal featuring an ornate letter *D* for Dreamland.

"Wedding invite?" the guy who had just moved into the garden apartment asked, also checking his mail.

"Oh, no," Cassie replied as the doors opened. "Just an over-the-top fashion show invitation."

He nodded his approval and then waved as the doors closed.

Cassie carefully cracked the wax in half, trying to keep as much of it preserved as possible. The envelope opened four ways instead of the traditional bifold, and there she was, front and center, fierce and fabulous, strong and sexy.

The angle Reid had shot her from made her look like she was on top of a mountain of gorgeous bodies, all outfitted in Dana's ethereal, sassy, and risqué designs. In the photo, Cassie had a whip in one hand and a tight grasp on her long, pop-star-esque ponytail, while Sam and Kit looked up at her. Their bodies looked banging— Kit was delicate and svelte, while Sam was all lean and compact curves.

And Cassie thought—no, she knew—that her body, extra pounds, dimpled thighs, visible tummy line, and all, looked fucking bomb.

Reaching her apartment's front door, Cassie heard the familiar distant sound of a vibrating phone from the depths of her messenger bag. Once she was inside, she caught the call on the last buzz.

"Well, supermodel? What do you think?" Dana said over the wails of a child. "Hang on a minute. Flo, would you just latch? There you go."

Cassie smiled warmly at the thought of Dana with her baby girl, Florence Mary Hayes-Sakai, safely at home after a harrowing birth. But their girl wasn't to be outdone; Flo started breathing on her own and nursing like a champ within a few days of being in the NICU, and after another couple of days of observation, she was deemed ready to go home.

"How is my perfect lady today?" Cassie inquired.

"I'm fine thanks, and the baby's great, too," Dana quipped. "So, what do you think?"

"This invite is awesome. The perfect vibe, maniacal and beautiful at the same time," Cassie said. "And the idea to throw a body-positive pool party on the top of Soho House over Memorial Day weekend—peak Chicago glam."

A pause passed between the two friends, which started out comfortable but then grew strained.

"But?"

"But nothing, D. I'm just taking it all in, I guess."

"Have you talked to him since the gallery opening?"

"Since the date of your child's birth?"

"Whatever. Have you? Answer me."

"You know I haven't."

Cassie didn't mean to let a full two weeks go by without contacting Reid. The way she felt after seeing him at her show had been exhilarating and sexy, and they fell back into their old beat immediately. He knew he had done a shitty job explaining his actions regarding the campaign, but Cassie felt like Reid was being genuine with her. Could she really blame him for wanting to help his brother? Someone whom he never thought he wanted a relationship with until now?

Well, yes. She could. And she did. He was still going to get the art director credit, and she was relegated to being the model. At least they weren't going to list her as his assistant or something like that.

"I know you want me to talk about everything, and we will, I promise. But I don't know what else to say, I told you everything."

"Sure, while I was hopped up on drugs and extreme baby-birthing hormones," Dana shot back. "But I have something that will make you feel good."

Cassie sat up straight. "Go on . . ."

"I had a vision recently, around four a.m., feeding this one—*OW*. Baby fingernails are like tiny knives when they sink into your tits."

"She heard you complaining about her," Cassie said.

"Anyway, I saw the most beautiful silver sequin caftan, and it's by a brand that I modeled for years ago, when I first started blog-

ging, I think. And I called in a few favors with the people I know
there and . . ."

"And what?" Cassie knew whatever Dana had in mind for the
show, it would be stunning. And they had a little over a month to
get everything planned out perfectly.

"I'm going to make you shine."

Normally, Reid arrived at these events late, but he decided to be
punctual and supportive of the job—and woman—he was proud of
and arrived to the Dreamland party early.

Not hearing from Cassie after Dana's delivery had been a disappointing blow, and after their interactions at her show, Reid was in
a funk. But he took a page from Cassie's book and threw himself
back into his work. He took on more projects than usual, including
an engagement photo shoot for one of the bike shop guys, and it was
more fun than he remembered. He edited images quickly and hand-
delivered proofs, prints, and mock-ups to his clients, who were local
and not too far for him to ride his bike.

Reid helped Russ pack up the house in Tinley Park, and they
made a plan for some final updates to make to it more appealing
before putting it on the market. Hopefully, once it was cleared out,
cleaned up, and landscaped, it would sell quickly. And with summer unofficially starting Memorial Day weekend, house-hunting
season was about to kick up a notch.

So, really, Reid arriving early to this shindig wasn't too out of
his new character. He did abide by the rules and wore dark gray
board shorts and a simple black polo shirt. He doubted he'd get in
the pool, but he decided to make an effort to support Dreamland.

He was doing everything he could to appear calm because he knew Cassie was coming.

Earlier that week, Rebecca casually brought Cassie up in a conversation about the guest list at the Dreamland celebration. When Reid deliberately did not comment on Cassie's attendance, along with the rest of the Buxom Boudoir team, including Dana and Riki, Rebecca harrumphed into the phone.

"Are you okay?" Reid asked. "Are you choking?"

"Not a chance in hell, Reid. I've got a bet going in the office, and I need to know if you and Cassie are a thing or not."

"I will neither confirm nor deny the status of my relationship because of an office bet."

"What about to an old friend?"

"Oh, we're friends now?"

"Look, buddy, I went out on a limb for you when it came to this campaign—"

"I didn't ask you to do that. In fact, I asked you not to do that, and now Cassie isn't speaking to me—"

"So you *are* a thing?"

"Were a thing. I haven't heard from her in a while."

"Dude, you really fucked up if she's done with you."

"Yeah, I did." *With a lot of help from you and your team of executives calling the shots.* But he kept his negative thoughts to himself.

Because now, Reid wanted everyone at this party to know he was taking things seriously, and above everything else, he wanted Cassie to know he was serious about her.

After checking his watch for the millionth time and seeing it was still ten minutes before guests were supposed to officially arrive, Reid remembered why he always came late to these things. Being early at parties was not fun.

"Hey, Reid," Russ said as he walked up to him. He'd found a bright red Hawaiian shirt somewhere that was about a size and a half too small, but Russ pulled it off by keeping it open and revealing a tight white tank top. "Sorry I'm late. Wait, actually, I'm early. You should be congratulating me."

Reid ignored his brother's request. "How was work?"

Russ was now working at Simone's full-time, running food and clearing tables during the day and helping stock the bar at night. It wasn't the most glamorous of jobs, but Reid was happy he could depend on James to give his brother a job and that his brother hadn't ruined things, yet. He hoped this was the start of a stable and meaningful time in Russ's life. And Reid was glad he was going to be a part of it.

"Great. I'm learning a lot, but it's mostly being at the other servers' beck and call, or waiting for someone to ask me to lift something heavy behind the bar," Russ answered, fidgeting with his collar. "I think I may like the restaurant business."

They spoke a bit longer about Russ's job when a familiar loud cackle rang out from across the pool. More and more people began to file onto the rooftop deck, clustering together with other people they knew. Dana's laugh, however, filled the entire room and then some, and a cheer rang out when they all realized who it was.

"It's our first date since the baby, so you all better get excited," she called out, and was received with another loud cheer. Dana and Riki walked in, looking ever the stylish duo. Dana was in the black one-shoulder swimsuit with one of her sheer robes on as a cover-up. Riki actually wore an outfit similar to Reid's, but naturally, she looked much cooler than him. They both smiled in his direction as they walked into the party and started greeting people individually.

Reid was talking to a Luscious Lingerie executive, who was excitedly telling him about the record set of preorders Dreamland had received like he hadn't heard it already. He was in the middle of pretending to be surprised at the amount of underpants they had already sold before the official on-sale date when Cassie walked in, surrounded by an entourage of models from the orgy scene, including Kit and Sam.

He swore he heard someone audibly gasp right before applause started. Russ let out a high-pitched wolf whistle, similar to the one Sam used to get everyone's attention, but his was more appreciative. Reid found himself clapping as well, never once taking his eyes off Cassie.

She was covered in sparkles—from her skin glistening with some kind of shimmer, to the long, shiny, silver earrings that hung from her ears, to the tinsel fringe caftan that swayed with every step. The deep V-neck and high leg slit in the wrap dress revealed she was wearing a black latex bikini with intricate straps that accentuated her chest and showed quite a lot of leg when it peeked from behind her dress. Reid couldn't take his eyes off her.

Play it cool, Montgomery. He decided to keep his distance, but not too far. He wanted to see how she'd react.

Cassie made the rounds, greeting adoring fans, who were mostly wearing swimwear or lingerie, showcasing a myriad of beautiful body types, skin tones, and fashion senses. While there were some attendees dressed like they were going to the office, some guests did actually go in the pool, and others looked like they were about to walk an haute couture runway. The best part of it all? Everyone was happy and at ease. Maybe it was the open bar, but Reid suspected seeing Cassie—a successful, powerful, full-figured, Black business owner and model—gave them the confidence to embrace their individuality. What anyone else thought didn't matter because they felt great and wanted everyone to know it.

Reid feigned interest in yet another business conversation when he saw Cassie staring at something as she stood near the bar. He followed her eyeline and saw that she finally noticed it.

The Sputnik chandelier photo.

While waiting for a beverage at the bar and making small talk with a local boutique owner, Cassie had been thumbing through the Luscious Lingerie catalog that would be mailed out to customers that week. There were also mini chapbooks of photos from the entire Dreamland campaign placed on tables and across the bar as an exclusive advance look for the partygoers. Reid and Rebecca had put them together at the last minute, because the images wouldn't all be on display that night—so he knew exactly which photos should be featured at the party.

After Cassie saw the Sputnik chandelier from where she was standing, she started scanning the rooftop while attempting to keep up with the conversation happening in front of her. Behind the bar was a three-series set, all from the first day she made Reid stand still in the sunlight, the light moving as she did, changing the way his leather jacket looked in different angles, showcasing the textured seams and tiny fibers from being worn in. All over the rooftop, there were photos of light bulb filaments, champagne flutes filtering light through bubbles, shadows impossibly crossed with themselves, and they were all the vision of Cassandra Harris.

He purposely asked the LL events team to place the photos where people would naturally gather so they could see that the model who inspired them to feel comfortable in their own bodies could also inspire them creatively. With the help of Cassie's mom, each photo had a small card on the frame, with the information to order original artwork or prints through the Glen Gallery.

Just as Cassie was reading one of these cards, Reid made his move to approach her.

"Hey."

"What is all this?"

"Some really cool artwork by this photographer I know."

Cassie kept looking around the room, and Reid had to stop himself from wrapping her in his arms. He busied his hands by shoving them in his pockets and looking at his simple black Vans and her very tall, very bright purple platform sandals. When he finally looked up at her exquisite face, he was met with a gentle but stern look gazing back at him.

"If this is some sort of grand gesture, Reid, it's great. It's really nice," Cassie said, picking up a nearby catalog of the Dreamland campaign, chock-full of searingly hot images of her—pictures they took together, which she'd guided him to take.

"Did you see the flip-books?" Reid offered, holding up a small square chapbook. Cassie started to page through it, but after a few pages, realized it was meant to be flipped quickly. She let the pages zip through her fingers and was mesmerized by the movement of the entire orgy photo shoot. From the foot stomp that started everything, to her fierce stance, to the interaction with the models— it was cheeky, silly, and the perfect gimmick to give away at this event.

"Rebecca really is a genius when it comes to this stuff, isn't she?" Cassie said, taking the photobook and putting it in her pocket. "But like I was saying, this party is great, and it's gratifying to see my artwork used outside of the gallery, so thank you for this."

"You're welcome."

"But it's not enough."

Reid nodded. "I know it isn't."

Cassie carefully studied Reid's face. "What do you mean?"

"I'm sure you've heard about everything with the house from Sam, who heard it from my gossipy brother."

"I may have picked up on a few things, and I think you did a good thing helping Russ." Cassie said. "I just wish it hadn't been at my expense."

"Me too."

"So, what now?"

"Well, before things get too serious, I want you to know I called in a few favors for this party. Walk with me," Reid said, hooking her arm with his. "Over there is the entire team for window displays at Macy's, along with a few people from Saks. They love your photos.

"And here we have talent scouts from *Chicago* magazine, *Chicago Bride*, and pretty much every major ad agency in the city. Can you believe they all wore bathing suits? They love your natural light photography and want to talk more about what you think for feature spreads.

"And then next to the bar, naturally, are a bunch of TV and radio people. They want new photos of anchors and on-air talent. Oh, and a couple of them wanted to book you for tips on body confidence and what to bring to a boudoir photo shoot."

"Reid."

"Cass." He stopped walking when he felt her hand curl around his bicep and squeeze.

"This is more than just a few favors."

"I know. And they're all here to meet you. And not just because I asked them, but because I sent them links to your portfolio and business website, explained how hard you work at any and every-thing you do, and told them that whenever they think of me for a project, they should call you first. And then I told them that my life was better because you are in it." He started walking again, needing to keep moving before their emotions got the better of them. "And then right here is where we'll stop and hopefully have a short chat before everyone in this party starts clamoring for a moment of your time, Harris."

Cassie gasped—he had led them to a small alcove, away from the pool and the music and the food, where a series of photos, some taken by her and some taken by Reid, showcased their entire relationship. From the first photos she took of Reid's jacket, to out-takes of her laughing with Kit and Sam on the rooftop, to a few pre-cious baby photos of Flo, they gazed at the photos clipped to string perfectly at eye level. And not too far away sat Cassie's parents, Dana, Riki, Kit, Sam, James, and Russ, all smiling back at them.

"How did you do all of this?"

"With a lot of help from everyone here. You've been working nonstop, so there was some serious behind-the-scenes planning."

"You're welcome," Dana called out, followed by self-applause from the entire group.

"Let's give them a minute alone, shall we? There you are, dar-lings, come find us when you're done," said Kit.

Cassie gave hugs to everyone as they left the alcove, and she was thankful for a few seconds to process everything that had just hap-pened. She was touched by the lengths Reid had gone to make a difference about the events that took place at the final photo shoot.

She wasn't sure she was ready to forgive him, though, or that this wonderful party was going to be enough.

"This is really amazing," she finally said once they were alone. "I can't believe how thoughtful and careful you've been. I appreciate it all."

"But?"

"But it doesn't change the fact that you still took—or were given—credit for the job I did. The job that was mine," Cassie held up a Dreamland catalog. "I admit, I turned to you and leaned on you when I was overwhelmed and needed help, and yes, you did take these pictures, but this Dreamland campaign was my vision. And since the beginning, you've taken things from me, too. Be it job opportunities, explanations for everything, or . . . my heart."

She held her breath for a moment and continued.

"I just don't know if I can do all of this and still find a way to let you back in."

Reid nodded, and took the Dreamland catalog from her. Turning to the inside back cover, he held it back out to her. "Check the credit, Harris."

Cassandra Harris: *Art Director, Model,*
and Badass Warrior Goddess

Reid Montgomery: *Shutter Pusher*

"I called Rebecca two days ago, pretty much as these catalogs were being printed. She probably got in trouble, but she went ahead and made the change. And you should see a completion bonus from LL any day now. Something about exceeding a preorder goal. That's what it'll say."

"Oh, Reid," Cassie said, hugging him, dropping the catalog and not caring one bit who saw them. "What about the work on the house? And everything with your brother?"

"Russ is teaching me to hustle. I'm taking on extra projects, some weddings and family photo shoots. Mostly hipsters," he said, rolling his eyes and smirking. "I also have it on good authority that Buxom Boudoir needs a new office assistant."

"Look, Montgomery, you're not off the hook completely," Cassie said, arching an eyebrow, mimicking Reid's smirk. "But I don't want to let what we had go."

"Me, too. I love you, Cass."

"I love you, Reid."

Taking his hand in hers, Cassie pulled Reid close. Smiling, laughing, sighing, and tearing up a little bit, she leaned up for a kiss. Just as Reid's lips met hers, they heard a loud, exasperated groan.

"*Ugh*," began Sam from across the room, but before she could finish it on her own, everyone chimed in:

"Get a room!"

Laughing with their friends, Cassie and Reid joined the party, and started whatever would come next, together.

EPILOGUE

―――

s it supposed to pinch this much?"

"Arch your back more."

"It hurts! Why? Why would you wear this if it hurts this much? Ouch—hey!"

Cassie dug a very spiky, very tall, oxblood-red stiletto heel into the middle of Reid's chest. They were at the Buxom Boudoir studio, sitting on the chaise longue, positioned directly in front of one of the large windows to let in as much bright light as possible. Cassie had found the perfect model for her latest campaign: Dana's shoe line for Luscious Lingerie's new footwear division.

Cassie had to admit, finding a reason to put her very hot, very photogenic boyfriend in a corset, hot pants, and fishnet tights with garters was one of the best ideas she had ever had. Perhaps only bested by the fact that she cast herself as the foot and leg model, and she was currently sitting on top of him wearing very sexy heels, doing everything in her power to help Reid forget about the corset and make sultry faces at her camera.

"Quit complaining, Montgomery, and think about that thing I did last night."

Reid looked up and smirked.

Click.

"Which thing?"

"You know . . . that thing with my tongue."

Reid's smirk became a scintillating smile, and Cassie took a photo that she wanted to both keep to herself and put on a billboard over the Kennedy Expressway.

Cassie scrolled through images on the viewfinder. "Maybe we should paint your nails? Something is missing. Something . . . more."

"I'll give you something more."

"You'll give me whatever I tell you to, Mr. Model," Cassie said, rolling her eyes.

Reid adjusted his corset.

"Would you stop moving the corset? I need it laced just so."

"I cannot last much longer in this. And these tights are itchy."

"I distinctly remember you agreeing to wear lingerie if it turned me on, once upon a time."

"I remember agreeing to wear very tiny, sheer underpants. Not a torture device."

Cassie gave Reid an overexaggerated sad face and went back to her camera. "Yes, maybe nail polish in the exact same shade as these shoes. I have a few options, of course. Dark and moody, right? That'll look great with your hands on my legs."

"I think I'm good for today; nail polish can wait until tomorrow, right? We've been at it all day, and I think my ribs have actually moved from how tight this thing is."

"Just wait until you see what I have planned for the principal photography for *my* lingerie line. Corsetry and fishnets for days. Also, do you really want to complain to me? An *actual* lingerie model?"

"Yeah, I do . . . and there's something under the couch," Reid said, loosening his corset and grabbing the hoodie that was on the floor nearby.

"What does that have to do with anything?"

"Harris."

"Montgomery."

"Cass," he said as he zipped his sweatshirt. "Reach under your end of the couch."

Without leaving his gaze, Cassie set her camera carefully on the floor and felt under the chaise. She felt her eyes grow wide. She pulled her hand out and held up a small, black velvet box.

"Reid."

"Cass."

She held the box in her upturned hand, both a smile and tears dancing on the edge of her expression.

"Reid, what is this?"

"Cassandra Harris," Reid said, sitting up straight, and pulling Cassie closer to him, so they were nestled together. "I love you. You make me strive to be better because you're the best person I've ever met. Even when you make me wear a corset. And I want to spend the rest of my life with you. Will you marry me?" Reid took the box from Cassie's hand and opened it, pulling out a gorgeous black diamond solitaire engagement ring—dark and moody and perfect for his girl.

Cassie took a deep breath. "On one condition."

"What's that?"

"You wear the corset on our wedding night." The look of confusion on Reid's face quickly melted into a genuine smile when Cassie exclaimed, "Yes, of course!"

Enveloping him in her arms, crushing her mouth to his, and toppling them both over onto the rug that cushioned their fall, Cassie kissed the man who was now her fiancé with wild abandon. While she couldn't wait to call and text her family and friends, Cassie was content right where she was, entwined with the man she loved. She knew they'd have a lifetime of photo shoots in natural light, wearing corsets and fishnets and proving that against all odds, they could find and deserve love.

ACKNOWLEDGMENTS

Writing a book feels so singular when the actual writing is happening, but then suddenly you are thrust into a world where there are so many important pieces to the puzzle, each one unique and very important to the final big picture.

Thank you to Ashley Herring Blake, agent extraordinaire, for believing in my story and loving these characters as much as I do. Your guidance and insight led to these shenanigans getting published. AHB—you're a dream!

Thank you to my editors, Liz Sellers and Cindy Hwang, for your dedication and wonderful suggestions that made this book shine. I could not have had better leaders throughout this process.

Thanks to the entire Berkley team! Everyone's time and care with every detail on every page on behalf of my work is insurmountably awesome, and I am forever grateful. Emily Osbourne, Colleen Reinhart, Leni Kauffman, and Daniel Brount: my book looks and feels amazing because of you. Dache' Rogers, Fareeda Bullert, and Daniela Riedlova: thank you for telling the world about my book. Megha Jain and Erica Ferguson: thanks for making my story make sense!

To my friends: you all are the inspiration for the fabulous friend group at the heart of this novel. There are bits and pieces of you in Cassie, Dana, Sam, and Kit. Honestly, you make my world go around.

To the residents of Romancelandia: you give me life, keep me sane, and I want each of you to know you're wonderful. This book would not be here without the countless reviewers, librarians, booksellers, and READERS who give their support to books they love. Thank you!

Growing up, I was always that kid who wanted to stay inside and read instead of play (reader, I am still that kid). Thanks to my parents, Gary and Cheryl, for indulging me in this preference. Thanks to my little brother, Alex (who is much, much taller than me now, but is still pretty great), for sticking to our agreement. He knows what this means. A special shout-out to my sister-in-law, Erica, for sending me a copy of *Bird by Bird* after I told her I really wanted to do this writing thing. And hello to my nephews, Oliver and Miles, too! To *all* of the extended Jackson/Dresser family members—thank you.

To Ivy Evelyn, wise beyond her years, for inspiring me to be better every single day. When you were five years old, you told me to "just write the book." So I did. I love you, Ivy-girl! Thank you for being you.

And thanks, above and beyond, to Zach Dresser, for smiling and nodding when I brainstormed out loud, bringing me copious amounts of coffee and snacks (and wine), and building the desk I sat at for months while writing this book and where I'll write all the others to come. You're the very best, and I couldn't have done this without your unwavering support, love, and devotion. I love you always and forever.

The Accidental Pinup

Danielle Jackson

DISCUSSION QUESTIONS

1. Cassie is an accomplished photographer, but she has never modeled before when she finds herself on the other side of the camera. How do you think she handles the sudden change in plans when her dream of the campaign was within reach?

2. Boudoir and pinup photography have grown in popularity in recent years, empowering all forms of beauty and personal expression. Have you ever had/considered having a sexy photo shoot?

3. Despite a difficult upbringing, Reid has made big strides professionally. Meanwhile, Cassie, who owns her own studio and has achieved some success, hasn't made the professional moves she knows she's capable of handling. How do you think the challenges they both faced affected the people they have become? How do they overcome their differences?

4. Cassie has created an awesome team of coworkers and friends at her photography studio, Buxom Boudoir. Out of Dana, Sam, and Kit, which of Cassie's friends would you want to hang out with most? Talk about a time in your life when your friends really went above and beyond to help (or challenge) you.

5. Reid and Russ have a strained relationship, and as Reid gets to know his brother better, he wonders if his distance, both emotional and physical, hindered Russ when he was growing up. What do you think of Reid's decision to "spy" on Cassie to ultimately help his brother?

6. The fun and dynamic Chicago setting for this novel offered some local flair beyond the usual touristy spots. Where would you visit—from this story or otherwise—if you could spend a weekend in Chicago? Do you have any favorite books or movies set there?

7. Cassie and Reid have vastly different relationships with their parents. Discuss the differences and how you think these relationships shaped them as people.

8. Body positivity, body confidence, and even body neutrality are all important movements to accept bodies as they are, no matter their size, and are incredibly important to Cassie and her work. How does Cassie's perception of her body change throughout the story? How does Reid's reaction to her in lingerie make her feel? How did it make you feel?

9. Discuss Reid's final grand gesture at the body positivity pool launch party for Dreamland. Do you think it was enough to warrant Cassie's forgiveness?

Danielle Jackson is a contemporary romance author, avid reader, lackluster-yet-mighty crafter, and accomplished TV binge-watcher.

Once upon a time, she was a publicist in publishing and continues to cultivate her love of books and reading by chatting with the best authors in the business as the event coordinator at an independent bookstore and as the cohost of the *Fresh Fiction* podcast. She also moderates panels, interviews authors, and hosts a romance book club.

Danielle lives in Chicagoland with her very own romance hero husband, darling daughter, and two tempestuous cats.

CONNECT ONLINE

DanielleJacksonBooks.com
🐦 DJacksonBooks
📷 DJacksonBooks